THE GIRL IN THE WALL

Emily Slate Mystery Thriller
Book 9

ALEX SIGMORE

Dark Woods Press

Prologue

"I DID IT! I DID IT," Jessica says, out of breath as she scrambles into my car, slamming the passenger side door behind her. "I actually did it." She says it like she can't believe it herself.

"Really?" I ask. "Everything we talked about?"

"Yes, now go." She glares at me, waiting for me to act.

I'm frozen by indecision; I didn't think she'd go through with it. But now that she has...my heart rate picks up. It means everything else is on as well. It means we can do this, and it all wasn't just talk. I turn my eyes to the road and hit the accelerator. The car jumps once, and for a second Gwen Stefani singing about spiderwebs is drowned out by the squeal of the engine, pulling my little car down the road out of sight of Jessica's house. It's not dark enough to flip on my lights yet but I want to get out of sight of the house. I can't believe this is going to happen. My whole body feels like a surge of current is moving through it. Is this what it's like to hope?

"What did he say?" I ask, trying to keep the nervousness out of my voice. I notice Jessica is breathing hard, her chest rising and falling. I find myself staring at her tits, straining to break out of her white cotton tank top. Who would have thought she could have developed so quickly? Not that I'm complaining.

"He just gave me a bunch of crap about being a disrespectful daughter and how I never appreciated everything he did for me," she says, pulling her loose brown hair back into a ponytail with the scrunchie on her arm. "You know how he is."

My hands grip the steering wheel tighter, my knuckles going white. "I know exactly how he is, my dear." She turns to me, a big grin on her face. "What?"

"I love it when you do that," she says. "Sometimes you speak like you're from a different era. You're *so* not like all the other guys at my school."

I stifle a laugh. "I would hope not."

"What makes you do that? Or is it just something that happens when you get older, like paying taxes?"

I arch an eyebrow. "I'm only what, six years older than you? The way I speak is a choice, not a requirement."

"Still, I like it," she says. Her breathing is coming back down, the adrenaline from the night's events wearing off. "So, what now? Can we grab something to eat? I didn't think I'd be hungry after that. In fact, I thought I'd be sick to my stomach, but it just felt so...so *good* to put that bastard in his place for once."

"He definitely deserved it," I reply. "How about I treat you to something nice?"

"Great," she says, cranking up the radio and putting one foot up on the dashboard of my Chevy Impala. The song switches over to Bush's *Glycerine*. I love that song. She's got on cut-off jean shorts, which leave little to my imagination. She didn't have those on earlier today; she must have changed before she had it out with him. *Perfect.* This couldn't have gone any better. I half expected her to run out and tell me she couldn't go through with it, that everything we'd been working on for the past few weeks was all for nothing.

But she didn't. She pulled through. And now he's going to regret this day for the rest of his miserable life. I'll make sure of that.

I pull in to the only drive-in Fernview has left, because it means we don't have to get out of the car. I want to get her back to my place as soon as possible. I can already feel my pants growing tighter just looking at her. This was the deal; she cuts ties, we head back, and we start our new lives together. We'll have to go somewhere; I haven't planned out where yet because I didn't want to get ahead of myself. The Impala only has about ninety thousand on it; it can still get us anywhere we want to go. We won't be able to get her a proper ID for another year or so, but until then we'll manage.

God, I just wish there was some way for me to watch that bastard wallow in his own self-pity. Him and his entire family.

We eat quick, and I don't reach out when a dab of mustard from her hot dog drips down onto her tank top. She curses, wiping it away to leave a yellow stain and I watch the whole thing with glee. I can hardly contain myself. This is really going to happen. The whole time I can't keep the images of her tight little body wriggling all over me.

As soon as we're done eating, I drive us back to my place. It's nothing fancy; and doesn't need to be. Plus, it's not like I can afford much more on my salary. But in our new life together we'll find a better place, a bigger place. Maybe even something by the water.

After we pull up, I linger in the car a minute, watching her get out, and eyeing those shorts as they hug every inch of her ass. I can barely contain myself as I imagine what the next few hours are going to be like. There's no backing out now; she's already come this far. Now I can finally let my imagination loose. I can start planning for the future. Things are going to be better; for everyone.

Well, everyone except for Jessica's father. But fuck him. Him and everything about him. He'll finally know what it means to be on the receiving end for once. And he'll be sorry. *Ugh,* I want to see it so bad. To watch that man melt down from the inside. But I can't. We have to leave. We can't stay here after what she just did. If we stayed there would be too much blowback, especially when everyone figures out she and I have been together all this time. This town is too small; everyone knows each other. They just won't understand our relationship. No one does…small minds and small people. I need to start planning. We can only stick around here for so long before someone realizes I'm not living alone anymore. And there's no doubt in my mind her father will do everything to find her.

"Here, allow me, miss," I say, unlocking the door and stepping aside, holding open the screen for her.

"Why, thank you." It comes out sounding like words from a little girl, and I have to remember that she's still so young. She has so much to learn. Fortunately, I'm here to teach her. I can tell her everything she needs to know.

"Wow," she says, when she gets inside, but I can already hear the hesitation in her voice.

"What's wrong?" I ask.

"What? Nothing, it's…it's great." She takes a few tentative steps in, but something *is* wrong. She's acting like she's been called to the principal's office, standing off to the side, holding herself tight.

"This is your home now too," I say, offering her the couch. I take a second to wipe it free of crumbs. "I want you to feel comfortable here."

"Thanks," she says as she perches herself on the edge of the couch, looking around the room. I follow her gaze. What is she *looking* at?

"Jessica, what's wrong?" I ask, using my authoritative voice. The one she always responds to.

"Nothing, it's just…I just thought it would be a little

cleaner, that's all." Her voice has grown smaller, like she's afraid to speak.

"Cleaner?" I ask, looking around. It's clean. There aren't roaches running around the place and I make sure every spill is cleaned up immediately. Maybe the carpet is a little dingier than she's used to, and the furniture more lived in, but that's all I can afford. I'd like to see her do this well on her own and tell me it's not clean. This is what happens when you grow up in a middle-class home, you just don't appreciate when someone has had to work hard for everything they have. Not all of us were given everything growing up, *Jessica*.

"Here, let me get you something to drink," I say, heading to the kitchen. My boner is well and gone now, but I'm not going to let that spoil the mood. She just needs some time to acclimate. I grab two beers from the fridge and pop the cans, returning to her. "You've had this before, right?"

She takes the can and looks at the label. "Natty light? Yeah, I think so." She takes a sip but the immediate revulsion on her lips is palpable. She looks like she's about to throw up but manages to swallow it with a lot of difficulty.

I grimace, then snatch the can from her and return to the kitchen.

"I'm sorry," she calls out. "I just wasn't ready for it. Let me try it again."

I place my hands on the countertop, shaking my head. This is not how I imagined this going. Not at all. "No, you don't like it. I'm not going to make you drink something you don't like."

She gets up. "I'm sorry. I just…" she looks around again. "I'm not sure what I was expecting."

I round the bar, coming back into the living room. "What, not good enough for you?" That familiar tingle at the base of my neck is back. I've never felt that in her presence before. I've never had a reason to.

"No, it's not that," she says, but I can already see it in her eyes. She's more stuck up than I thought. I'd hoped she wasn't like her father, but it seems like some of that's genetic. But I'm not worried. I can still fuck it out of her. *Play nice*, I remind myself.

"C'mon," I say, taking her by the arm. "Let's head to the bedroom. You'll feel better in a few minutes." But as soon as I pull at her I feel the resistance. She doesn't move from the spot.

"I…I think I'd rather just go home," she says, her voice trembling.

"Home?" I ask, incredulous. I jerk her arm, pulling her closer to me. "How can you say that? After everything we planned. Everything we've—*I've* sacrificed? Are you telling me you want to go back to *him*?"

"No, it's not like that," she says. "He absolutely deserves this, I just…I'm not sure I'm ready."

"You said you were ready before. Was that a lie? Were you lying to me, Jessica?" I'm using my authoritative voice again. I can't seem to help myself. Because she's pissed me off and I'm doing everything I can to keep from lashing out at her. How *dare* she? After all I've done for her, she wants to go home?

"N-no." She's trembling. Is she afraid of me? "I didn't lie. I thought I was ready. But now I think I was wrong."

"Listen to me," I say, jerking her closer again, pulling her in so our faces are mere inches from each other. "You and I are going to have a life together. We've planned for this. There's no going back now, you've already set everything in motion." That anger is bubbling up; the kind I usually reserve for her father and people like him. But this time it's more…visceral.

"I-I can still go home," she says, her voice growing smaller by the minute. "He's my dad. He'll forgive me."

"You're telling me you're willing to forgive *him*, for every-thing he's done to you? To me? How could you?"

"Please, you're hurting my arm," she says. The smaller her

voice gets, the more I like it. I have power over this girl, and I can do whatever I want with her. She's no match for me. Seeing as how she's willing to go back to my sworn enemy it seems fair that I still have my revenge. In a single moment she's destroyed everything; the future we had together, all our dreams, all our hopes.

I deserve compensation for that.

I pull her through the back hallway, throwing her onto the bed. She's like a rag doll, no fight in her at all.

"Please," she says, sobbing now. Oh yes, I like this very much. I can feel my boner coming back. This is unexpected, but I'll take it.

"This is *your* fault," I say, closing the door behind me. "We could have had everything. Maybe in time you'll figure it out. Until then, I'll just have to teach you about the consequences of your actions." I unbutton my pants, pulling down my zipper and exposing myself to her. She turns away, the revulsion on her face making me even angrier.

"Don't tell me a little *bitch* like you hasn't ever done this before," I growl. "Do I have to tell you how to do *everything?*"

I walk closer to her, pulling my pants down a little further to give her better access when all of a sudden I feel a pain explode across my groin as she headbutts my dick, smashing it into my balls in the wrong direction. My knees slam to the ground and I fall as Jessica scrambles up, running for the door.

"You little *bitch*," I manage to yell, working to pull my pants back up through the pain. By the time I get back to my feet she's already out of the bedroom and at the main door, trying to get the handle unlocked. Fortunately for me this house is old, and it's the kind that doesn't have a latch, but instead needs a key to open either side. She seems to realize this at the same time as she hears me coming for her and runs to grab my keys from the counter. But I reach her before she can fit the key into the slot and wrench her back, throwing her down.

Her back hits the coffee table at a bad angle and she cries out. I shove my keys into my pocket and go after her again as she tries to scramble back from me.

"Stay away from me, you psycho! I'm going to tell my father *everything*."

Oh, how I wish she hadn't said that. This is going to require more drastic measures.

I'd say she'll regret those words, but she won't have the chance to. Ever again.

Chapter One

I TAKE a deep breath and glance at the clock at the upper right-hand corner of my screen. Two hours. It feels like it's been twenty. What can be taking so long?

"Em?"

I look up to see my best friend and fellow FBI Agent Zara Foley glaring over the top of her computer screen at me. It's the look that tells me whatever I'm thinking is probably plastered all over my face right now. "What?"

"You look constipated."

That breaks my concentration and I actually laugh, though it's more from nervousness than the comment being funny. "I didn't realize I was being monitored."

"Have you even *met* me?" she asks. "Besides, you need to relax. Go get a cup of tea or something."

"I need something a lot stronger than tea," I grumble.

Now it's her turn to laugh. "I'd love to see Wallace's face if you just brought your own bottle to work, kept it in your desk drawer there."

I shrug. "It's no worse than what I've seen some of these small town cops do," I say.

"Yeah, but they're not working in the J. Edgar Hoover

Building." She stands, holding out her hand for mine. "Here, let's take a walk around the gym. Burn off some of this nervous energy."

I shake my head. "I'd rather stay here. If I go down there I'll just be worried that I'll miss the call."

"Uggghhh," Zara says. "Fine. But I can't watch you fidget and fret anymore. You're breaking my concentration, and I've got like, ten cases I'm trying to work through. Can't you do anything to distract yourself?"

I stand, shaking out my hands. They've been clammy all day. And focusing on work has been next to impossible. Usually that solves most of my problems, but today is the day I'm due to hear something back from the handwriting analysis lab in Quantico. They've been analyzing the letter that arrived at my apartment over a month ago in my dead mother's hand-writing. At first I had blown it off as a joke or someone's attempt to extort me. But after seeing what ignoring a problem for too long can do to someone—a community even, I've decided I can't ignore the letter.

My mother died seventeen years ago. I attended the funeral. I saw them lower her casket into the ground. There's no way she's alive, so whoever is doing this, is looking to get my attention.

Well, they have it now.

"Hey there…fellow…agents." I glance over to see Special Agent Nadia Kane approaching. She's carrying a laptop under one arm and a file folder in the other. But the way she said it made it seem like she decided to approach us then thought better of it in the middle of the sentence. She and another agent, Elliott Sandel, assisted on the case in New Hampshire. With the four of us working together, we were able to uncover our killer and wrap things up before anyone else was hurt. I had originally suspected them of monitoring me on my boss's behalf, seeing as Wallace doesn't exactly trust my judgement a hundred percent of the time, but they both proved themselves to be competent and trustworthy during the case.

Still, I'm not sure I'm ready to let them into my inner circle yet. Zara insists I can't keep myself closed off forever and at some point I'll need to talk to someone other than just her or my boyfriend, Liam, but I'm not so sure.

Dealing with people is hard when the topics of discussion aren't work-related.

"Hi," Zara says, chipper as ever. I just give Agent Kane a friendly wave. "New case?"

"Just came down the pipeline," she replies. "Is it just me, or does your division always get this busy at this time of year?"

Agent Kane is a transplant over from counterterrorism. She, Sandel, and a dozen others were moved into our department once it was discovered my boss's boss, the Deputy Director of the FBI, was a mole for a secret, underground organization. Despite exposing him, the outgoing administration thought it would be best if the FBI was reorganized to try and reestablish public trust. It's been almost two months so far and I don't know how well that's going. It's above my pay grade. I'm just trying to get through the days at this point.

"Em?" Zara asks.

"Hmm?"

She looks at me like she expects me to respond. Then I remember, Zara wasn't here last year, she was still in data analysis. She only graduated as a field agent a few months back. I was the only one of us here this time last year. "Honestly I think it has more to do with the reorganization than anything," I tell Agent Kane. "It usually gets busier during the holidays, but we're a good week past Christmas now. It should be slowing down."

"I hope it does soon," Kane says, though she still seems to be pulling back a little. I can't tell if she regrets beginning this conversation or not. "Wallace is running us ragged."

"Too bad we can't have a post-holiday party since we

don't get time to celebrate," Zara says. "Can you even imagine?"

Kane laughs, and I have to admit the image is a little funny. A bunch of strait-laced, serious-as-death FBI agents attempting to let loose? Talk about a buzzkill. It'd be like Men In Black with a bunch of people standing around, looking uncomfortable as hell as festive music played.

"Maybe it's better we don't," I say. "For everyone involved."

"Well, good chatting, but I need to get on these," Kane says, holding up her stack of files. "Have a good day."

"Thanks, you too," Zara says. Once Kane is out of earshot she turns to me. "We really gotta work on your people skills."

I roll my eyes. "My people skills are fine, thank you. How many perpetrators have I interrogated? How many families have I had to comfort?"

But Zara won't let me get away with it. "That's different and you know it. None of those involve you personally. You can put up that compartment wall inside your head and playact if you have to. When it comes to genuinely connecting with people, you struggle."

"Thanks," I say. Like I didn't already know that.

Her face softens. "Em, sorry. I just...sometimes I worry about you."

"Me? I'm fine," I say. "I wasn't the one whose legs were cut to shreds by those barbed wire traps."

"Psssh," she says, waving me off. "Those were superficial, and you know it. And quit turning this back around on me. We're talking about you."

I'm about to keep arguing with her because as crazy as it sounds, this is actually better than waiting around for the handwriting results. But before I can say anything else, my phone rings. I can see from the flashing light that it's an internal call. I grab the receiver, hoping it's the analysis lab. "Slate."

"Come into my office for a moment, please," my boss, Fletcher Wallace says.

"Yes, sir." I hang up then shoot Zara a look. "He beckons."

"Do you think it's about the results?"

I shake my head, walking fifteen feet to his door. As far as I'm aware, Wallace doesn't know about the handwriting request, seeing as that was more of a personal issue. However, if anyone does raise a stink, I have a pretty good track record with nefarious people undermining me and possibly compromising this office, so I doubt it's going to be an issue.

"Yes, sir?" I ask, sticking my head into his office.

"Slate," he says, glaring at me over the tops of his horn rim glasses. Fletcher Wallace is all business, and ever since he took over from my last boss, Janice Simmons, he's run this division as tightly as anyone could reasonably expect. Though we didn't get off on the best foot, I feel like we've come to an understanding. At least, that's what I like to tell myself.

And yet, something inside me tells me to needle him just a bit, which I like to do by not coming all the way in his office when he calls for me. I don't know why, but it really seems to annoy him and as long as I keep getting that reaction, I'm gonna keep doing it.

"Close the door, please," he says for probably the hundredth time that I've done this. Still, I keep my distance and don't sit, hoping to make this a quick meeting. The guys from analysis could call up any minute. He glares at me a moment, then a hint of resignation crosses his face, telling me that he's not going to fight it this time. I might actually be wearing him down.

"I thought you should know, I just heard from the District Attorney. James Hunter has changed his plea to guilty."

For a second I'm thrown off-balance. "What?" I'm genuinely stunned, so much that I steady myself on the chair in front of me. Hunter was the man who has plagued my life for the past six months, starting when he ordered the death of his son and my husband, Matt. After that it was a cat-and-mouse game with him involving his other son and wife, and an international assassin. Amazingly, I was the only one left standing when it was all said and done. But from my conversations with him I'd assumed he'd always pronounce his innocence. I figured he'd force a trial, which would mean I'd have had to go on the stand and testify. Something I hadn't even allowed myself to begin thinking about. But by changing his plea, he's negated all of that.

"To all the charges?" I ask.

He nods. "Just came through this morning."

"Then…" It takes me a moment to mentally process what this means. "It's over. It's all over."

Wallace gives me another nod, this time his features softening, but only by an infinitesimal amount. Zara thinks I'm cold and closed off? This man is the world champion. "He'll be going in front of a federal judge in a few days for his sentence."

"That's quick," I say.

"High profile case, and the D.A. wants this wrapped up as soon as possible. New president, new administration, new everything. The director understands his job is on the line and doesn't want this hanging over their heads." Personally, I try to stay out of politics as much as I can. Though, seeing as Congress is the one that is ultimately in charge of our division, that's not always possible.

I'm not sure what to say. "Thank you for letting me know."

Wallace levels his gaze at me. "Slate, I want you taking the next two weeks off."

It takes me a second to realize what he's said. My mind is

buzzing with the consequences of Hunter's plea change. "I'm sorry?"

He removes his trademark glasses and folds his hands on the desk in front of him. I've never seen him without them. "This isn't a suggestion. It's an order. You've been going full throttle ever since I took this position."

"I don't consider desk duty full throttle," I say, though I regret it the moment the words leave my lips. Neither of us has mentioned my almost-transfer a few months ago.

He bristles, but when he speaks again, his voice is still even without any anger or malice. "And from what I understand, you've been maintaining that level ever since you came back to duty after the loss of your husband."

I stiffen, unsure how to respond.

"You need a break, Slate. As much as you don't want to admit it."

"Is now really the best time?" I ask. "We have all these new cases coming in."

He takes a deep breath, as if he's steadying himself. "Believe it or not, I know what I'm talking about. You should know better than anyone that you can't burn this hot and not flame out. When was the last time you took any leave?"

I open my mouth to answer, but it takes me a minute to come up with the answer. "Maybe a year…" When I was almost fired for nearly blowing a huge case…right after Matt died.

He nods. "It's been long enough. You've accrued the time, and you're taking it. I've already cleared it with Dr. Frost."

"But I'm in the middle of this embezzlement case," I tell him. "I can't just drop everything."

"We'll manage," he says. "We need you at your sharpest, not worn down to the bone because you haven't taken a break. I don't want to see you back in this office before MLK Jr. day."

My heart is already picking up the pace. "But sir——"

"No butts. Take the rest of the day to note your progress on your current cases, then head home. Go on a vacation, get out of town for a while. You don't need to be here for the sentencing. Hasn't Hunter interfered with your life enough?"

His last sentence hits me, and I realize that man has been the architect of everything bad that's happened to me in the past year. As much as I'd love to put him behind me, I'm not sure I can miss the sentencing. I want to see the look on his face when he learns how long he's going to be in prison. And then I never want to see his face ever again.

But at the same time I see what Wallace is doing. He doesn't want me here to cause the Bureau any problems—he thinks I'm too emotionally compromised to handle it.

"You sure you don't have another killer you need me to chase down?" I shoot him half a smile, so he'll think I'm joking, but I'm really not. Getting through the holiday season without Matt was hard enough, but thankfully I had work to keep me busy. But these weeks that come after it, when all the lights have been taken down and everyone is just trying to survive until spring...how am I supposed to deal with that?

"Leave me a detailed report, you can email it if you need to. Then go." I can see there's no changing his mind. I head for the door. "And Slate," he says. "If I see you back in this office before I see the Peace Walk down Pennsylvania, you'll be on suspension. Clear?"

"Clear," I say, resigned to my fate.

I trudge out of the room and head back to my desk, shooting Zara a look. "What is it?" she asks.

"Wallace...he—Hunter..." There's so much I can't even find the words to explain.

"Hey," she says, coming around her desk, taking hold of me. "It's okay."

I give her the rundown of everything Wallace just laid on me. I think the revelation about Hunter is hitting me harder than I expected.

"A break will do you good," she whispers while still holding me by the side. "Believe it or not, this is good news."

That's easy for her to say. But every time I'm alone all I can feel are the ghosts of everyone and everything I've lost. I'm not sure how I'm going to handle not being able to focus on work for two weeks.

"Emily!" We both turn to see Liam rushing over. His eyes are wide. "I just heard back from the guys in analysis. Your results are in."

"Oh, right," Zara says, giving me a sheepish smile as she releases me. "Guess who called while you were in with Wallace?"

Chapter Two

"THERE SHE IS, THE LEGEND HERSELF." I can't help but smile
as I enter the FBI's crime lab in Quantico. It was an hour
drive down here, but when I called down to get the results
from my submission, I was told to come in personally. The
crime lab is notorious for taking a while to fulfill requests
seeing as what they do can't be rushed. It doesn't matter how
many people they hire for these positions, sometimes the work
just takes time. It's been almost three full weeks since we made
the initial submission.

The man before me is in his mid to late fifties, clean-
shaven and wearing a white coat with a purple bow tie as the
only hint of color anywhere on his person. I've heard of John
Dyer, PhD. before, but I've never had the pleasure of meeting
him. He's probably the FBI's best analyst regarding handwriting and fingerprints, and I only just learned that he took
on this project personally when it came through the pipeline.

I hold out my hand. "Dr. Dyer, it's a pleasure to finally
meet you in person."

"The pleasure is all mine Agent Slate," he says, taking my
hand. "Tell me, how many cases have you sent my way since
you began your career here?"

"I'm not sure," I say. "I'd have to check." Dyer is one of those people who automatically puts you at ease. He's relaxed, easy to talk to, and has a stellar reputation in the Bureau. I'm glad Hunter's corruption didn't reach down this far. Though just thinking of the man makes me remember I don't have to worry about him anymore, which is strange to say the least.

"I'll tell you." Dyer shoots me a wide smile. "Exactly four. Most agents that have been with the Bureau have sent me dozens of cases by now. But not you. You're something of a rarity around here. Word of your exploits still reach us though." He shoots Liam a wink.

I feel my cheeks redden. "I'm not sure what to say."

He produces a big smile. "It's not a condemnation at all. You're out there, doing the hard work. I have to say that we're all very proud of you down here at the lab. You and Agent Foley both."

"Thank you," I say. So much praise…I'm not sure what to do with all of it. Though I know he means well, I just don't do great responding to things like this. I turn to my right. "I assume you know Agent Liam Coll? He just joined the Bureau a few months ago from Stillwater."

Dyer holds out his hand. "Coll, good to meet you in person. We've had a few conversations over the phone and email, though I've always wondered what you looked like." Dyer is a bit of an eccentric, I'm learning.

"You too, sir," he says, though his face reddens when he realizes what he's said.

"Sir, ha! No one around here calls me that. Though I appreciate the sentiment." Dyer turns back to me. "The reason I took on your request personally was because we receive so few from you, Agent Slate. Most of my days consist of signature comparisons to make sure people haven't forged documents. Your request was a welcome reprieve."

"Glad to hear it. But you could have emailed me. I don't want to waste your time—"

"Nonsense," he says. "It's no waste. The results are…well, they're results. It's better if I can talk you through them in person."

I exchange a glance with Liam. "Is that bad?"

"Depends on how you look at it. Come with me," he says, leading me through the crime lab. It's been years since I've been down to the lab. Though Liam just completed his training across the way not that long ago. Dyer takes us through a few different areas where people look up, acknowledging him as he passes. He gives a friendly wave in return.

Finally, we reach what I assume is one of the analysis labs. There are six different stations, each with equipment I couldn't even begin to understand. But the place resembles a mad scientist's workspace with glass devices and metal trundle arms everywhere. Two other people are working on projects of their own, each of them using large magnifying glasses mounted on a gimble.

Dyer leads us over to the long table at the end of the room. It's well-lit and covered in a dozen different instruments. "Sometimes the old ways are the best ways," he says, removing what I recognize to be the letter I received from a manilla envelope. There's a small tear in the top of the letter where I almost tore it in half before throwing it away. Sometimes I can be too impulsive for my own good.

"I took the liberty of copying all the samples you sent us of your mother's handwriting for records," he says, removing another set of documents from a separate folder. "But these are the originals. You're welcome to have them back after I show you what we've found."

Dyer takes one of the real documents from my mother, which happens to be a note she wrote me when I was eleven. It was little more than a note telling me she was going out to the store and would be back soon, and somehow it never got thrown away. After she died, I made sure to keep it in a safe place. I wanted to have everything I could have of hers at the time. I remember finding one of her hairs months later, just lying there, on her table in the bedroom. I grabbed a plastic baggie and sealed it inside. Maybe that was weird. But grief does weird things to people.

Placing the note under one of the two magnifying glasses beside each other, Dyer slots in the letter I received under the other glass. He then offers me the seat so I can take a look for myself. "Most of what we're looking for in handwriting comparison is consistency. Obviously, no one is going to write every letter the same way every time. And usually, especially now in the digital age, handwriting tends to change over time. As people use it less and less, their handwriting tends to get worse and worse as they get older. But I digress." It's easy to tell this is a subject that excites him, just hearing him speak of it tells me this man is definitely in the right job.

"It's not an exact science. And there are plenty of ways people can try to trip us up and forge handwriting. Have you ever heard of Konrad Kujau?"

Both Liam and I shake our heads.

"Well, look him up sometime. Fascinating stuff. But for our purposes, just be aware that sometimes forgeries slip through. We've come a long way in analysis, but it will never be perfect." He points to the two samples under the magnifying glasses. "What we're looking for here is letter form, which will be how the person shapes the letters; line form, which is how much pressure the writer places when writing, as well as the speed at which they write, and finally, formatting. The space between the words, letters; how the writer structures their margins and whatnot. Look here." He uses a long black stick with a sharp point on the end to indicate a lowercase "A" on the letter I received. "You can see the curve of the letter, and how much pressure was used. Now look at this." He indicates an "A" on my mother's note. "See the darkness of the lines? How the shape is nearly identical?"

I nod. "So does that mean it's genuine?"

"That's just one letter. Take a look at a few more. See any differences?"

I take a few minutes looking over the two samples, going back and forth between each one while Liam looks over my shoulder. "The 'l's' don't look quite right. And this one 'g' is different."

"Not a bad eye, Agent," Dyer says. "Some of that can be explained away. The writer could have been in a hurry, or under a great deal of stress. What I want to point out by showing you this is that if this is a forgery, it's a good one. About ninety percent of the documents match, across multiple samples."

"So that means there's a ten percent chance my mother *didn't* write this?" I ask.

He winces. "I'm not sure if I'd say that. All I can tell you is there's a chance the same person wrote both of these samples. I can't say that for sure because like I said, this isn't an exact science. Ink doesn't carry DNA we can analyze, unfortunately. It's possible a skilled forger could have created this one, but they would have needed access to your mother's handwriting in order to study and practice. It's not unheard of."

I allow a frustrated breath to escape my lips. I was hoping the crime lab could give me an answer one way or another, but it doesn't seem like that's going to happen. "Thanks anyway. I appreciate you taking the time to look."

Dyer gathers up all the documents again, taking care to slip each of them in their own envelopes. He then hands them back to me. "It was my pleasure. And I have to admit this was indulgent on my part. I've been wanting to meet you for some time. I'm glad I finally had the chance. If you ever have any other projects that need our attention, we're at your service." He holds out his hand and I shake it again.

"Thank you. I'll be in touch."

Liam takes a moment to thank him as well before we head back out.

"He was nice," Liam says, with only a hint of sarcasm in his voice.

"Go ahead, say it," I grumble as we make our way back through the lab.

"I think you have a fan club." He's trying to wipe the smile from his face and failing miserably.

"We don't need to go that far," I say. Though I was surprised at the response from Dyer. Maybe they are just really bored down here and were happy to finally look at something that wasn't fraud or embezzlement.

Once we're back outside, the late-day winter sun nearly blinds me and I have to fumble the inside of my pocket for my sunglasses, slipping them on. In the process I drop one of the envelopes, but Liam snatches it from midair before it can land on the wet ground.

"Okay, Jason Bourne," I tease as he hands it back to me.

"What can I say? I have a secret set of skills no one knows about." He shoots me a wink.

"Good, cause we're going to need them if I'm ever going to figure out what this is all about."

We get back to the car and he pauses after opening the driver's side door, looking over the roof of the car at me. "What are you thinking?"

I toss the documents into the backseat. "That this is still a forgery, but it's one by someone who knew my mother well enough to copy her handwriting. Like he said. They have access to things of hers—something that allowed them to practice."

"Who would want to do that?" he asks.

I shake my head. "I have no idea. And unfortunately, I don't think we're going to find the answers we need here."

He screws up his face. "What do you want to do?"

"I don't know, but according to Wallace I can't do it at the office."

"Em," he says, his voice softening. "Taking time off isn't a bad thing. Why don't we go somewhere? Get out of D.C.?"

"Can you even do that?" I ask. "I'm pretty sure Wallace wants all hands on deck, especially with me out of commission."

He shrugs. "Let me at least check with him. Can't hurt."

I shake my head. "Yes, it can. If he feels like you're slacking off this early in your career, he could mark that against you. If it was Janice I'd say go for it. But this is Wallace we're talking about." I sigh. "I'll just stick around, take Timber to the park on the days it isn't frigid out there. Maybe Zara can introduce me to some video games or something."

"Em—," Liam says, but I stop him before he can get started. He knows when he's lost the battle.

"C'mon," I say, getting in the car. "I just want to get home."

I zone out the whole way there, my mind wandering from one topic to another, all of them surrounding my mother in some way or another. Before I know it, we're home and I can't remember the trip at all.

"I'll grab your mail," Liam says as I head for the door. "You get settled."

"Thanks." I head up the stairs and as soon as I slip my key in the slot I can already hear Timber on the other side of the door, panting excessively. He practically bursts through the door to welcome me and I have to give him a full rubdown before he'll stop spinning. I toss my things on the counter and check the note from Tess, the dog sitter.

"Looks like you were a good boy today, as always," I say, hanging my coat on the back of one of the stools along the counter. "As if you'd ever be anything else."

I'm just slipping my shoes off when Liam comes in, though his face is paler than normal and his features are drawn. "What's wrong?" I ask, suddenly on edge.

He holds up a single envelope from the mail. "It's another one."

Chapter Three

WHILE LIAM WORKS ON DINNER, I find myself in my bedroom, going through boxes of my old things. On my bed Timber watches me intently. I haven't pulled any of this out since before Matt died; it all ended up getting packed away and stored when I moved here, and it's been in the back of my closet ever since. But when I needed actual handwriting samples from my mother, I ended up cracking the seal. But now that another letter has arrived, I decided I need to go back and look for anything that could give me a clue as to what these letters are about.

The second letter sits off to my side. My initial reaction had been to burn it, but I'd taken it from him after pulling on a pair of gloves, even though I knew there wouldn't be any prints on it. Together Liam and I opened it carefully, inspecting the short note. Like the first one, it was brief and cryptic:

Precious Emily,
You don't know the pain I've carried around all

these years. Pain that could have been prevented.
If only they had listened.
— Mom

I have to admit I'm a bit unnerved by its appearance. The first had arrived via courier, this one seems to have been delivered with the regular mail. Now that whoever is sending these knows they're coming to the right place, they're not being as careful. I'll take this in for prints, but I'm sure that like the first letter it will be clean. Unless the sender has made a mistake somewhere which, is the only way I'm going to find out who is sending these things at this rate.

I take a deep, calming breath and turn my attention back to the pile in front of me.

I've never taken the time to organize these pictures, but since I seem to have nothing but time on my hands, I've decided not to put it off any longer. Maybe they can give me some indication of who could be doing this to me. Ideally, I'd like to scan them into my computer for safekeeping but, let's be real, that won't ever happen. Best I can do is slot them into smaller boxes and label them so I can access them easily when I need to. I doubt this is going to be the last letter I receive.

It's funny, almost all of the pictures I own are from before Mom died in oh-four. I guess either we just stopped taking them or everyone got digital cameras that year for Christmas and physical photos stopped being a thing.

Either way, I pick up a picture from a trip the three of us took to Williamsburg. It was in the middle of summer, in a place that likes to pride itself on authenticity—hence no air conditioners. It's easy enough to see the frustration on Mom's face. Her long, black hair is pulled back into a messy pony and sweat runs down her cheeks under the visor. Dad, however, looks pleased as a peach. He's got a big grin on his face, his moustache which would later turn full gray still a dark brown to match his sideburns. His arm around her and both of them with their hands on my shoulders. I was only nine at the time, and barely reached their torsos. My hair was a lot longer then, I remember it being a point of contention between me and Mom. How I complained about what a pain in the ass it was all the time, but she insisted I'd appreciate it later. I never quite understood that since hair keeps growing, but now I don't mind it longer.

It was a fun trip, from what I remember. Despite the heat, we had a good time. It was often like that, the three of us. I was always surprised my parents never had another kid, but they'd always joke I was more than enough of a handful and if they had another one they'd have to find a third parent to take care of them. I guess that's all they knew how to handle, seeing as Mom was an only child as well. Dad had a brother, but he was older and died in the war before Dad was out of high school. So I guess when the two of them found each other, they were effectively only children themselves.

I find myself staring at the pictures of Mom over and over again. I don't really have a good one of her handy. It's that digital photo thing again—there are no pictures of my mother on the cloud. Pulling my phone out, I snap a few images of the pictures in front of me, saving them in a new folder in my photo albums. Surprisingly, I feel a little better.

I look over at the files I've brought back from Dr. Dyer and the analysis lab. I understand they can't give me an answer with a hundred percent accuracy, but at the same time, I'm disappointed. I had hoped giving the letter to the lab would at least give me an answer, but all it's told me is whoever is impersonating my mother is doing a damn good job of it.

I stare at another picture of her. She's the only one in the picture, standing in front of a lake somewhere. She's younger, probably close to my age now. I would have only been a year or two old. And though there's a smile on her face, she looks almost…sad. Maybe I'm reading too much into it, but she looks…wistful, longing, in some strange way. I flip the picture over but all I see on the back is the date. September '93. Yep, little Emily would have been just under a year at that point. I wonder why I'm not in the photo. Or Dad. She's just…alone.

"Hey, Em, dinner's ready," Liam calls from the kitchen.

I extricate myself from the pile, staring at the mess I've made. I'll deal with this later—it's too much to try and pack up right now. As soon as I'm up, Timber's off the bed, around the corner and sure to be right under Liam. I think that dog loves food more than anything else.

"Smells delicious." Garlic, saffron, combined with rich butter and an aroma I can't place but makes my mouth water. It all makes me think Liam has gone all out this evening.

"Take a seat," he says, indicating the breakfast nook table that's normally covered in my crap from work. He's cleaned it off, found candles from *somewhere*, and set two places, complete with wine glasses.

"What's all this?" I ask.

He comes over, pulling my chair out for me and waiting for me to sit down before he dramatically unfurls a napkin, placing it in my lap. "Everyone deserves to have a good meal after a hard day."

"You really didn't have to go to all this trouble—" I begin before he shushes me with a kiss that sends a tingle down my entire body.

"Yes, I did," he whispers. "You needed it."

"Maybe we should just skip dinner," I whisper back.

"No way. I've got this thing to the perfect temperature. It's now or never." He heads back into the kitchen with a towel over his shoulder as he plates the food. Before Liam came into my life, I cooked twice a year. Christmas and Thanksgiving. And that's if you count making a green bean casserole as cooking. But ever since we began dating, he's been spoiling the crap out of me with delicious food. I don't even care that it's all going to my waist. Okay, yes I do, but it's almost worth it.

Seeing as I don't have anything to do for two weeks I can add in some extra cardio time.

He sets the plate down in front of me and I have to physically stop the drool from leaking out of my mouth.

"Pan-roasted pork loin with potatoes and garlic, with a side of broccoli and for dessert, an apple pie crumble," he says proudly.

"Where did you—*when* did you get all of this?" I ask.

"I ran down to the corner market while you were in the bedroom," he says. "It's only a five minute walk."

"Really?" I ask. I didn't even know that place existed. "I didn't realize I'd been in there that long." I pull out my phone, looking at the time again. I guess I was. "Thank you. This looks, and smells, incredible."

He takes an exaggerated bow. "Enjoy."

Timber has taken up his position right beside me, a big grin on his face as his tongue is out of his mouth and flopped over to the side. "No way," I tell him. "This is too rich for you."

"Ah, but we must not forget," Liam says, returning to the kitchen and coming back with a small bowl of what look like mashed potatoes. "Bland, but messy." He sets the bowl down and Timber looks at me a second before I motion for him to go ahead. In seconds he's destroyed the bowl, licking it entirely clean before returning to my side and looking back up at me.

I can't help but laugh at the speed with which he dispatched those potatoes. "Maybe if you're good you'll get another treat," I tell him.

Liam takes his seat across from me and lights the candles on the table. "Liam, really. Thank you. This is all too much."

He shrugs. "Well, I figured with Wallace up your ass combined with the news—or lack thereof out of Quantico you kinda needed it."

"Yeah," I say, "I kinda did." I don't waste any time cutting into the loin, and as soon as it hits my mouth there's an explosion of flavor like nothing else I've ever tasted before. I want to savor it, but it's so good I find myself trying to get one of everything on my fork as fast as possible. It doesn't take me long to clean my own plate.

I sit back, sated and full. "My compliments to the chef."

"Compliments received and accepted." He tosses his napkin at me. "But you gotta do the dishes."

I toss the napkin back. "What happened to spoiling me after a hard day?"

"Can't let you get too soft. First it starts with gourmet meals. If I keep this up, you'll be walking around in Louboutin's with a Prada bag in your hands."

I snort, almost spilling the wine I'm sipping on. Some of it goes up my nose. "Yeah, in Zara's dreams." I take a deep breath and look around. As good as the food was, it doesn't solve my main problem. What the hell am I going to do with myself for two weeks? Maybe Liam is right—maybe it would be good to get out of town for—

Before I can finish the thought my phone buzzes, indicating an incoming call. I grab it off the counter. And while I don't recognize the number, I do recognize the area code. "Hello?"

"Is this Emily Slate?" a gruff voice asks.

"This is, who am I speaking with?"

"This is Captain Reyes with the Fernview Police. We'd like a word with you."

"What kind of word?" I ask.

The captain pauses for a moment. "Are you still local— here in Fernview?" he asks. Liam mouths *who is it?*

The police in my old hometown, I mouth back. "I'm in D.C., why?"

"Would you mind coming down for an interview? We've got some questions for you." He's being cagey, like I would be if I was interested in speaking with a witness…or a suspect.

"Regarding what?" I ask.

"I'm not ready to speak about that over the phone, ma'am. But there is something we need to have cleared up here. If you wouldn't mind coming down, I'm sure we could be done in under an hour."

"Captain, this seems highly irregular," I tell him.

"I'm aware, which was why I waited until today to call you. I figured with the weekend we'd have a better chance of speaking with you in person." *Man, what is it with everyone needing to see me in person all of a sudden? Doesn't anyone send emails anymore?*

"I don't know," I tell him. "It's a four-hour drive one way."

"I'm aware, Ms. Slate. But like I said, this is of some urgency."

I let out a frustrated breath, while Liam looks on, concerned. It's almost nine p.m. The captain sure has picked one hell of a time to come calling. "Let me think about it. Can I call you back at this number?"

"I'd appreciate it, Ms. Slate," he replies.

I hang up, then give Liam the short of the call. He stares at me a minute, thinking. "I don't know, sounds…odd. Why not just tell you what he wants on the phone?"

I shake my head. "It's obviously something he wants kept under wraps. Which means whatever it is hasn't hit the media yet." Despite that, I google my hometown anyway, looking for anything out of the ordinary. But the news stories are all mundane.

"Well, what else do you have to do?"

"Hmm?" I ask, looking up.

"You've got all this time. What else are you going to do?" he asks. "Might be a good chance to get out of town for a little while. Visit some old friends. Let's face it, being here has been…stressful." I know he's thinking about the second letter.

I glare at him under hooded eyes. "In all the time you've known me, have I ever talked about my hometown?"

"Umm…" he says, screwing up his face.

"Yeah, I'm not big on going back there." I take another sip of wine.

"Bad memories?"

"Bad everything. All I ever wanted to do was get away from that place. And I finally did. I got out of there as soon as I could, went to college, applied to the FBI and started my life here. The only time I ever went back was for Dad's funeral."

"Okay. Just a thought. But I'll warn you now, it's beefaroni tomorrow night. I can't make this kind of masterpiece every day." He gets up to start washing dishes.

I smile. "I thought I was on dish duty."

"Eh, I like cleaning."

"I don't know what I did to curry favor with the gods in my past life, but whatever it was, I need to do it again," I say, gathering up my own dishes to help him. We clean everything quickly, then I practically pull him to the bedroom, where I have to shove the pile of pictures to the side, effectively destroying what progress I'd made on them. Oh well, it's worth it, considering the vigor with which both of us perform. I swear Liam's cooking is like an aphrodisiac.

Usually I'm zonked after sex, but I can't seem to relax my mind. Liam falls asleep almost immediately, but I just lie there, staring up at the ceiling. Finally, I get up and head back into the kitchen, rummaging for leftovers. Timber follows dutifully along and I remember I still need to take him out, despite the fact it's twenty degrees out there.

Grumbling, I pull on my big coat and slip on some boots, taking him out into the night air. It's crisp, and strikes at my lungs, causing me to take deep breaths. Why would the captain want to speak with *me*? What could be of such importance and secrecy that he calls me at nine on a Friday night, asking me to make the drive down to my hometown?

As Timber and I get back inside and I shrug the coat off again, I realize my mind isn't going to let this go. Thinking back to the pile of old pictures on the floor, I realize it offers a good opportunity at the same time. Going back to my hometown might give me the chance to investigate these letters a bit more. I know it's a long shot, but if I'm going to find out who sent them, the place I'd probably start would be the place I grew up. Where I knew Mom the best. Maybe once I see what the captain wants I can go speak to some of my parents' old friends, see if anyone else knows anything about this.

I retrieve my phone from the bedside table and return to the living room so I don't wake Liam. It's almost eleven, but I call the number back anyway.

He answers on the first ring. "Ms. Slate?"

"Captain Reyes. I've thought it over," I say. "I'll be there tomorrow."

Chapter Four

AFTER A QUICK BREAKFAST, I'm on the road before eight. I don't want this to take any longer than necessary though I doubt I'll drive all the way back tonight. It's going to take me a little time to speak with the people in town and I'm hoping whatever Captain Reyes wants won't take more than an hour or so. Still, there's a little prickle on the back of my neck about the whole situation. I don't like going into a situation blind, but at the same time, how bad can it be? It's *Fernview*, not L.A. The most exciting thing to happen there was that year half the town flooded from that hurricane.

About an hour into the drive, I call Zara, mostly because I'm bored.

"Helloooo," she says in that annoyingly happy way she always does.

"Morning," I reply. "I wanted to give you a heads-up. I'll be out of town for at least a day or two."

"Ooo, that sounds fun," she says. "You and Liam booked a romantic getaway? Let me guess, a log cabin halfway up a mountain where no one can hear you guys grunting and grinding all day long."

"No, good guess, though. I'm heading back to Fernview

for the day. I got a weird call last night from a police captain down there. He wants to speak with me in person about something."

"That is weird. Why can't he just ask you over the phone?"

"That's what I said. But he's insistent we only speak in person."

She's silent for a moment. "Do you think he knows you work for the FBI?"

"Why else would he call me specifically?"

"I dunno. When's the last time you even spoke to anyone you grew up with?"

I take a minute to think. It's been a while. A long while. "I'm not sure. I can't even remember who that could have been. I mean...I see what some of them are doing on social media, but for the most part I've left that part of my life in the past."

"Then this isn't a happy trip," she says.

"Not particularly, but I'm hoping I might be able to find out something about these letters." I give her a quick rundown of the results from the lab yesterday as well as the surprise that was waiting for me when we got home.

"I wish I could have gone with, but with all these extra cases piling up, I'll be lucky if I get a day off before Valentines."

Damn Wallace, why does he have to take me off the job now, when I'm needed the most? "I'd be there if I could, but our illustrious master has decreed I'll be canned if I show my face in the office."

"I wouldn't let him hear you call him that," she laughs. "What did Dr. Frost say?"

"I haven't spoken to him about it," I say. "I figured time off from the job meant time off from therapy as well."

She snorts. "You're gonna pay for that one when you get back."

"Probably. Hey, keep an eye on Liam and Timber while I'm gone, would you?"

"Sure, is everything okay between you guys?"

"Yeah, it's nothing like that. I just…I worry about Liam sometimes. He's always so intent on making sure I'm heard and being conscious of my feelings I'm afraid his problems could be lost in the shuffle. I just want to make sure he's not holding a bunch of stuff in." I put on my blinker and pull into the other lane, passing a slow truck in front of me.

"You know me," she says. "I'll just go up and ask him straight out."

"Z, that's not what I mean."

"Yeah, but wouldn't that fix the problem?" she asks. "Instead of all this dancing around?"

I purse my lips; despite the fact she can't see me. "He might just shut down or pretend like everything's fine. The goal is to get him to open up."

"Fiiine," she huffs. "He staying at your place while you're gone?"

"Yep, keeps me from having to pay the dog sitter extra for overnight."

"Well, have a good trip. You'll be back tomorrow?"

"That's the plan. And then maybe I can drag you away from work long enough to give you a break."

"Deal," she says. "Be safe."

"You too." I hang up and turn my attention back to the road. I know I shouldn't worry about Zara, but she's like a sister to me and I'm not sure I'd be able to handle it if anything happened to her. Not to mention the fact she's only been a Special Agent for six months and is already handling a large caseload. I know Wallace really believes in her; I just hope he's not putting more on her plate than she can handle all at once. Poor Liam is still assisting other agents and hasn't even received his own cases yet.

I take a deep breath and switch on one of my driving

playlists, though I tune out the music almost immediately. The drive down to central Virginia is neither remarkable nor pretty. This time of year, it's just a bunch of evergreens mixed with bare branch trees lining both sides of the road as far as the eye can see. Every now and again I'll pass a house or a turn-off that cuts through the middle of the highway, but it's a boring drive for the most part. The last time I came this way I was headed down to take care of all of Dad's affairs, including arranging the funeral. Being an only child meant everything fell to me, and since Dad wasn't particularly close with the rest of his family, I really had no one to help me out. Just a few of his friends or friends of the family who offered plates of food at the reception. It had been eerily similar to Mom's funeral, at least what I can remember of it. I was so shocked at the time I think I blocked most of it out, but I don't recall there being a big to-do about it. She was there one day, gone the next and by the end of the following week, it had all passed like nothing ever happened.

At least, that's how it seemed to everyone else. But my world had been shattered. I don't think I felt normal ever again, not in the same way. Eventually I had to learn to live with it, but I just remember wanting to shut everyone and everything out back then. It's part of the reason I wanted to get away from Fernview so soon—there were too many memories of Mom. It just seemed easier to start over with a blank slate somewhere else. Somewhere I didn't know anyone, where no one was aware of my past.

And then when Dad went it felt like I'd abandoned him; left him all alone in Fernview to die alone. I know that wasn't really the case, but it felt like it and I'd just written the whole place off. It was a small town, full of small people and I didn't belong there anymore.

After nearly four straight hours of driving, the little town finally comes into view. It's nestled into a small valley with a large lake off in the distance—ostensibly where everyone always spent their summer vacations. I've never been a fan of lakes. Oceans, yes. Lakes are too...enclosed.

The town itself isn't much bigger than twenty-thousand people and has a small downtown area, part of which is visible as I come in on the highway. The tallest spire is a church—the First Presbyterian of Fernview. Most of the town is rural, spreading out to farms and large swaths of nothing but trees.

The further I drive into the town, the more my memories begin to come to the forefront. Taking a joyride with some of my high school friends in an empty lot that's now part of a strip mall; the place where Mom used to take me when she got her hair cut and I'd have to sit and wait for her in the front office, the pool where we used to go swimming, all boarded up and empty from the looks of it. It seems Fernview has moved on, though I can't tell if it's for the better or not yet.

On a whim, and because I'm on this side of town, I decide to take a detour and drive past my old house instead of heading straight for the police station. Maybe it's because now that I'm finally here I'm feeling a bit more nostalgic than I have in years, or maybe it's because I just want to see what the current owners have done to the home I grew up in.

My old house sits at the end of a long, winding street about two miles long, and there's only one way in or out. Which gives me the opportunity to see the rest of the neighborhood and how it's changed over the past five years. Most of the houses around here were built in the fifties and sixties, and as far as I can tell, they haven't changed. Occasionally, I see where someone has sold off some extra land to stick another house in between its neighbors, but other than that it's all about as I remember it.

Finally, as I reach the bottom of a small hill and crest another, my old house comes into view. It's off to the right, a two-story brick colonial with a stone entrance. But before I even get a good look at the house I can tell something is wrong. Yellow caution tape surrounds the house and is strung across the driveway, keeping anyone from pulling in or out. Two police cruisers sit on either side of the driveway. I roll down my window and an officer from one of the cruisers approaches.

"Sorry, ma'am, you'll have to keep moving. We need to keep the street clear."

I don't hesitate in showing him my badge. "What's going on here?"

He eyes the badge a minute, then motions one of the other officers over. I immediately recognize him. Owen Tate, one of the star football players at my old high school and big time dickhead. He already looks like he's in a sour mood when he comes over to see what his buddy wants.

"She's with the FBI," the other officer tells Tate.

Tate looks at me a minute, then my badge. "Well, well, look who finally showed up," he says. "Captain's looking for you."

Chapter Five

"Tate," I say. "So nice to see you out of your shoulder pads. Now tell me what's going on here."

He shakes his head, a little smile on his lips. "Sorry, under orders not to discuss it with anyone, FBI or not."

"Dammit." I blow out a frustrated breath and pull my car behind the other cruiser before I get out. He's as hardheaded as he was back in high school. Nothing could ever be easy—no, he has to go and make things as difficult as possible. It's people like him that made me want to leave here in the first place.

"Look," I say, approaching them again. "I think I deserve some answers. Why all the caution tape? What happened here?"

He holds his hands up like he's innocent of all this. "Talk to Reyes. I'm not about to break his orders just because you tell me to."

"C'mon, Owen," I say. "I know you know this used to be my old house. I'm just looking for a straight answer."

"Do you want me to call it in?" the other officer asks.

"Call what in?"

Tate shakes his head. "Nah, I don't think Emily will be a

flight risk, since she's part of our magnanimous federal government." He turns back to me. "Though I would head down to the station if I were you. Captain's waiting."

"A *flight risk*?" I ask, incredulous. But he just wiggles his eyebrows at me before he turns and heads back to his squad car. I haven't seen Owen Tate in over ten years, but time hasn't been kind to him. What little hair he has left is already starting to go gray and the massive bags under his eyes tell me he's either working too hard or drinking too much. If this little encounter has told me anything, it's the latter, given what I know about him from high school.

Obviously I'm not going to get any answers here, but I linger a moment, looking at my old home. Other than the caution tape and a new coat of paint on all the non-brick areas, the house looks the same from the outside. It has a generous front yard, plenty large for young Emily to run around with no dangerous streets around where I could have been hurt. I think it was one of the reasons my parents bought this house, knowing I was on the way.

Finally, I get back in my car and make a U-turn at the end of the street where it hooks left and heads-up and around the block before circling back around farther on down the road. As I pass Tate and the other officer he shoots me a smug little wave. Did he *know* I was going to be here? He certainly didn't seem surprised to see me. I wonder how much Captain Reyes has told the rest of the troops.

Obviously more than he was willing to share with me.

I head back up the hill, but before I reach the crest I remember something and throw my car into reverse, backing back down until I'm in front of a house five units down from my own. Due to all the growth in the neighborhood between houses—probably another reason my parents wanted to move here, the seclusion—I'm positioned so Tate and the other officer can't see me. I park out in front of the small one-story white siding home, remembering it from my childhood. It doesn't look any different either.

As soon as I reach the front door I give the door a few taps, not the heavy knock Zara always gives me shit about. The last thing I want to do is scare the occupant inside to death.

A full minute later I hear a latch on the other side slide and the door opens to reveal a small, frail-looking woman in a wheelchair. She's wearing spectacles that remind me of Coke bottles but greets me with a wide smile. "Yes?"

"Mrs. Holloway?" I ask.

Her eyes perk up at my mention of her name. "Wait, Emily?" she asks. "I can't hardly believe that's you. Come in, come in." She wheels herself back out of the way, surprisingly adept with the wheelchair. I'm surprised to see her in it; her front steps don't have a ramp. "Close the door for me, would you?"

"I don't mean to intrude," I begin, closing the door and following her down the hallway. It's old hardwood and I can see the small tracks the wheelchair has made over the years as she's gone back and forth over them.

"It's no intrusion, I'm delighted to see you," she replies, wheeling herself into the living room. "How long have you been in town?" She indicates I take a seat on the pristine loveseat which is one of four different seating options in the room. It's just as I remember it as a kid. Everything has a pattern, and is some shade of pastel. Even the walls, which are covered in the same yellow wallpaper, though it's a little more faded now. Mrs. Holloway is about the same as well, except for the wheelchair. She always was the tiniest woman, which is why I liked her; she was the only adult I knew that was close to my size when I was little. To see her in the chair makes me wonder what must have happened. But just as I'm about to ask, she hoists herself out of it, keeping one hand on the furniture until she makes it to the loveseat opposite me. She still has some mobility after all.

"Um…I just got in not more than half an hour ago."

She adjusts her glasses. "Well, it's wonderful to see you again. I'm so sorry I missed your father's funeral. I'd just had my accident and it was difficult to get out of the house."

"What happened if you don't mind me asking?"

"The stupidest thing an old person can do," she says, half laughing. "I went down the stairs. But I missed a step and went *all* the way down, landed right in the basement on a broken hip. It hasn't been the same since. I tried getting around without that damn thing, but it just hurts too bad." She makes a motion to the wheelchair.

"I'm sorry to hear that," I say. "I don't blame you for not coming. But I do remember you sent flowers."

She gives me a wide smile. "You always were the nicest girl. Your parents did a good job with you, something I always reminded them of." She looks around me through a doorway which leads to her kitchen. "If you want something to eat or drink, help yourself. I'd get it for you, but the damn thing is acting up today."

"No, that's okay," I tell her. "Thank you, though. I wanted to know if you knew what was going on down at my old house. I caught Owen Tate and another officer down there guarding it."

"Oh, *that*," she says. "I guess you would be interested in it, seeing as you used to live there and all. I never thought you should have sold it. The people who moved in after you were so noisy. Thankfully they didn't stay very long, maybe ten years or so. Sold it to a nice family up from North Carolina. But you and your parents were always my favorites. Remember when you used to come around selling wrapping paper for your school? I'd always buy at least three rolls even though I never needed it. But you were just so *polite*, how could I not? I think it's probably still up in the crawlspace some-

44 · ALEX SIGMORE

where if you need some paper. I haven't wrapped a gift in
years."

"No, that's okay," I tell her, chuckling. I do remember
those days. Mrs. Holloway would always invite me in, give me
something tooth-meltingly sweet and listen to my pitch before
agreeing to buy more wrapping paper than she ever needed.
"You were always my best customer."

"I miss those days," she says. "Now most of the neighborhood kids have grown up and moved on. Just us old fogies left.
Though a nice young couple just moved into your old house
about a month ago."

I furrow my brow. "Wait, that's not the family from North
Carolina?"

She shakes her head. "No, it was the strangest thing. They
were just gone one day, like they hadn't even been here. Sign
was out front listing the house for sale again. Though it didn't
take long before someone snatched it up. It's a beautiful
home."

"Who lives there now?" I ask.

"I think their names are Pade? Or Parnell? I'm not really
sure, to be honest." She taps the side of her head a few times.
"It isn't what it used to be up here." She pauses a moment.
"Oh yes, you were asking about the police. Well, apparently
when that young couple went to do some renovations on their
home, they discovered a body."

I almost sputter. "I'm sorry, a *body*?"

She nods, leaning forward, conspiratorial. Mrs. Holloway
has always been known to have the inside information on
everything that goes on in this town, so I'm not surprised
she knows. It was why I decided to come here. "Word is
they found it in one of the walls as they were tearing it
down."

"But, but...that's..." How could that be possible? A body
in *my* house? How could I have not known about that? Did
Mom and Dad know? Just the thought of having lived there so

long with a body behind the walls is enough to make me shudder.

"I know, it's quite the event," Mrs. Holloway continues. "They're trying to keep a lid on it, but I heard from Burt McLean down the street that they've gotten the mayor involved. Things like this just don't happen in Fernview."

I sit back, the plastic on the loveseat crinkling under me. "Tell me about it. A *body*. Do you know anything else about it?"

She shakes her head. "I just know they've had someone on guard at the house ever since they found it."

"When was that?" I ask.

"Thursday, I believe," she replies. "It's been the most exciting thing to happen to this neighborhood since Marge Hetwood's home hair curler blew up," she says with glee.

"You're not wrong there, it certainly is exciting," I tell her. I'm reeling from the implications. No wonder the captain wanted to speak with me. He wants to know if I know anything about why it was back there, since I'm the only living person left in my family.

"I don't want to take up any more of your time," I tell her, getting up. "I really should be going."

"So soon?" she asks, the disappointment clear on her face. "Oh, well, I suppose a young woman like you doesn't need to be wasting her time with an old lady like me. You've grown so much it's hard for me not to think of you as a little girl anymore." She manages to maneuver herself back into her chair faster than I would have thought.

"Thank you for the visit," I tell her. "I'll be sure to stop back by before I leave."

"Oh, honey, you don't need to do that," she says, waving me off. "Don't worry about me, I've got everything I need here. That is, unless you just want some good old-fashioned gossip talk."

"Thank you, Mrs. Holloway, really." I take her hand, it's

frail and a bit cold, but she gives mine an appreciative squeeze.

"It was my pleasure, dear," she says as I reach the door. "I forgot to ask before you go, what are you doing these days?"

"Oh, I live up in D.C., working for the FBI."

Her face lights up. "You're kidding. My, your parents would be so proud of you."

I can't help but feel a prickle at my eyes. Neither of my parents ever got to see me become an agent, though Dad at least knew about my desire. One of the hardest days of my life was when I finally graduated and there was no one there to celebrate with.

"Thanks." I give her a big smile. "It was great seeing you, Mrs. Holloway."

"You too," she replies. "If you find yourself back this way, don't be a stranger."

I bid her one last goodbye then head back to my car. As easy as it would be to slip back into a sense of nostalgia about this place, I need to be firing on all cylinders. A body found in my old house. How long had it been there? And who put it there? I have a million and one questions.

Fortunately I know where I can go to find some answers.

Chapter Six

IT TAKES me less than ten minutes to get into Fernview's downtown and to the police station. On the way I called Liam and gave him the rundown of what's going on here. He reminded me not to go off on anyone until I had all the information, which was probably good advice. Sometimes I tend to jump the gun. But I'm not about to sit back and let them accuse me or my family of having anything to do with this. And I'm not running either. Reyes needs to give me the full story.

I don't waste any time getting out of the car and heading inside, noting the last time I was in this building was when Mom died. Dad had to come down to the station to answer a few questions and I remember insisting that I come with him, though he wanted to leave me with Mrs. Holloway or one of the other neighbors. I see now that I was probably scared he'd leave me too and I'd be all alone which was why I didn't want him out of my sight for those first few weeks after.

Inside it's much as I remember it, though it's strange seeing the place as an adult and mentally comparing it with all the police stations I've been in before. It's just another small-town police station, nothing really special about it. But when I was a kid, it was intimidating as hell. Though now, I'm able to reform the image in my mind. Instead of the stark and scary building I'd seen then, the image in my mind shifts and now I see it as just another building. It's funny—I hadn't thought about this place in years, and now to see it makes me feel silly for being frightened when I was a kid.

"I'm here to see Captain Reyes. I'm Emily Slate," I tell the officer on desk duty at the front. He nods and puts in a call through his headset.

"Just one minute, he'll be right out," he says.

I take a minute to prepare myself, while I try to look like I don't have a care in the world. No wonder Reyes called at nine p.m. He was hoping to throw me off a little, thinking I'd be more pliable on a Friday evening, maybe with a drink or two in me. He was betting on getting me down here, interrogating me rather than trying to ask questions over the phone or come up to see me in person. And the only reason it worked was because someone else happened to send me a letter out of the blue.

I've learned that coincidences are usually anything but. This *has* to have something to do with the letters, I'm sure of it.

"Ms. Slate?"

I turn to see a man in a captain's uniform come out. He's probably got about six inches on me, though he's relatively thin, his uniform hanging off him. His complexion is on the darker side, and he sports a black moustache that's trimmed neatly. Deep lines on his face tells me he's not new to this job. "Captain Reyes."

I extend my hand and he takes it, holding on for a second. "You're with the FBI?"

I nod. "I see you've spoken to Tate."

"He radioed in to let me know you were on your way," he says, taking a deep sigh. "Well, I guess this changes things."

"Expecting to interrogate me?" I ask and he finally lets go.

"*Interview,* Agent Slate. Nothing more."

"Strange way to ask for an interview," I tell him.

Finally, his face breaks into a smile. "Okay, you got me. I guess I can't get out of this one. Guilty as charged. We've had something of a situation develop here and I need some information from you. Though now my half-baked plan is out the window."

"I assume you mean the body."

If he's surprised, he doesn't show it. "Then you know already. Either you're very good at your job or I need to get my handcuffs." He says it like he's half joking, but I catch an undercurrent of seriousness there.

"The former. I spoke to one of my old neighbors. She filled me in since your officers wouldn't."

He visibly relaxes. "Sorry. Protocol, especially if you were a suspect. But I'm beginning to think you might have made that drive for nothing."

"Don't tell me you actually considered me a suspect," I say. "I was a child in that house."

He gives me a noncommittal shrug. "You never know. Parents can swear their children to secrecy. If the child is young and impressionable enough, they can keep that until their grave."

"Care to give me the details of the case?" I ask. "I do have almost five years experience with the Bureau."

He nods, motioning for me to follow. "Sure, as long as you don't mind sitting in one of our interview rooms."

"Wouldn't be my first time in one," I tell him.

He chuckles and leads me back through the security door. "How long have you been in Fernview?" I ask.

"About six years. My family moved here after a stint in Cincinnati, which, if you've ever been then you know. I was looking for a quieter place to raise my kids. When the position opened up, it seemed like a good opportunity. Been here ever since."

"Yeah, I guess it's a good place to raise kids," I say.

"You were born and raised here, weren't you?" he asks, holding open a door for me that says *Interview Two*.

"Yep. Moved to NoVA after high school."

"Didn't want to stay around?" he asks, his tone nonchalant.

"I just thought it was better to get out of town when I had the chance. I guess it felt like if I didn't get out when I did, I'd be stuck here forever," I admit.

"I understand that," he says. "I used to feel the same way when I was a kid. I think there's something about being young and wanting to explore the world that's inherent in all of us." He gestures to one of the chairs in the interview room and I take a seat.

"So, what can you tell me about the case? Do you have an ID on the body yet?"

He takes the seat across from me. Strangely, there is no file folder in his hand. I guess he really was planning on interrogating me. "This is not the kind of thing I was hoping to see when I came down here from Cincinnati." He looks like a man who hasn't slept in about two days, and given what I know about the situation, I wouldn't be surprised if that was actually the case. "I got the call Thursday afternoon; I was in the middle of signing off on some permits to close a road here in downtown for a birthday party if you can believe it."

"And you didn't expect to have to deal with the body," I say. "I know how that goes."

He shakes his head. "I still can't believe you're with the FBI. You don't look old enough to have been in the Bureau for very long."

"I hear that more than I care to. But I'm an experienced agent. And trust me when I tell you I've seen more than my fair share of these things."

He inclines his head toward me. "All right. Here's what we got. On Thursday afternoon Kim and David Page were in the middle of doing some home demolition for a new kitchen that they wanted to put in your old house. But when they went to demolish one of the walls David accidentally smashed into something soft with the sledgehammer. At first they couldn't figure out what was going on until he tore away more of the wall and saw the body all wrapped up in plastic and duct tape. Then they called me."

"Do you have a positive ID yet?" I ask.

"We do, it's Jessica Ashford." He pauses a moment to let the words sink in.

That's a name I haven't heard in a long time, and not one I expected to hear today. Jessica Ashford disappeared back in 1998 and was never heard from again. Something at the back of my neck tingles again. That thing warning me about coincidences. This can't be an accident.

"You know her?"

"She was my friend's sister," I say. "I mean, we weren't friends back then, back when Jessica disappeared, but we became friends later...after I learned about what happened."

"I read the original report," Reyes says. "Her parents filed it the day after she went missing, and an investigation was done. But not a very thorough one. The prevailing theory at the time was she was a runaway."

I nod. "That's what I remember hearing. But Judy, Jessica's sister, never believed it. She and I would talk for hours about what happened. Since I never knew Jessica I couldn't say, but Judy was sure she wouldn't have run away from home, and she wouldn't have left without telling her."

There's a knock at the door, and it opens before Reyes can say anything. Owen Tate sticks his big, bald head inside, glaring at me. "Captain," he says. "I thought you weren't going to begin the interrogation until later."

Reyes turns to him glaring. "She's in the FBI, she's not a suspect."

"Just because she's in the FBI doesn't mean that she

couldn't have had something to do with this," Tate says. "It would be a good cover."

"You can go back to your desk now, officer," Reyes says, his voice stern.

Tate shoots me another look before backing out of the room again and closing the door behind him.

"Sorry about him. He can be a good officer, when he hasn't been on a bender for the weekend. But help is hard to find in a town this small and sometimes you have to go with what you've got."

"It's fine," I say. "He and I never really got along well in high school anyway."

His eyebrows arch. "I didn't realize you two went to high school together," Reyes says.

"He was a few years ahead of me. But in a town like this pretty much everyone ends up knowing each other," I say.

Reyes chuckles. "I guess that's true." He pauses for a moment, looking down at the table, then back at me. "I hate to have to ask this, but I wouldn't be doing my job if I didn't. You don't know anything about Jessica's body in the house, do you?"

"No. I hope if I was going to hide a body, I'd be smarter than to hide it in my own home." I say it jokingly, but I'm not sure it comes across.

"And your parents couldn't have had anything to do with this either, right?"

I squint, trying to figure out the best way to answer this. Obviously, it's ludicrous to even suggest my parents had anything to do with hiding a dead body in our house. But since neither of them are around to defend themselves, I'll need to prove beyond the shadow of a doubt they couldn't have had anything to do with this. Otherwise Reyes will continue to consider them suspects, no matter what I say. Hell, he might even think *I'm* still a suspect. "Where was the body found exactly?"

Reyes pulls out his phone, scrolling through something on the screen. "The wall that was demolished was on the main floor, between the kitchen and the living room."

I sit back. "That wall must've been installed after we moved out of the house," I say. "As far as I remember, there wasn't a wall between the kitchen and the living room when we lived there."

Reyes scrolls through his phone some more. "And your family moved in in nineteen-ninety-two?"

I nod. "And we moved out in two-thousand five. After my mother died."

He gives me a look of sympathy. "I'm sorry to hear that." Though from the tone of his voice he doesn't sound very sorry. I'm sure he's had to say that more times than he can count, and at some point it just becomes automatic.

"If that's true, then that means she was placed in the home sometime after you moved out." He heaves a deep sigh. "I'm sorry to have wasted your time, Agent Slate. I had hoped you could shed some light on the situation."

"I wish I could help more," I say. "But it seems like it happened after my time."

Reyes stands, nodding. He reaches out his hand again and I take it, giving it a shake. "Thank you for coming all the way down here. I'm really sorry you made the drive. Turns out this could have been a phone call after all."

"That's all right, there's something I needed to take care of while I'm in town anyway."

"An FBI case?" he asks.

"No, just a personal matter."

He pauses another moment. "How long are you going to be around?"

"I'm not sure, why?"

"It would be helpful to have an FBI agent close by in case we needed some assistance," he says. "It isn't often we have to deal with something like this, your experience could be invaluable."

I have to admit, the prospect is intriguing. To find out what happened to Jessica all those years ago would be really satisfying. But I'm not here to work, I'm here to find out who sent those letters. "I'll probably be here for another day or so," I say. "You can call me if you absolutely need to." I reached into my pocket pulling out one of my business cards handing it to him.

"Thank you. I'll try not to bother you while you're on vacation. But in the event, something else comes up, it'll be nice to know you're close by."

I nod toward the door. "I'm not sure Tate would agree."

"Then it's a good thing he's not the captain."

Chapter Seven

Reyes leads me back down the hallway, going over the finer points of what it's like to be a police captain in Fernview today. I'm only halfway listening; my mind is still back on Jessica and the fact that they found her in my old house.

Jessica disappeared in early nineteen-ninety-eight, and we didn't move out of that house until halfway through two-thousand-five. Which means somehow she found her way back into Fernview long after she disappeared. Maybe she really was a runaway, and she tried to get back home. Or maybe she ran in with the wrong crowd or got herself into a bad situation that she couldn't get herself back out of. It's just strange to me, how she could've ended up only back here, of all places. I don't like the idea that someone was sadistic enough to put her in my old house and as much as I hate to admit it, I'm really starting to wonder if I should stick around and help out Reyes with the case.

I'm so deep in thought, that I almost run into a young woman with long, reddish hair, standing off to the side, speaking with another officer. "Excuse me," I say. "I wasn't watching where I was going."

She looks up and I notice her eyes are almost the same

color as mine, they're just a little bit deeper blue. "That's all right," she says. "We all get deep inside our own head sometimes." Her tone is soft but reassuring without much hint of emotion. I give her a terse smile, then continue along and follow Reyes back to the front of the station.

"Again, I'm very sorry to have brought you all the way down here Agent Slate," he says, his face reproachful. "If I'd realized you were in the FBI—well, we would have both saved ourselves a lot of trouble."

"I understand," I say, smiling. "It might be something I would've tried too, had I been in your position."

He holds up my card. "I'll be in touch if we have any new developments. But if you find yourself so inclined, feel free to offer any advice."

I give him a quick wave on my way out of the building. I need to call Liam and give him an update on what's going on. I'm sure he'll tell me I should stick around since apparently I have nothing better to do at home.

I would like to get a look at the inside of the house though, it's been so long since I've seen it. I wonder what's changed. Obviously, sometime after we moved out, new owners decided to erect a couple of new walls, which strikes me as a little odd. I assume Reyes is going to be talking to the next owners of the house since they're probably the ones who added the wall where they found her.

As I'm lost in thought I don't see the shape running up until she's almost on top of me. I take a few steps back instinctively feeling for my weapon only to realize that I don't have it on me. When I'm not on duty, I don't wear it. Something Dr. Forest suggested to help me get over the feeling of being watched by Camille all that time. His position was I needed to be able to let my defenses down and allow myself to experience the world. But that's not much comfort when someone is rushing you out of nowhere.

"Emily?"

It takes me a second after being startled, but as soon as I get a good look at her face, I recognize her immediately. "Judy?" Judy Ashford. Jessica's little sister and my one-time best friend. Before I know it, she pulls me into a hug.

"Oh, my god. What are you doing here?" she asks. "Are you here because of Jessica?"

"I am, actually," I say as she lets go. It's strange to see her now—I was just thinking of her, but as she looked when we were kids. Though, Judy looks almost exactly like she used to back in high school. Long dark hair pulled back into a high ponytail, a prominent chin, and dark green eyes. Her cheeks are a little hollower than I would've expected, and her eyes are tinged red, probably from crying. "I just finished speaking with Captain Reyes. Judy, I'm so sorry."

She nods, shuddering a little as her emotions take over. "I just can't believe it," she says. "Did he tell you where they found her?"

I nod. "I'm sure they'll find whoever did this, but I promise you we didn't have anything to do with it."

Confusion crosses her face. "Why would *you* have anything to do with it?"

I frown. "Because I used to live there."

She takes a step back. "That's right, I'd forgotten."

I nod. "That's what Reyes wanted to talk to me about. He wanted to know if I had any information that could help the case. But I told him that we moved out of that house right after Mom died, before that wall was ever built."

"Oh," she says. "I guess it makes sense he'd want to talk to you." Though there's the ghost of something on her face that wasn't there before. She's more on edge now; guarded. Any warmth that was there when she first saw me is gone. "That's kinda weird, isn't it? Both of us living in the same house?"

I furrow my brow. "What? No, you lived in that house over near Oakdale. I remember, we used to sit up in your room; you had a nice view of the houses below."

She shakes her head. "That was my mom's house. They were divorced, remember? My dad bought your old house after you guys moved out," she says.

That prickle on my neck is back. I almost state the obvious but stop myself in time. "How come I never knew that?" I ask instead, though my mind is firing on all cylinders. Jessica Ashford was buried in the walls of her father's home. *No coincidences.*

She shrugs, like it's no big deal. "It was a messy divorce. But the only times we ever hung out was when I was staying with Mom." She looks back at the police station. "Did they tell you anything? Do they have any suspects?"

I shake my head, trying not to interrogate her myself on the spot. "They didn't give me any specifics, just wanted to ask about when I lived there. Though Owen Tate wasn't too happy to see me."

She lets out a small laugh, but it's forced. "No, he wouldn't be." She pauses, as if searching for words to fill the awkwardness growing between us. "What are you doing nowadays? I don't even know where you live."

"I'm up in D.C.," I say. "Working for the FBI."

Her eyes go wide. "Really? But...they didn't call you down here to help on the case?"

I shake my head. "When they called, they didn't even know I was with the Bureau. Reyes was treating me like a suspect."

"Huh," she says, thinking. "They brought me in yesterday. I was in there for probably an hour with my dad. I think it wore him out too much, I had to take him back home." Her attention is split—I can tell she's thinking about something else while trying to hold on to the conversation. It's something she used to do when we were kids too.

"How is your dad?" I ask. "Still fiery as ever?"

That brings her back and she shakes her head. "No, he's calmed down in the past few years. I think when Jessica never came back it began to take a toll on him. And I wasn't enough to keep him going."

"Jude, that's not true," I say. "Your dad loved you."

She gives me a sardonic smile. "Not as much as he loves his first daughter, apparently." She looks at the station again. "Anyway, I've got to run. I wanted to check with Reyes to see if there are any updates on the case. Are you headed back to D.C.?"

"I…um…yeah, probably tomorrow," I tell her.

She leans in and gives me another quick hug. "Well, great seeing you. Be safe." She heads off, leaving me alone on the sidewalk and I'm struck by how abrupt that was.

I can't believe I didn't know Judy lived in that house after we did. Or, at least, she lived there during the times she wasn't staying with her mom. Maybe I did know and I blocked it out; I remember being so glad to be out of that house and getting the chance to start over in a new place without all the memories of Mom everywhere.

Heading back to the car, I speed dial Liam. "Yello," he says after the first ring.

I give him the full rundown of the story, including the part about Jessica being returned to the home where her father and sister were living.

"Well, that's weird," Liam says. His voice is a little distant and I can tell he's propped the phone between his ear and his shoulder.

"Tell me about it. Imagine finding out the sibling you thought ran away had been in your house all along." Something about that bothers me. Whoever killed and wrapped her didn't take her back to the home she grew up in. No, they made sure she was in the same house with her family. Does that mean she had been buried in her old home and moved? Or did she die later, and had been placed in my old house because it was convenient? My mind is a tornado trying to figure out what could have happened.

"It's like something out of a horror movie," he replies. "So are you going to stay and help?"

I purse my lips. "I don't think so. I'm here to find out who sent these letters, not solve some cold case from fifteen years ago."

"Yeah, but it's *your* house, Em. You've got a personal stake in this."

"Not anymore. It stopped being my house after Mom died. It hasn't been mine for fifteen years."

"If you say so. Any luck on finding out who sent the letters?"

"I haven't even had a chance to look yet, I've been at the police station all afternoon."

"Got any ideas of where to start?" he asks.

"I guess I'll check in with some of Mom's old friends. If anyone knows anything, they should. That is, if I can find anyone." I wait for him to respond, but he doesn't say anything. "How are things up there?"

"Busy as always, I came in early this morning, and don't worry, I made sure Tess is scheduled to check on Timber if I'm not back by at least three—which, given the mountain of work Wallace has thrown at me today—doesn't look likely."

I chuckle. Maybe I should be grateful Wallace insisted I take some time off. "Anything I can help with?"

"Seems to me like you have your hands full down there." Grumbling, I utter something under my breath I'm sure he won't catch. "Em, did you consider this whole case might have something to do with those letters?"

"It was my first thought as soon as I saw the cops surrounding the house," I tell him.

"Then why are you fighting this so hard?"

I let out a long breath. "Because it's *Fernview*. I don't like being here. It feels like a step in the wrong direction."

"It's not like you're moving back there forever. Find a hotel, set up shop, and do what you do best. Investigate.

Everything will be fine here. I promise not to burn your apartment down while you're away."

"Awfully bold of you to assume you're allowed to stay," I tease.

"I suppose I could just kidnap your dog and keep him at my place," he shoots back.

I roll my eyes, suppressing a smile. "Fine. Just don't drink all the good liquor."

"You mean that pot swill you keep in the back cabinet?"

"You better get back to work before Wallace finds out you're taking personal time on the phone. I have his number on speed dial."

"Yeah, yeah," he replies. "Back to the grindstone. You be careful down there."

"Oh, and tell Zara not to work too hard either," I say, smiling.

I can hear the smile in his voice. "Glad you're concerned for at least one of us."

I don't want to hang up, but I'm not one for long good-byes, either. Finally I let him go and turn back to the matter at hand. As usual, he's right. I don't want to admit it; but I should probably stick around and find out what I can about this case. The fact that Jessica was buried in my old house and a letter was sent to me in my dead mother's handwriting can't be a coincidence. That's one too many strange events with one thing in common.

Me.

Chapter Eight

I SPEND the rest of the afternoon re-familiarizing myself with my hometown. While it's mostly the same, the details from my childhood are fuzzy, and it takes a little while for my memory to catch up. I'm working off the memory of a nine-year-old, heading to the homes of people I haven't seen or spoken to in almost two decades. But when I was little, many of these places were regular stops for me. Mom always seemed to have a close group of friends that saw each other regularly, and I was usually along for the ride, stuck in the kids room with children I didn't know very well and never kept in touch with.

But I remember the homes.

My first three stops are all duds. My first stop was supposed to be for Betty Ennis, but I can't remember which house she used to live in on the block, so I don't bother knocking on any of the doors. She was always so prim and proper, and always wore an A-line skirt, like she was out of the fifties or something. And she made the most amazing banana bread. She had two sons, both around my age, but I can't remember their names anymore. Betty wasn't Mom's closest friend, but her house was closest to ours; I just can't remember which one it was. I make a note to do some research later to see if Betty still even lives in Fernview.

The next two options, Susan Walker and Amanda Phelps no longer live in the homes they used to when I was a kid. These homes are full of new families, who have no idea what happened to their old owners. Resigned that I'm not going to have any luck, I find a hotel close to downtown and book myself a couple of nights, just in case. I spend the rest of the evening scouring through Facebook and social media, looking for anyone who might have known my mom who still lives in Fernview. But the pickings are slim. It seems I wasn't the only one with the idea of leaving town.

Ironically, the only person who looks like she's still local and who was also close with Mom was Judy's mother—Nadine. And given what that family is going through, I'm not about to go accost her while they're grieving the news about Jessica. Maybe in a few days.

Frustrated, I head out to find something to eat, settling on a place I never tried while I lived here, but looks good enough now. They serve mostly fried foods and very little that anyone would consider healthy, but at this point I don't care. I'm in a fried food kind of mood. After a quick meal I head back to the hotel, hoping tomorrow will be better. Though as I'm falling asleep I can't get the image of a body, wrapped in plastic, standing between two support beams out of my head.

Sleep doesn't come easily.

THE FOLLOWING MORNING, I HEAD BACK TO THE POLICE station to speak with Captain Reyes about the letters. I doubt he'll be able to give me any assistance, but I figured it can't hurt to ask. Maybe someone reported receiving a letter themselves, who knows? But also I have to admit I'm curious about how the case is proceeding. Despite my reasons for coming down here, it's taken all my willpower not to hyperfocus on it all morning.

I skip breakfast in lieu of some coffee from a small kiosk in a local strip mall called *Java the Hut*. Just like when I used to live here there's a line about five cars long before I get there, though it moves fast. I opt for a hazelnut blend before heading on to the station. It's not bad—not as bad as I was expecting. I know I give my hometown a bad rap, but it's really not so terrible. I think I was just so desperate to leave this place I was willing to write the whole thing off.

When I get to the station, Reyes isn't in yet, but the desk sergeant allows me into the back. I guess having a federal badge allows me some perks after all. Instead of waiting for Reyes in his office, I head over to the bullpen and take a seat, ready to do a little people-watching. I normally wouldn't do this, but I'm beginning to enjoy seeing this place in a new light. Plus, it might give me a chance to needle Tate a little more. I hadn't realized just how easy it was to fall back into old habits here. I know people and they know me; I don't have to start brand new with everyone.

After a few minutes I spot the same woman I almost ran into yesterday. She's at the other end of the bullpen, a pair of earbuds in as she works studiously on something at one of the empty desks. Whatever it is, she's using good old pen and paper, not a laptop like everyone else around here. Her earbuds virtually disappear into her reddish-orange hair. It's thick, but not excessively wavy and falls down past her collar. Though it does make her stand out.

At the exact moment I realize I'm staring at her she looks up and locks eyes with me, neither surprised nor angry, from the looks of it. I know it's too late to pretend like I wasn't staring and I offer her a quick smile before going back to my coffee. She looks left, then right, as if she's seeing if anyone else is watching her, then gathers up her materials and crosses the bullpen, taking a seat beside me. She pops her earbuds out and stows them in a shoulder bag she's carried with her.

"You're the FBI agent, aren't you?" she asks.

I set my coffee down, nodding. "Emily Slate." I offer my hand and she takes it. "I'm sorry, I didn't mean to stare."

"Anna Forest," she replies before letting go. "That's okay. It's the hair, isn't it?"

"Was I that obvious?"

"No, but it does tend to happen. Luck of the genetic draw, I suppose. My mother is a blonde and my father's hair is as dark as yours."

I take another sip of my coffee. "It's been a while since I studied genetic selection in high school."

"Oh, it's very simple," she replies. "Someone like me is the result of two recessive genes in both parents. Of course, that's not counting my eye color. Odds of a blue-eyed, red-haired baby are about point-seventeen percent. As you can imagine, my parents were very surprised. I remember my mother making the hospital prove they hadn't switched her child with someone else's."

I chuckle. "I'm sure that made you feel good."

She waves it off. "By the time I learned about *the scandal* as she called it, I was too old to care."

I notice she's not wearing a uniform like everyone else here. "Are you a contractor?"

"Sort of, Forensic Psychologist," she says.

That causes an eyebrow raise. "In *Fernview?*"

She shrugs. "I grew up in Boston. Decided I wanted to live somewhere more peaceful, at least for a little while. Fernview was about as far from home as I could get, aesthetically speaking."

"You mean a backwoods town without a skyscraper in sight?"

She smiles. "Something like that. Are you assisting on the Ashford case?"

"Not...officially. I'm here for personal reasons, though Captain Reyes did ask for my assistance should I feel the urge. I figured I'd come in this morning for an update."

"Excellent," she says, her eyes lighting up. They almost look like a brighter shade of blue than they were yesterday. "I'm curious. Do you have a lot of experience with these sorts of cases? I know the FBI covers a wide variety of subjects."

"That's true, we do. But I've seen more than a few cases where we've tried tracking down an unknown killer. They seem to be popping up more and more often these days."

"That's good news," she says, leaning closer. For a second I'm confused that she means it's good news there are more serial killers out there but before I can clarify she continues. "Then I have to ask. In your experience, do killers who behave this way do it out of a sense of need, or desire?" My confused look causes her to pull back a little. "What I mean is, does this type of behavior normally stem from events in the killer's past that they couldn't control, and thus they take the opportunity to compensate for those events by hurting others? Or is it perhaps purely psychosomatic, a result of some physical abnormality in the brain?"

"Umm," I begin, not sure where to begin. "Well, I need to—"

"Agent Slate?" I look up to see Captain Reyes coming in, his own cup of coffee in his hands.

I stand, greeting him. "Captain."

"Reconsidered my offer?" he asks.

"Sort of," I say. "But I was also hoping you could help me with a personal matter."

"Great. I'll do what I can. I see you've already met our brilliant Dr. Forest. Come on into the conference room, I'll get you squared away." I'm about to stop him to tell him I was just curious about the case but before I can, he turns to the other side of the room. "Hodge!" A linebacker-sized man looks up from a box of donuts on his desk, one already in his mouth.

He shoots the captain a single-finger gun, then closes the box and heads our way.

Well, at least I'll get the basics of the case. I turn to the woman. "Pleasure to meet you." Dr. Forest gives me an appreciative nod before going back to whatever she was working on. Though I can tell she wanted to pick my brain a little more. I catch a glimpse in her notebook, and it looks like a drawing of a dragon.

I follow Reyes down the hall, past his office to a medium-sized conference room, with an oval-shaped table and six chairs. Hodge meets us there, holding the door open for me with a hand coated in sugar powder. "Agent Slate, this is Detective Bill Hodge. He's been on the case since day one."

Hodge gives me a nod. "Pleasure," he says, his mouth still full of donut. He walks around to the other side of the table, plopping himself down.

"Hodge here has been with the department for what, fifteen years?" Reyes asks.

"Seventeen," Hodge says, leaning back. With arms like those he looks like he could bench press a truck, though his affinity for donuts shows around his waistline. He's wearing a faded suit jacket, the elbows wearing thin. I take the seat across from him.

"Here's what we have so far," Reyes says. At the front of the room a screen appears on the whiteboard, and I look back, seeing the projector mounted into the ceiling, providing the picture. "Obviously Hodge is up to date on everything, but I'll give you the whole picture from the beginning." He motions to the door. "You already met Dr. Forest. I asked her to consult on this case, given the potential for mental instability. She's still working on her assessment."

It looked to me like she was working on her art.

"We can't ignore the fact that Jessica Ashford's body was found in the same home her father and sister lived in for almost ten years. Hodge thinks it's significant." The larger man shoots me a wink.

I turn back to Reyes. "You already interviewed Judy and Jake Ashford. I'm assuming you came to the same conclusion you did with me?"

"I haven't ruled out Jake Ashford as a potential suspect yet," Hodge says. "Feel free to question him yourself."

"And Judy?" I ask.

Hodge turns to Reyes. "We're not looking at her as a suspect at this time."

"That tracks with what I know about her," I say.

Reyes snaps his fingers. "That's right. You two know each other, don't you?"

"You do?" Hodge asks, sitting up. "How?"

I glance across the table. "I was born and raised in Fernview."

"Wait a second. Slate? You're Margaret Slate's daughter, aren't you?" I nod. "I see the resemblance now. I worked her case, you know."

"I remember," I say, though it's a little fuzzy. I thought he looked familiar, but I wasn't sure. I recall a large man about Hodge's size asking my dad a bunch of questions after Mom died. "You thought my dad had something to do with it."

"Nothing like that," he says. "Your dad had a mental breakdown in the hospital. We brought him here to help him calm down. Talk him through it."

"What?" I ask. "No, he didn't."

Hodge finishes his donut. "I can assure you he did. It's no big deal, it happens when spouses lose their partners unexpectedly."

"Don't tell me about losing your partner unexpectedly," I say through gritted teeth.

Hodge's eyes go wide. "I didn't mean anything by it. Just that I helped him through it. I remember you being here, you wouldn't leave his side."

I find I'm having a hard time controlling my breathing. Suddenly the room seems a lot smaller and a lot more cramped than before. A mental breakdown? I don't remember anything about that.

"Agent Slate?" Reyes asks. "Are you all right?"

I look up and realize I've clenched both fists tight enough to leave indentations on my palms. I immediately relax them and look at both men, all too sure of what they're thinking. I'm not going to lose control here in front of them; but I am going to get to the bottom of this.

"Of course," I say, taking a deep breath. "Let's...keep going."

Both men look relieved not to have to deal with a *hysterical* woman. Reyes clicks something on the podium and a picture appears. I'm taken aback for a minute, because it looks just like I imagined it would last night when I was trying to get to sleep. A body, wrapped entirely in blue plastic and duct tape, squeezed in between two support beams in a wall. There's a small electrical switch not far from the body, and the back wall behind her is untouched. But the side of the wall we're looking at has been completely torn away. I recognize the flooring; that's definitely where the kitchen meets the living room.

"This was how the scene looked when we pulled the rest of the wall down," Reyes says. "You can see here is where Mr. Page's sledgehammer impacted the body." He points to the upper right shoulder. "He didn't puncture the plastic, but we think he did some damage to what remains of the under-neath. The body is at the coroner's office right now, being examined."

"How many people have lived in the house since I moved out?" I ask, trying to block out the weird sound Hodge's breath makes when it exits his nose. It's like a mouse blowing a whistle.

"Three families. The Ashfords, the Carvers and now the

Pages," he replies. "The Carvers moved back to North Carolina about a month ago; I still haven't been able to contact them. And we've obviously eliminated the Pages. They're younger than you and would have been children when Jessica went missing."

"Any other suspects?" I ask.

"Not yet. We're trying to keep a lid on this, but like you said, in a town this size, word is bound to travel. Soon enough the local news station will pick it up. I'm hoping to make some progress before that happens." Reyes flips through a few more pictures. Each show the crime scene in more detail, along with Jessica's still-bound body.

"How did you ID her so quickly?"

"She still had her driver's permit in the pocket of her jeans," Hodge says.

"Really?" I ask. "Then the killer wanted us to know who she was. They're proud of their work, and wanted it showcased."

"Dr. Forest came to the same conclusion," Reyes says. "You may want to speak with her to get her take on things as well."

I examine the picture more closely. "I don't guess you were lucky enough to get any fingerprints off the body?"

He shakes his head. "No such luck. We're still trying to figure out exactly when she went into that wall. Thanks to you, at least now we know it was after two-thousand-five."

"Do you even know when the wall was built? It might not have been there when the Ashfords lived there either and this could all be nothing more than a coincidence."

"We're still working on that," Hodge replies. "But you're right. It's just as possible the Carvers installed that wall when they moved in."

"Have you interviewed anyone else?" I ask.

"I went around the neighborhood a couple of days ago

with another officer, we didn't get very far," Hodge adds. "I've got a lot of cases that need my attention."

Ah, the truth comes out. Finally. Reyes can't afford to move this case to the backburner, but at the same time, he doesn't have time to properly investigate. No wonder he wanted me to stick around.

"The benefits of a small police force, huh?" I ask, shooting Reyes a look.

Hodge's mouth turns into a frown. "I'd be happy to send you the case files if you think you can do better. With you being in the FBI and all."

"Sure," I say, standing. "I'd love to take a look. In fact, I'll be happy to get started on this right away. Here's my information." I toss my card on the table. "Send me everything you've got." I head out of the conference room before either of them can say anything else.

"Agent Slate!" I hear Reyes call after me.

The nerve of that man. I don't know what it is, but I know if I stayed in that room any longer I would have exploded. Hodge strikes me as the kind of man who always thinks his initial impression of something, or someone is right. He's not the kind of detective who likes to dig a little deeper. And to say my father had a mental breakdown? I know for a fact that didn't happen; I was with him the entire time. He was upset, sure. But a *breakdown*?

"Agent Slate, wait, please."

I turn to see Dr. Forest running after me. "Are you going to assist on the case?"

Only now do I realize what I've agreed to in my haste. Now I have to work with Hodge, or at least speak with him in some capacity. I'm not usually so reactive; but I don't take kindly when people talk about my family. "I guess I am."

"That's very generous of you. Though if something like this happened at a house where I used to live, I'd want some answers too."

"It's not entirely about that," I begin, thinking back to Judy. I know what it's like not knowing what happened to your loved one and wanting to find the truth. If someone could have done that for me with Matt, I would have paid just about any price. I can't leave her without answers if I know I can help.

Dr. Forest seems to sense I'm going to say something else, but she doesn't push. "We could really use you. No offense to Detective Hodge, but between you and me I think his attention is split at the moment. He's dealing with a lot of other cases, and he isn't really focusing on what he already considers a cold case. I've had some time to work with him and I know how he operates."

I take a deep breath, counting to ten. While I understand detectives have a lot of cases on their plates—the FBI is no different—I can't imagine not giving a case my everything. "Well, I'm not like that. Reyes said I should get your opinion on the case as well."

"I'd love that," she says. "I run a small practice here in town, so I'm not available all the time, but I'm sure we can work something out." She sticks out her hand again. "Welcome aboard. I'll make sure the captain comps all your food and expenses. It's the least he can do."

"I appreciate that," I say. "And do me a favor. Make sure the rest of the force knows I'm here on a *voluntary* basis. I don't need a bunch of accusations about the federal government coming in and taking cases away from hardworking police officers."

She gives me a quick smile. "You got it."

I head back out to my car, shaking my head. I didn't even ask Reyes about the letters—but there will be time for that later. Zara is never going to believe this.

Chapter Nine

THE FIRST THING I do after leaving the station is get a fresh cup of coffee from *Java the Hut*. I feel like I'm going to be visiting the kiosk a lot over the next few days. The second thing I do is head back out to my old house. Despite my reservations, I'm in *Emily* mode now and I actually find it a relief not to be thinking about those letters again. At least now I should be able to look around and get a sense of the place. I don't really expect to find anything after fifteen years, give or take, but I want to stand back in the house, see if I can't put myself in our killer's head. Maybe Jake Ashford really did kill his daughter. Part of the reason I never saw Judy when she stayed with her dad was because he was always such an asshole.

This time when I pull up to the house there's only one other squad car there. As soon as I get out of the car, the officer in the other car gets out as well to meet me.

"Are you the FBI agent?" he asks.

"That's me," I say. "Is the house unlocked?"

"No, we keep it locked during the day unless someone needs access. I got the key here though. I can take you through, if you like." The officer is young, eager. I don't know if he's fishing to get into someone's good graces or if he really is just trying to be helpful, but it would be better if I take a look at the house alone. I'm bound to be overwhelmed by emotions once I'm in there, and I don't need anyone seeing me going through that.

He nods and fishes a pair of keys out of his pocket. "Take as much time as you need. Reyes has me on duty all day." He tosses me the keys and I nod my appreciation.

Since the driveway is still blocked with the caution tape, I step under it and make my way up the long walk. As I expected I'm hit with a flood of emotions and memories, hundred different images coming to me all at once. The first day I got off the school bus and came running up the driveway to my mother's waiting arms. Riding my bike up and down the driveway, my dad so proud that I no longer needed training wheels. The day the toy I ordered finally came in the mail and I tore back up to the house, box in hand, so excited. Back when you ordered something in the mail, and it took six weeks to get to you. Prime shipping has really spoiled all of us.

I walk around to the back of the house inspecting the backyard, but everything looks normal. Not that I would expect it to look any other way, but I like to keep an eye out. I haven't had time to start building a profile on our killer yet, and it's possible he may have left other clues around the house for us to find. Things that only people who lived here might notice. But as far as I can tell, the backyard is almost exactly the same as it was when I used to live here. That in itself seems kinda odd, considering the number of times this house has changed hands.

I pull on a pair of nitrile gloves before opening the back door with the keys. Once I'm inside the house I'm struck by the smell of fresh paint. The back door itself opens right off the kitchen, which is wide with a large island in the middle. The island is covered in cardboard boxes, appliances, and dishes that are still wrapped in plastic. It looks like the Pages didn't get very far unpacking. A body was probably the last thing they expected to find when they bought the place.

Immediately I see the wall in question. Watching where I step, I take a close look, and can tell exactly where the photographer took the picture I saw earlier. The only difference now is Jessica's body is missing, and there is fingerprint dust all over almost every surface. The wall itself is still open and exposed on this side and I can see electrical wires and plumbing running between the beams. It's funny, with this wall here the kitchen looks entirely different. It doesn't look like the kitchen that I grew up in at all. Given that, and all the other decor changes this really doesn't even feel like the same house. Those memories I expected to be hit with don't come, and I'm able to look at this place just like any other crime scene.

Thank goodness for small blessings.

I take my time inspecting the scene, going over every inch of the area looking for any clues that the original investigators might have missed. One thing I notice is the wall seems to have a little bit more depth than a wall would normally have. I assume this was done on purpose in order to make sure her body would fit. Which means whoever did this has some expertise in construction and/or engineering—or at least planned for this and it wasn't just convenience sake that she went in there. Then again, we could be looking at more than one perpetrator here. It's always possible that the killer had a partner, as that would've made it a lot easier to hide the body. And if Jake Ashford was responsible for this, I'll need to look into his known associates to see if anyone has prior construction or building experience.

I spend the next few minutes walking around the rest of the floor looking for any other clues that might stand out. I note other changes that previous homeowners have made, most of which are cosmetic. Old wood paneling walls are gone, replaced by new drywall. Bathrooms no longer feature the same pink tile that was there when I was living here, and have now been updated with a tasteful neutral color. Structurally, I don't see any other changes other than the wall in the kitchen, which strikes me as odd. I would think if they were going to go to all the trouble of doing a renovation, they would do more than just add one wall. The first thing I need to do is establish exactly when this wall was built, and which homeowner had it installed.

Even though I probably don't need to, I take a look upstairs just to make sure that I'm not missing anything. The primary bedroom looks about the same, though the bathroom that's attached has been rearranged and updated. When I reach my old room, the flood of memories finally hits me. The main difference is that the room is now missing the carpet that used to be there, which has been replaced with hardwood floors. But other than that, it's exactly the same. My closet is still the same small closet where I would build pillow forts and hide inside them, reading at all hours of the night. My window still looks out over the backyard, and I take a minute to appreciate the view. It's familiar, but not exactly the same. I guess when they say you can't go home again, they mean it.

Deciding I've wasted enough time here, I head back outside and hand the keys back to the officer who was leaning up against his squad car watching me.

"Thanks," I say. "Just needed to take a quick look around."

"No problem. Did you find what you are looking for?"

"I did. Were you part of the team that canvassed the neighborhood?" I make a quick survey, noting there are six different houses within eyesight of this house. I wonder how many people still live here that might know something.

"No, that was Officer Tate and Detective Hodge." I'm not so sure I trust those two to have done a thorough job. Not to mention I'm still waiting on the case files from Hodge. It might be a good idea to double-check with the neighbors, start over from scratch and do it right.

"Okay, thank you officer…"

"Malone," he says, proudly.

"Thanks, Malone," I say, then head back to my car. I won't be able to narrow down a timeframe until I know when the wall was built, but if I can find a few neighbors who knew the Ashfords and the Carvers it will be a help. It's going to be a lot of houses; I wish Liam or Zara were here. At least it would make the work go a bit faster.

But what's really nagging at the back of my head is the fact that Jessica disappeared seven years before she could have ever showed up here. What was she doing in all that time? And what happened to her? I'll need to check with the coroner to get the details. Hopefully they've had time to properly examine what remains of her body.

Once I'm back in my car I check my email again, still seeing nothing from Hodge. Frustrated, I dial the number for the station, asking for him personally.

"Hodge," he says in the exact same tone as earlier.

"It's Agent Slate," I say. "Can you send over those files?"

"Hm? Oh, right. Sure, I'll shoot them over this afternoon," he says. "You know, Reyes wasn't too happy you stormed out of the meeting."

I take a moment and do my best to calm myself, but it barely works. "There was nothing else to say. Any chance I could get the files earlier? I'm about to interview the neighbors and I don't want to do work you've already done."

"You're wasting your time," he says. "Tate and I did that two days ago. I thought you Feds were supposed to be efficient."

"Did you cover everyone in the neighborhood? Including Mrs. Holloway who lives down the street?" I ask.

I hear him flipping through some papers. "No, we didn't get to her. Only the immediate houses in the vicinity."

"Then you're not doing yourself any favors. A lot of the

people in this neighborhood are close. How do you think I found out about the body in the first place?"

There's a pause on the other end, then a sigh. "Okay, I'll head down and bring the files with me. We can canvas the rest of the neighborhood together."

"No, that's not—" I begin but he's hung up before I can even get the words out. "Dammit," I mutter under my breath. That is *not* how I wanted that to go.

Chapter Ten

PART of me thinks I should just start without him, but if I'm going to be forced to work with Detective Hodge I probably don't need to antagonize him any more than I already have. Maybe I overreacted in the conference room and I just need to reset before he shows up.

But when a vehicle comes down and parks behind my car, it isn't a standard-issue police vehicle. It's a rusted, faded minivan that has to be at least twenty years old. One of the door panels is a different color than the others and I note some rust spots around the wheel wells. At first I'm about to praise Hodge's ability to find a car that's sure not to attract attention when I see it's actually Dr. Forest behind the wheel instead.

"Good morning again," she says, getting out of the vehicle. She holds a file folder in her right hand, and gives it over to me. "This is for you."

"Where's Hodge?" I ask.

"Emergency call came in, some fire on the other side of town. Looks like it could be arson. Reyes asked me to step in while Hodge deals with that." She's got on the same clothes as earlier, a pair of faded jeans and a screen-print T-shirt that's barely visible under her puffy overcoat. Her hair is loose, but neat and there's an air about her like she doesn't have a care in the world.

"Kids?" I nod to the minivan.

"What, this? No, I just happened to get a really good deal. They had a bunch of vehicles available in the police auction and I got it for a steal." She beams at me.

"Thanks for the files," I say, holding them up. "But you really didn't have to come all the way down here. I don't want to intrude on your Sunday."

"It's no problem at all," she replies. "Weekends are when I do most of my work for the department. I rarely get to see the other side of the investigative process. Most of what I do is sit in courtrooms, present evidence and build theories to help the detectives. It's all very boring and mundane."

I chuckle, flipping through the files. As Hodge said, they only spoke to a few different neighbors. Not a thorough job at all. "Well, I get to find out who's lived in this neighborhood the longest. It's riveting stuff."

"Do you need some help?" she asks.

I frown. "You don't want to spend the rest of the day going door to door, do you? Odds are there's nothing here. I'm just trying to be thorough."

She shrugs. "It's not like I have anything else to do. Plus, I figure if we're going to be working together, what better way to get started?"

I'm not about to refuse free help, though I do find Dr. Forest a little overeager. But I know what she's feeling. Every time I'm stuck behind a desk all I want is to get out of the office too. God knows I've been in that situation more times than I'd like to admit. "We've got about two dozen neighbors in the immediate area," I say. "And another fifty in the entire neighborhood. Odds are most of them probably haven't been around since two-thousand-five. So we need to go house to house, see who's lived here since then, and ask if they know anything about either the Ashfords or the Carvers."

"Got it," she says. "Any specific questions I should be asking?"

"Ask them if they knew the Ashfords or the Carvers well, if they ever visited the house, and what general sense they got from the people who lived here." I put my hands on my hips and take a look down the street. It's a lot of houses, which is good because it gives us a lot of opportunities for someone who may have seen or knows something. But at the same time, it's going to take forever.

"A general sense?" She asks.

"Yeah, you know, what did they think of their neighbors? Did they ever witness anything shady? Is there a particular memory or some behavior that they recall as being…off?"

"Oh, I get it." She looks up and down the street. "Do you want the odd numbers or even?"

"I'll take the odds." I point to the house across the street and two down. Hodge never got that far. "Starting with that one. Hopefully, with it being Sunday, most people will be home. If not, just mark the house as did not answer, and we will come back to it later."

"Sounds easy enough to me. This is kind of exciting, thanks for letting me assist."

I give her a quick smile. "You're the one doing me a favor, so thank you. If you run into any problems, just give me a ring." I hold up my phone.

We part ways and I head across the street to the house I used to stare at every day as a kid already feeling better about this. I'd much prefer to coordinate with Dr. Forest than Hodge.

The house is partially hidden by lots of untrimmed shrubbery, and there's a gravel driveway that leads up to the front of the house. I take the first few stairs and then rap on the door, stepping back in case they have a camera so they can see me clearly.

A few minutes later, the door opens, revealing a middle-aged man wearing a football jersey. "Help you?"

This is definitely not the same old couple that used to live here when I was here. I shouldn't say I'm surprised, because they were old even back then. I doubt they're even still alive. "Good afternoon," I say, holding up my badge. "I'm working on the investigation across the street. Would you mind telling me when you moved into this house?"

"FBI?" The man asks, his face twisting. "Jesus, must be serious. What the hell happened over there?"

"I'm not at liberty to say, sir," I tell him. "Just know that we're taking the utmost care in investigating what happened."

"Well," he says, stepping back and squinting. "I guess we moved in right around the time of the recession."

"Oh-eight?" I ask.

"Yeah, I think so. I'd say either oh-eight, or oh-nine. Sometime around there. It was the only reason we got this house because it was such a good deal."

"Did you ever meet your neighbors that lived in that house?" I ask.

"Which ones? Seems like that house is been changing hands every couple of years," he says.

"How about the Ashfords?" Even if he wasn't here in two-thousand-five, he lived here during a majority of their time here. It's worth asking if he knows anything.

"Yeah, I met them a couple of times. Nice enough people, though he was always something of a know it all. He'd always offer to help me work on my truck, then proceed to tell me what I was doing wrong to fix it. The daughter was nice though, not that I saw much of her after she went off to college. Honestly, I was kind of glad when he moved out of the neighborhood."

That fits with what I know about Jake Ashford. Seems like

you didn't need to be special to get the royal treatment from him. "And what about the people that moved in after the Ashfords left?"

"Yeah," he pinches his face. "I never really got to know them. My wife met her a couple of times, and I'd see him taking his trash in and out. I know they had a daughter, but they always kept to themselves. And they weren't here but a couple of years. Not the most outgoing of people. I like to think of myself as a friendly man, but sometimes you can just tell when someone doesn't want to interact with you, you know?" He seems almost offended, like the idea that his neighbor across the street not interacting with him is an insult.

"Do you happen to remember anything with either the Ashfords or the Carvers that you would consider strange?" I know I'm being very general here, but at the same time I'm not going to come out and ask if he saw someone dragging a dead body up the driveway.

"Strange?" He asks. "How do you mean?"

"I mean was there anything that stands out to you, that you thought at the time was a little odd, but it wasn't enough to make a big fuss about."

He takes a moment to think before drawing in a deep breath. "Now that you mention it, there were a couple of weeks, right after those Carvers moved in, where they had all the windows covered up with newspaper. I couldn't understand why they needed to keep the windows covered up for that long, especially if all they were doing was painting. Hell, I can get a room painted in a day if I absolutely have to."

"You say this was right after they moved in?" I ask.

"Yeah, I'd say about a month after they moved in. Kept the windows covered for months after that."

"Do you know if they were having any renovations done, maybe that's why they needed the newspaper up?"

"I guess," he says scratching the back of his head. "But I don't remember seeing any contractor trucks over there. If they were doing the work, they did it themselves. Guess that's not so strange nowadays."

"Anything else?" I ask.

"Not that I can remember."

"Okay, thank you very much," I say. "I appreciate your help." I turned to head back down the steps to the next house on the list.

"Hey, wait a second," he calls out. "What happened over there? Do we need to be worried? I've got a family here; I think I have a right to know."

"Don't worry, sir," I tell him. "You and your family have nothing to worry about."

He eyes me like he doesn't believe me, before finally closing the door. I have a feeling I'm going to be getting a lot of that today.

As I visit most of the rest of the houses, I'm met with the same story. It seems like the recession really did a number on this neighborhood. Most of the old residents were at retirement age and looking for a way out, and there were a lot of people looking to snap up cheap homes in an established neighborhood. I only speak to two different people who happened to live here before two-thousand-five, but neither of them know anything about either the Ashfords or the Carvers.

I speak to four other people who give me a similar story about the Carvers. It seems the family were recluses and didn't venture out much. People would see them coming and going from their house, but they never went out of their way to meet their neighbors, and they never attended any social events.

What little I get back on the Ashfords, is the complete opposite. Jake Ashford seemed to want to stick his nose in everyone's business. And he wasn't shy about telling people when he thought they were wrong. He rubbed a lot of people the wrong way to the point where I get the impression the neighborhood breathed a collective sigh of relief when he left.

I'm about halfway done with my side of the list, when I

get a phone call just as I'm leaving another house. "Slate," I say.

"Agent Slate, it's Anna. I'm here with a resident who insists she will only speak to you."

A smile crosses my face. I should have figured. "Mrs. Holloway?" I began heading to my car immediately.

"I see you're already familiar with her."

"We had the chance to talk yesterday," I say. "I'll be right over." I head down the street to Mrs. Holloway's house and park right behind Anna's minivan. When I get out, Anna meets me at the front door. It seems Mrs. Holloway has invited her in just to tell her that she wanted to speak with me.

"I figured it was easier to call you rather than to try and argue," Dr. Forest says.

"That was probably smart." She holds the door open for me and I step in catching sight of Mrs. Holloway in her chair in the hallway.

"Twice in two days," Mrs. Holloway says. "I really drew the lottery this week."

I smile. "I wasn't lying to you yesterday. I didn't realize I'd be sticking around for longer than a day or two. But Captain Reyes down at the police station asked for my help on this case so I figured I'd stick around."

"You always were a curious one, Emily." She shoots me a wink. "Now you and your friend come on in here and we'll have a nice chat."

"We don't want to take up too much of your time," I say, following her back into the same sitting room as yesterday. "I just have some follow ups about what you told me."

"You mean about the body," she says, shooting Dr. Forest a wink.

Forest raises her eyebrows. "You already know."

"My child, in my heyday I was one hell of a gossip. That just doesn't go away with age. In fact, it gets worse. I'm better connected than the CIA, as far as this town goes." She shoots me another look. "No offense intended."

"None taken," I say, sitting back on the plastic-covered loveseat. "Not my organization." This time, instead of moving to the loveseat opposite me, Mrs. Holloway stays in her chair. "Now, what can I help you with?"

"We'd like to know about your experiences with the people who lived at that house, after Agent Slate and her father moved out, of course," Dr. Forest says.

Mrs. Holloway thinks for a moment. "Well, like I told you yesterday, I never had much to do with the people that just moved out. They seemed nice enough, though," she says.

"The Carvers. But you said they moved out quickly?" I ask.

She nods. "They did. Sign just appeared at their house one day, and I noticed their cars were gone. Never saw them again."

"What about the Ashfords?" Dr. Forest asks.

Mrs. Holloway sets her mouth into a line. "You see that first cabinet in the kitchen there?" Dr. Forest and I turn at the same time, looking at the cabinet above the stove on the other side of the doorway. "Up there is a bottle of gin. If I'm gonna talk about Jake Ashford, I'm gonna need you to pour me a glass."

I suppress a smile and get up, heading for the cabinet. I shoot a look at Dr. Forest, but her brows are drawn in a disapproving look. Maybe I shouldn't be contributing to a ninety-year-old lady's drinking habit, but I'm not about to sit here and tell her she can't drink in her own home.

"Where are your glasses?" I ask.

"Right on the tip of my nose," she calls back, then cackles to herself. I search through the cabinets until I find a lowball. I pour her a small amount, then drop a few ice cubes from the ice maker into the glass, returning to the living room with it. She holds out her hand, greedy for the glass. "I wouldn't have blamed you if you'd gotten yourself one."

I give her a quick smile. "I'm more of a whiskey drinker myself."

"Never could stand the stuff," Mrs. Holloway says. "But my husband loved it." She drains the entire glass in one go, then sets it on the closest table. "Emily, dear, I don't know how much you remember about Jake Ashford, but he was just not the nicest person."

"So I've heard," I say.

She looks up at Dr. Forest, then to me again. "Now I don't like speaking ill of those whose life has—pardon the expression—taken a dump on, but it always seemed to me like Jake Ashford used the loss of his daughter as an excuse to be the most miserable son-of-a-bitch this neighborhood has ever seen. Excuse me. That's not ladylike but it's the truth. There were days when I'd find him at my door, telling me I needed to install a wheelchair ramp on my front steps to comply with some sort of city code, otherwise he'd be forced to report me to some department or another, despite the fact I never use my front door. I always go out the back. Oh, the horror stories I could tell you. Did you know that when Archie Winters had a heart attack, that man had the nerve to tell the rescue squad they were wasting their time because Winters was a smoker and he'd just be right back in the hospital in a month? Talk about a walking menace."

I exchange a glance with Dr. Forest. She gives me a small nod. "That seems to be the consensus we're getting from the other neighbors as well."

"Well, I may be a gossip, but I'm no liar," she says, giving us a curt nod. "I always felt so bad for that poor Judy Ashford. To have a father like that, always criticizing everything she did, everyone she spoke to...terrible. You knew Judy, didn't you, Emily?"

"I did," I say. "I ran into her again yesterday."

"Poor girl," Mrs. Holloway says. "How is she?"

"Um…fine, I guess," I say, shooting another look at Dr. Forest. I think we've overspent our welcome here. "One last question. Do you recall either Mr. Ashford, or the Carvers saying or doing anything you found…odd?"

She thinks a moment. "Other than getting into everyone else's business where he didn't belong? No. Then again, I'm an old lady. When you've lived as long as I have, not a lot looks odd to you anymore."

I pull out one of my business cards and place it on the side table, beside her drink. "If you happen to think of anything, feel free to give me a call. My personal number is on there."

"I absolutely will. It was such a pleasure seeing you again so soon, Emily." She turns to Dr. Forest. "And you, I enjoyed meeting you too, young lady."

"You're an interesting person to know," Dr. Forest says. "Thank you."

We say our goodbyes, then head back outside. "So?" I ask as soon as we reach our cars. "How have you fared so far?"

"Six houses with no one home. Everyone else is giving me a similar version of events. The Carvers were reclusive while Jake Ashford decided to be the neighborhood dickhead."

I chuckle. "That's what I'm getting too. Though the neighbor across the street did give me a good morsel." I tell her about the newspaper on the windows.

"Could have been used to cover up the wall construction," she says. "But then again, I'm no detective."

"You're doing a fair job of it," I say. "Let's finish up here and then I want to try and find these Carvers. Reyes said he hadn't been able to get in contact with them, correct?"

"Right," Dr. Forest says. "I believe Hodge put in a call down to North Carolina, but hasn't heard back."

"Seeing as he already interviewed Jake Ashford, I want to get a crack at them first before going back over something Hodge has already done. Who knows, maybe I'll get lucky."

"Would you be willing to grab dinner once we're finished here? It would give us a chance to compare notes," she asks.

"Sure," I say, a little hesitant, though I don't know why. Dr. Forest seems like a nice, capable person. And I can already hear Zara in my ear screaming at me that I need to keep making new friends, even if it is in a city I never plan on coming back to again.

"Great," she says. "I'll let you know when I'm done." She returns to her minivan as I head back to my car.

Twenty-five neighbors down. Twenty-five to go.

Chapter Eleven

WE ENDED up finishing a good five hours after we began. Between backtracking to houses that weren't occupied earlier in the day, and trying to get other, less cooperative neighbors to give us *anything,* both of us were wiped by the time we were done. Dr. Forest—who insists I call her Anna—took me to a vegan restaurant that definitely wasn't here when I lived in Fernview. I'm not much on vegan food, but it tasted good enough.

After a quick meal and finding out that she graduated near the top of her class at William James, I head back to my hotel for the night. She promised to have her full analysis of the killer for me tomorrow, once she's worked through her thoughts a little more. At least having her help today really cut down on the amount of time I had to spend knocking on doors. And thankfully I had the foresight to bring my work laptop which allows me to keep track of all my notes. And even though I have access to my Federal ID, I stop myself from using it here. I don't want to go down that rabbit hole if I don't have to.

As I lay back on the bed, I dial Zara, hoping she's off from work by now. She better be; it's almost ten p.m. But when I call, it just rings before going to voicemail. "Hey, it's me," I say. "Checking in. I wanna tell you what they've got me doing down here. And yes, before you say it, I know. I'm not supposed to be working. But this was kind of a special case. Anyway, call me back, I'll tell you all about it."

I hang up, then dial Liam.

"Hey, sexy," he says, his voice deeper than normal.

"Hey, yourself," I say. "Trying to woo me over the phone?"

"Just paying you a compliment," he replies. "How's your day been?"

"Oh, fine," I feign, before giving him the rundown of everything from Hodge's accusations to my dinner with Fernview's newest forensic psychologist.

"Wait a second," he says. "You're supposed to be investigating your letters. What happened to that?" His voice is light, like he's just giving me a hard time.

"I can't just sit around and do nothing," I say. "Judy just found out her sister had been buried in the walls of her own home. She's devastated." Maybe I'm embellishing here. Or maybe I just know what it feels like to lose your family and not have any answers. "I need to find out what happened here, if not for her own sake, then for mine. I'm not dropping the letter investigation; I'm going to do both at the same time."

"Sounds like a handful, but okay," he says. "You never do like to let a puzzle go."

I take a deep breath and roll over. "Tell me about your day."

"You mean searching through hours and hours of video for a vehicle in one of Caruthers' cases? It's riveting. Wallace has everyone working double duty."

"Better than being locked and handcuffed in a box?" I ask, a smile on my lips.

"Barely. At least when I was there I could get some sleep."

I scoff. "You did not sleep while you were captured!"

"Okay, no. But man, I wanted to," he says. "Where's an international assassin when you need one?"

"If you wanna get handcuffed again I can arrange that," I say.

"Careful. I've already got one *boss*. I'm not sure I need another," he jokes.

"What, Zara keeping you busy running her errands?"

"Actually, I meant Wallace. I didn't see Zara today, I guess she's out in the field."

I sit up. "At all?"

"I don't think so. But then again, I was sequestered behind Kemp and you know what a mountain of a man he is. I can barely see over his shoulders. She was probably just out working one of her cases or something."

"Yeah," I say, my mind immediately going to the worst-case scenario. But I pull it back. I'm not going to do that to myself.

We spend the rest of the time talking about our days, how Timber is holding up without me, and where we're going as soon as both of us get some time off together. But the entire time I can't quit thinking about Zara in the back of my mind. After I hang up, I shoot her a quick text, telling her to text me back when she can. I wait up for a little while, hoping for a response, but finally, I'm so tired I end up falling asleep with the lights on.

～

THE FOLLOWING MORNING WITH STILL NO TEXT FROM ZARA I'm starting to get worried. I shoot off a couple of texts to Liam for him to check on her for me today. He says he will, which at least makes me feel a little better. I'm just about to head out and find some breakfast when I notice Anna Forest's minivan parked in the hotel parking lot as soon as I exit the hotel. When I walk up to the driver's side window, I see her inside, drawing with what looks like charcoals on an art pad. Another dragon. I knock on the window, and she looks up, smiling. It takes her a second to pull out a wipe, cleaning her hands of the dark stains from the pencils before she rolls the window down. "Good morning," she says.

"Is everything okay?" I ask.

"I wasn't sure what time you got up, so I figured it would be better if I waited out here," she replies.

"For what?"

"Didn't you say last night you wanted to find the Carver family today? Interview them, since they were the only suspects that hadn't been contacted yet?"

I think back to our dinner the night before. "I did. But that doesn't explain what you're doing here."

She reaches under her art pad, then hands me a file folder for the second time in two days. "It took a little digging, but I managed to find them in Raleigh."

I look at the short report, giving their address and full names. "How did you get this?"

She shrugs. "I kept thinking about what all those neighbors said, how the Carvers closed themselves off from their community. While not conclusive, it could be indicative of abnormal behavior. I found myself fascinated by the opportunity to speak with them. And since I knew you wanted the same thing, I spent a few hours tracking them down."

"You didn't have to do that," I say. "I'm sure Hodge is done with the arson case; he could have done this for me. I didn't mean to keep you on the clock. Don't you have patients —a practice to attend to?"

"I'll be honest, I've only been in Fernview a few months and things are…slow. I've been working on a grant from William James but mostly I've been doing consulting work for surrounding police and sheriff departments. It's what's been paying most of my bills."

Now the minivan makes sense. "You had to know work

would be slim coming to a place like this. It isn't exactly a growing city."

"No, but I like the seclusion. And you're right, I did know. But the more I work with these different departments, the more I find what they do fascinating. I'm not saying I want to change careers, but I'd love to get more involved in the process."

"Is that your way of telling me we're going down to Raleigh together to interview Mr. and Mrs. Carver?"

Her eyes go wide. "No, I would never assume—I didn't mean to try and butt in—" she begins, looking flustered for the first time since I've met her. I'm glad to see she's not the impenetrable block of ice she appears on the outside.

"Anna, it's okay," I say. "I was just giving you a hard time."

She takes a breath of relief, though she still seems a little shell-shocked. "Really, Agent Slate, I wasn't trying to curry any special favor. I just wanted to help with—"

"It's Emily. And I know," I say. "You're fine. Actually, it would be nice to have the company. It's a two-and-a-half-hour drive each way. And you can finally give me your professional opinion on what kind of person we're chasing here." Wow, look at me, taking the initiative. Zara would be so proud. An uneasy pang hits my stomach as soon as I think of her again. I won't feel better until I hear from her or Liam.

"Emily, are you all right?" Anna asks.

I nod. "Just some stuff going on at home. Nothing I don't deal with every day." I glance at the interior of her car. It's an older model, with worn upholstery and the odometer is in the six-digit territory. "So, your car or mine?"

She looks around. "Yours might be better. I'm not sure I trust mine to leave the city limits. Once it breaks down, they might not be able to resuscitate." She gets out, a smile on her lips. "But that's what you get for two-hundred and fifty bucks, right?"

∼

THIRTY MINUTES LATER WE'VE HAD A QUICK BREAKFAST AT A drive-through and are on the road to Raleigh. It's almost a straight shot south, but there's no interstate here which means it's all state highways and back roads. And that means the drive isn't exactly smooth.

"You okay over there?" I ask, glancing at Anna. She's holding onto the "oh-shit" handle, looking straight forward in what I recognize as an attempt not to get sick.

"Mm-hmm," she says.

"Do you get motion sick often?" I ask.

"Usually it's not too bad, but I forgot to bring some Dramamine with me. I always have to take it before getting on a plane or a boat."

"Next place I see I'll stop so we can grab you some."

"You don't have to do that; I'll be okay," she says.

I suppress a laugh. "No offense, but I don't think you will. You're already looking a few shades paler. Just focus on one thing in front of us, and keep your eyes locked on it. It helps if it's something large and far away. Like a big tree, or the top of a mountain."

"Uh-huh, got it," she says.

We go a few more minutes and she begins looking slightly better, but I'm still going to stop as soon as we hit the next convenience store. "Why don't you give me the rundown on your analysis? Might help distract you."

"Right, that's a good idea," she says, finally letting go of the handle. She reaches into the back seat to retrieve her bag, but I hold out my hand.

"Maybe best not to read it. That's not going to help."

"Okay," she says, sitting back in the seat. "Well, our killer is someone who enjoys playing psychological games. I imagine they wanted to keep Jessica close, but not necessarily where anyone else would know where she was. She was easily identifiable, which suggests he's proud of his work, and wanted it showcased when found. I believe the coroner's report will give us some more information once it's complete, especially how she died. That will be a key factor in understanding this man. He's obviously someone who likes to exert control over others, to the most extreme point. So we're probably looking for someone with deep self-esteem issues. Which was why I asked you yesterday if you thought this was more of a nature or nurture situation."

"Oh," I say, thinking back. "I guess that is what you asked, isn't it?"

"Sorry," she says. "I can be a little...verbose sometimes. Great for writing proofs and for explaining concepts. Not so great when time is of the essence."

"Don't worry about it," I say. "You just caught me off-guard. But I think your theory is right on. Most of the time when I deal with guys like this, they're always trying to make up for something. Whether that's an inadequacy they feel is more of an issue than it really is, or something else. It's almost always about making themselves feel bigger than they actually are."

"So then you agree it's most likely a man," she says.

"That's what the data says," I reply. "Though I have had a few cases where I've run into a female killer. Those are always a little more complex."

"Can you tell me a little bit more about your other cases?" she asks. "I'd love to know what other sorts of individuals you've come across."

"Honestly, I don't like to spend too much time dwelling on them. Most of them were horrible, horrible people," I say. "If I could pay someone money to erase them from my memory, I absolutely would."

"Oh," Anna says. "I apologize; I should have realized. That was insensitive of me."

"No, it's just this job...it really shows you the worst of

humanity. And then when you think it can't get any more depraved, you're proven wrong." I take a deep breath. "Sometimes it's a lot."

"What do you do to cope?" she asks.

"Try not to think about it. And you know, hard drugs." For a second she looks appalled, until she realizes I'm joking and her mouth breaks into a grin. I get the feeling Anna Forest isn't the joking type.

"Do you have someone to talk to?" she asks.

"I do. The Bureau assigned me to a therapist a few months ago."

"And has it helped?"

It would probably be more helpful if I didn't keep trying to sabotage the process every time we meet. "Yes?"

She snorts, then covers her mouth and nose in embarrassment. When she's recovered, she turns to me. "Believe it or not, I hear that a lot. Sometimes the relationship between therapist and patient isn't a good fit. Don't be afraid to seek out someone else."

I nod. "Thanks. I'll try." Ahead of us I catch sight of the first convenience store I've seen in half an hour. Thank God. I need a distraction from this conversation. "Here we go. Time to get you fixed up."

Chapter Twelve

WE REACH RALEIGH BEFORE ELEVEN, heading to the address Anna provided. As we drive up, I can't help but notice the well-manicured lawn and the mulched beds lining the walkway. No doubt in the spring and summer they are filled with all varieties of flowers. The exterior of the house is painted a warm, welcoming shade of yellow, with white trim and shutters. The shingled roof looks to be in good condition.

There is a two-car garage attached to the side of the house, with a driveway leading up to it. The windows are all spotless, and there are several trees in the yard providing shade. The front porch is spacious, with a swing and a couple of rocking chairs inviting guests to sit and relax.

Overall, the house has a cozy, homely feel to it, with just the right amount of charm and character. It looks like the kind of place where anyone could easily imagine raising a family or hosting dinner parties with friends. Picture perfect, in almost every way.

It's almost too perfect. There's not one stray toy on the lawn, no errant water hoses left out and it looks like all the hard surfaces have been recently scrubbed as they're a few shades lighter than the surrounding houses.

"It's like a postcard," Anna says as we get out of the car. We've already discussed our strategy going in, and I'm doing my best to keep my game face on. There's a possibility the people living in this house may have buried a body in their old one; I can't allow myself to get distracted.

"Just follow my lead," I tell her.

"Do you think they're even home?" she asks. "On a Monday morning?"

"I hope so," I say. "I really don't want to try and track down where they work too."

I ring the doorbell, taking a look around the porch. There are no signs indicating someone lives here, no personal items of any kind. It's possible they just haven't gotten to it since supposedly they've only been here a month or so. Still…seems strange.

A few minutes pass before I finally hear the door rattle. A second later it opens to reveal a young girl, probably no older than twelve, with almond-shaped eyes and dark, silky hair. She's dressed in a blue dress that goes up to her collar and cuts off at the sleeves. Like her hair, it's silky smooth, without a speck of dust on it whatsoever. To me it looks like she's headed out for a night on the town, as ridiculous as that sounds.

"Hello," Anna says. "What a beautiful dress. Are your parents home?"

"Wait right here, please," she says, heading back through the house, though she leaves the door open.

"Thanks," I whisper. "Her dress threw me. Usually when I meet kids they're screaming or covered in some kind of goo."

Anna chuckles. "No problem. It is kind of odd, isn't it?"

Now that the door is open we can see into the house, and the interior matches the exterior. There isn't a scuff, mark, or bit of dirt anywhere that I can see. And the hallway before us is free of any furniture, save a small table right inside the front door. But even that seems to have been organized with the utmost care.

"Oh, I'm so sorry," a woman says, coming around the corner. She looks like an adult copy of the child; except she's wearing a different type of dress which is green. And she's in high heels. "I was in the basement and didn't hear the doorbell. If you're selling something, I'm afraid we don't have any interest."

I notice the little girl hasn't reappeared with her mother. "Are you Naomi-Ling Carver?"

She furrows her brow and folds her hands together in front of her. "Yes," she says, hesitant.

I show her my badge. "I'm Special Agent Emily Slate with the FBI. This is Dr. Forest with the Fernview Police Department. May we have a moment of your time?"

She opens her mouth, then closes it again, then opens it a second time, looking almost like a fish trying to catch its breath. "What is this all about?"

"It would be easier if we could come in and speak with you," I say, sensing her hesitation. Already I don't like the direction this is going.

"Very well," she says, stepping out of the way. "Come in. We can speak in the parlor."

I walk a few feet in and realize that when Mrs. Carver says *parlor*, she really means the small room at the front of the house. It's tastefully decorated, and minimalistic. A few pieces of art hang on the walls, but I don't see any pictures of her or her family. This could be anyone's home.

Anna and I take a seat on the small couch while Mrs. Carver perches herself on the edge of a wingback chair. "I have to admit, I've never even spoken with the FBI before," she says. She's coming across as more nervous than I was expecting. Maybe we really do have something here.

"Did you and your family reside at four-nineteen Heritage Road in Fernview?"

"We did, yes. In fact, we just moved." She fidgets in her

seat. "May I ask, how did you find us so quickly? We didn't leave a forwarding address."

I exchange a quick glance with Anna. "I did some digging and knew you used to live in North Carolina. It was just a matter of narrowing down the city. And since you used to live in Durham, I didn't think it was a stretch to search Raleigh."

Mrs. Carver bites her lip, then glances at the hallway. She's about as jumpy as a rabbit on cocaine and I fear she's going to fly up and push us out at any second.

"Ma'am, is there something wrong?" I ask. "You seem very anxious."

"No," she says. "Nothing's wrong. I just don't understand what you're doing here."

"We're investigating a murder," I say, keeping my voice neutral. Her eyebrows raise in surprise, though I can tell this is not the bombshell she was expecting.

"A *murder*? In Fernview?"

"We're not sure yet," I say. "But the body was found in your house."

"Mom?" All three of us turn to see the girl standing in the doorway, her eyes wide.

Mrs. Carver stands and leads her out of the room. "Come, Ellen, keep working on your studies. We'll talk about this later." She's back in the chair within seconds. "I'm sorry, she's homeschooled. Usually, it's just the two of us here by ourselves."

"Is your husband at work?" I ask.

She nods. "He just accepted a job at Insight Dynamics. He's an engineer."

"Where did he work while you were in Fernview?" I ask.

"A company called Techtopia; they were a startup that went under." She glances back at the doorway again, probably to make sure the girl isn't still listening in. "I'm sorry, I don't understand how someone could have been killed at our house."

"I never said she was killed there, Mrs. Carver. Her body was found between the walls. The new owners uncovered her during some home renovations."

Her hand goes to her heart and she sits back. "My God. Are you serious? Which wall?"

"In the kitchen, right beside the door that went into the cellar."

"How long was she in there?" Mrs. Carver asks.

"We were hoping you could answer that question," Anna says.

"*Me?* I didn't have anything to do with that. We never did anything to that house; that wall was already there."

"You're sure about that," I say.

She nods, adamant. "Absolutely. We didn't expect to stay in Fernview for long. But it turned out Bert's contract with Techtopia went on longer than expected. But we never did a thing to that house, other than paint a few rooms."

"Were you ever away from the house for an extended period? Maybe on a vacation?" I ask.

Again, she shakes her head. "No. We don't take vacations." I purse my lips and look at Anna again. She's wearing a similar expression. What kind of family doesn't take vacations?

"Is there any way someone could have gotten into your house, opened up the wall and hidden the body inside without your knowledge?"

"I don't see how. Even if they had, Ellen is allergic to drywall dust. She would have been coughing and sneezing up a storm if someone had torn open a wall. We would have noticed immediately."

"I see," I say, feeling a bit deflated. Whatever she's hiding, I'm not sure it's related to the body. And if she is telling the truth, that means the body had to be hidden in the house sometime during the Ashfords' tenure.

I lean forward. It's time to push a little. "Mrs. Carver, I

can't help but feel like you're not being entirely honest with us here."

"W-what?" she asks. "I don't know anything about a body, I've already told you."

"But you are very anxious about something," Anna says. "Your pupils are dilated, and your breathing is short and labored."

"How would you react knowing you lived in the same house as a dead body for five years?" she asks, defensive. She's holding herself as tight as a wound rubber band.

"You exhibited those signs before we even told you about the body," Anna adds.

Finally, a tear escapes her eye and she wipes it away quickly. "Please, you have to understand. We are good citizens; we pay our taxes. We would never do anything to hurt the country that has given us so much."

I exchange another look with Anna. "I'm sorry?"

She lets out a long breath, and deflates into the chair. "My husband and I are here illegally. We were brought over as children. It wasn't our choice. We have worked our way up from virtually nothing. If we're sent back, Ellen will have no one. We have no family here."

I hold up my hand. "Mrs. Carver, are you telling me you moved because of your immigration status?"

She nods, wiping her eye again. "Bert was contacted by someone over the phone—we don't know who it was—but they said if we didn't pay them fifty-thousand dollars they would reveal our status to the authorities and have us deported."

I pull out my phone, taking notes. "When was this?"

"About two months ago," she says. "We were so scared we didn't know what to do; we don't have that kind of money just sitting around. Eventually we decided it would be better if we just left, hopefully whoever it was couldn't find us again."

"Did they call you on your home phone or cell phone?" I ask.

"The house phone," she says. "It was a Tuesday morning, I believe." Even though she's told us, she's practically shaking, her thin hands with perfectly-manicured nails trembling.

"And you thought we were here to deport you?"

"Why else would the FBI show up on my doorstep?"

Okay, that at least explains her behavior. I'll need to look into her story more though, just to confirm. I doubt two illegal immigrants with a child would have anything to do with a body. No wonder they weren't very social. They've been living with this fear for who knows how long? "Have you tried for your citizenships?"

She nods. "Of course, but we've been on the waiting list for years now. I can already tell you we wouldn't have any trouble passing the tests. I'm just glad Ellen isn't facing the same stigma."

"She was born here I take it," I say.

"In two-thousand-nine," Mrs. Carver says.

This is looking more and more like a dead end. "Give me a little time to investigate this," I say, holding up my phone. "I'll see if I can't find out who threatened you."

"You're not going to arrest me?" she asks.

I shake my head, standing. "I have no interest in your citizenship status. Like I said, we're trying to find out who killed the girl who was found in your wall."

She stands as well, still trembling a little. "Thank you, but please, don't pursue it. If we just keep our heads low, our day will come. We just need to be patient."

I don't like the idea of not finding out who was threatening them, but then again it's far beyond the scope of this investigation. "If I do, I'll make sure it can't come back on you."

That seems to be good enough for her and she nods, appreciatively.

As we reach the door, I turn back. "Oh, there was one other thing. Did you ever cover your windows in newspaper when you lived there?" If I'm going to catch her in a lie, this is my last chance.

She gives me a sheepish smile. "Oh, that. When Ellen was six she contracted some rare form of sun poisoning. She couldn't be exposed to any UV rays otherwise she'd break out in hives. It took us three months to find a treatment that would finally allow her to go outside again. Newspaper was cheaper than curtains for every room in the house."

I give her another nod. "Thank you for your time, Mrs. Carver. Sorry to have disturbed you."

As soon as we're back in the car, Anna turns to me. "That was *not* how I expected things to go."

"Yeah," I reply. "Me either."

Chapter Thirteen

"Do you believe her?" Anna asks as we get back on the road headed for Virginia.

"It's not the most peculiar story I've ever heard, but it is strange." I rub my temple. "I'll have to do some investigating when we get back and see if her story checks out. Based on the way she was acting; she sure is scared of something."

"So once you find out she's telling the truth, are you gonna find out who threatened her?" Anna asks.

"If I have the time, but right now I need to focus on this case. If it turns out both her and her husband really are illegals, then I'll probably have to put it on the back burner. At least until I find out who stuffed Jessica in that wall." I glance over, wincing. "Sorry, that was disrespectful."

"Does this sort of thing happen a lot? What I mean is, do you often find cases going off in tangents like this, perhaps in ways you didn't anticipate?"

She's watching me intently, and I can't help but feel like I'm being psychoanalyzed a little. "Why the sudden interest?"

"I told you; I don't get to see this side of things very often. It's interesting to me to learn the process. It's like trying to figure out a puzzle, and I don't know about you, but I love puzzles."

I smile. "Yeah, I like puzzles too. But not the kind you have to put together out-of-the-box. Those drive me nuts. It feels like I'm doing the work someone has already done, making a picture when I already know what it will look like. I much prefer the type of puzzle that I don't know what the answer is until I find it."

She sits back, her gaze out the front windshield, watching as the trees fly by. "That makes sense. I'm glad to see that you're not like some of the other detectives that I've encountered, people who have been in this job too long."

"Yeah? Care to enlighten me?"

She gives me a wry smile. "If I could do it without violating doctor-patient confidentiality. Then yes absolutely. But then again, you'd probably be able to figure out who I was talking about just from context clues."

I smile. I like Anna Forrest, she's witty, but in an unconventional way. She's also a little withdrawn; one of those people you can tell is really thinking about what she's going to say before she answers. "My gut tells me Mrs. Carver was telling the truth. I don't think she or her family had anything to do with Jessica being in that wall. They just happen to be socially reclusive. Which didn't do them any favors with their neighbors."

"So then, what does that mean?" Anna asks.

"It means, that we need to go back and talk to Jake Ashford again. He's been our prime suspect from the beginning, hasn't he? Didn't Detective Hodge think he was the one responsible?" I think back to the hastily written notes I read in the file after Anna delivered them. Hodge hadn't singled Ashford out specifically, but he had circled his name a couple of times and was interested in a follow-up interview.

"I believe that was the detective's initial impression," Anna says. "Given what I know about the man, it may not be a stretch. Based on the information I found, he's what most people would refer to as 'a grade-A dickhead'. Nobody likes this guy. He pushes and shoves to get his way, and usually does. Then his daughter ends up in the walls of his own house? It seems too much to be a coincidence."

So Anna has her own theories about Jake Ashford. But I don't think she's telling me everything she thinks. "You didn't say anything earlier."

"It's not my place. I'm not the detective, I'm just a helper."

"Listen, if we're to be working together, I need to know that you feel you can be open and honest with me. You have expertise, I want to hear it."

Anna shifts in her seat uncomfortably. "Okay. From what I know about the man and what information I learned from Detective Hodge and some of the other people in Fernview, I believe he exhibits a classic case of narcissism. Everything I've been able to find points to the fact that Jake Ashford believes it's his way or the highway. No matter what the subject matter. And when people argue with them, he tends to get combative. I haven't met a person yet who has told me he's an easy person to be around. I have to imagine having a father like that isn't easy either."

Interesting. "Have you spoken to Judy? Alone?"

"No, I haven't had the chance. Hodge has been there the entire time."

"Did you give this assessment to Hodge?"

She chuckles and shakes her head. "He never asked."

Why am I not surprised? "Okay, well I guess we should probably inform him of our progress. Maybe Hodge can do some legwork for us, check on the immigration status of the Carvers. At least that will help us eliminate them from suspect pool."

"Are you sure you want him knowing they're potential illegals?" Anna asks.

"That's a good point. Maybe we'll leave that checking to

us." I pause a second. "There's actually someone in my office who can do that research. She won't say anything." Only now I realize I still haven't heard back from Zara. My heart does another one of those little flippy things that I don't like. I pull out my phone and I speed dial Liam. He picks up on the first ring.

"Hey there," he says, his voice chipper. "How's the investigation going?"

"Fine. Have you heard back from Zara yet?"

"No, but I checked with Wallace. He just informed me that she's out working on the case, undercover. We have to wait until she contacts us."

Dammit, I knew it. God, I hope she's being safe.

"As soon as you hear from her you let me know." I can't believe she didn't tell me she was going on an undercover assignment. It must've been very sudden.

"Will do."

"In the meantime, I need you to run a I.S. check for me. I need you to look into the immigration status of Naomi-Ling and Bert Carver of Raleigh, North Carolina. I'll shoot you over the address here in a second."

"Okay." He pauses. "Why?"

"Just trying to eliminate some suspects."

"Do I need to look for anything else?"

I glance over to Anna. She's looking at me, concern on her face. I know she's thinking about whoever threatened the Carvers, but I can't deal with that right now. I need to keep my focus on Jessica. Maybe once all this is over I can go back and investigate some sort of this extortion ring, if that's what really happened. "Nope, that's it just that for now. The sooner you can get back to me the better."

"You got it. I'm sure I can pull up their information through the PIA's."

"Thanks, Liam, talk soon." I hang up and then one-handed text him the address that we just left.

"Friend at the FBI?" Anna asks. I nod. "Seems like you guys are pretty close."

"To be honest, he's my boyfriend too." I look over at her, sheepishly.

"I could say something about spending so much time with your significant other, but I'll refrain." She shoots me that smile again, and as the silence fills the car I feel like that's the closest thing to a joke I'm going to get out of Anna Forest.

AFTER ABOUT AN HOUR, I GET A TEXT BACK FROM LIAM confirming the Carvers are illegal, but they haven't been flagged by ICE yet. I know he'll hold off until I give any further information so there is no risk of him leaking their information to the authorities.

"Looks like the Carvers were telling the truth," I say, reading the text string again. "If that's the case, then they definitely didn't have anything to do with Jessica."

"Should I notify Hodge we're going after Ashford? He can probably get over to his house and detain him if you need him to," Anna asks.

I shake my head. "Not yet. We don't have any reason to hold Jake Ashford yet, this is just a hunch. I want to talk to him first. We don't want to spook him. If he really did have something to do with this, he's already on edge."

Anna wrinkles her nose. "Who else could it be? I highly doubt Judy would have killed her sister and put her in that wall. At least that wasn't my impression from my initial assessment of her."

"I thought you hadn't interviewed her," I say.

"I didn't. I just watched the recordings of her and Hodge."

We pass an old farmhouse that's partially collapsed from age. I think back to her original question. "It's possible anyone could have had access to that wall. A contractor could have come in and installed it before the Ashfords even moved in. Maybe the realtor had the place renovated before going on the market. Or they could've had it worked on while they were living there which would've given access to dozens of different people. What we need to find out, is if Jake Ashford really has the temperament to kill his own daughter."

"And when that wall was built," she adds.

"That too. You can call Hodge and let him know we're prepping to interview him. At least give the office a heads-up."

She doesn't waste any time. "Hello, Deborah? It's Anna. Y—yes, I did get the basket, thank you." Anna shoots me a quick glance and a smile. "I need to speak to Hodge, is he still in? Every time I call his main number it always goes to voice-mail. Sure...yeah, I'll hold." She covers up the end of the phone. "She got me a fruit basket for Christmas. I had to give most of it away, it was so—" She turns back to the phone. "Yes, I'm still here. Oh...he's...oh. What about Reyes? Really? The whole department?"

I furrow my brow and give her a look, but her concentration is on the phone call. "Okay, yes, thanks." She hangs up. "Hodge, Reyes and half the squad is out on this fire case."

"Really?" I ask. "That's weird."

"I thought so too. Maybe everyone's just getting over excited; not a lot happens around here. I thought Jessica was going to be the biggest thing this week. But I guess everyone wants to see the big fire."

"Guess so." Well, no matter. It isn't like we need any backup; we're just headed to talk to a sixty-five-year-old man. I doubt we'll run into any problems.

I really like having Anna along. She's a calming presence, whether she knows it or not. "What happens if Ashford isn't in a talking mood?"

"We'll cross that bridge when we get to it."

By the time we get back to Fernview and pull onto Jake

Ashford's property, the sun has just disappeared behind the Blue Ridge Mountains in the distance. After moving out of my old home, Ashford moved to a large tract of farm property on the edge of town. He doesn't have a driveway, just a large yard littered with gravel, grass growing up between the rocks. A blue Chevy sits off to the right, in front of an old lean-to that's about to collapse.

The house itself sits in front of us, a two-story farmhouse up on a brick crawlspace. A porch stretches across the front and wraps around the left side, leading to a side door. The lights in all the downstairs windows are on. "Has he ever met you in person, at the station maybe?" I ask.

"I don't think so. I don't remember seeing him in person, why?" she asks.

"Just curious." We'll need to be careful here. With Ashford's temperament, he could shut down before we even get started. I've already decided how I'm going to approach this—friend of the daughter, play it up all innocent.

Anna follows me up the steps and I knock on the door. After a few minutes I hear rustling. A bolt shoots and the door swings in. For a second I'm confused. I thought we'd come here to find an aging Mr. Ashford—as I used to know him—but the man at the door doesn't look a day over fifty. His dark hair is peppered with smatterings of gray, and his face is lined, but not wrinkled. He's leaning on a cane in his right hand, but his eyes are still sharp and hold an air of suspicion. "Yes?" he asks.

"Mr. Ashford, do you remember me? Emily—Slate?" I ask.

Recognition dawns on him. "Emily…Judy's friend, right?"

"Right," I say. "How have you been?"

"Well, to be honest, Emily, it's been pretty fucked here since Thursday." I have to force my face to remain neutral. I forgot how brusque he could be.

"I was very sorry to hear about Jessica," I say.

"Yeah," he replies, then seems to notice Anna. "Who are you?"

"Mr. Ashford, I'm with the FBI," I say, getting his attention again. "I'm assisting Fernview PD on this case. This is Dr. Anna Forest, who is consulting. There are a lot of people trying to find the person responsible for this."

"They damn well better be," he says. "Well? Do you want to come in or did you just stop by to stand on my porch?" he opens the door wide enough for us.

"Thank you," I reply, taking his cue. Anna follows in silently. She's kind of like a cat, moving around a space, not touching anything, not making any noise, but studying it all in detail.

"You have some updates on the case?" he asks, and I notice he's got a pronounced limp, even with the cane. Still, he moves quick, leading us into one of the rooms off the main hallway. It's been set up as a study. Without even slowing down he heads for his desk, where a bottle of brandy sits, open. A small glass sits beside it, alcohol leaving a ring on the leather top. He takes a seat behind it and pours himself one...or maybe this is number five.

"We'd just like to ask you some more questions," I say.

"What for? That detective already spent two hours interrogating me." He downs the glass.

"Did he ask you about the wall where she was found?"

He looks up. "What?"

"The wall. You had it installed, right?"

He sneers at me. "What does—what are you implying?"

"I'm just trying to establish a timeline," I say. "Information from the previous owners shows the wall wasn't there while they lived at the house. And the people who bought the house after you had a little girl who is allergic to drywall. They couldn't take the chance of installing or demolishing walls."

"So you think I did, is that it?" he pours another glass, his bottom lip pronounced. "Typical of a woman to jump to conclusions. You think I killed Jess, then shoved her body in there for what? To help keep my house warm?" He downs the glass again.

"Mr. Ashford…" I begin.

"Get out," he says. "Get the hell out of my house. Friend of Judy's or not." It's as I suspected; his emotions are running too high to get anything out of him. That combined with his normal temperament has turned this into the shortest interview I've ever conducted.

"We'll come back later," I say, heading for the door.

"The fuck you will," he yells after. Glass smashes against one of the walls in the room we just left, and I pick up the pace, indicating Anna follow close. We reach the door and show ourselves out.

As we reach the bottom of the stairs, I see a pair of headlights pulling into the parking area. The car pulls up beside ours and a second later Judy steps out.

This just got a lot more complicated.

Chapter Fourteen

My one-time best friend steps forward, caution on her face. "Hey, Emily, what's going on?"

"They accused me of killing your sister, that's what," Ashford says from behind us he comes out on the porch, leaning up against the railing, the bottle still in his hand. It must've been the glass that met its untimely demise.

"That's not what we said, we're not here to pin blame, just gather information," I tell Judy, putting my hands out. With Ashford so volatile, I'm sure having Judy here is only going to complicate the situation.

"I thought you were headed back to D.C.," Judy says. "And who is this?"

"Judy, I'm Dr. Forest; I'm a forensic psychologist who has been helping on your sister's case," Anna says. She doesn't move to shake Judy's hand, but her voice carries an air of authority I haven't heard from her before.

"Forensic psychologist?"

"That's right. Due to the nature of your sister's...case, the Fernview Police Department thought it was prudent to bring me in."

"I know what they're doing," Ashford says again taking

another swig. "They bring in all these fancy experts so they can pin it all on me."

I turn to Mr. Ashford. "Mr. Ashford, no one has accused you of anything. All we wanted to know was if you knew when the wall in your house was built."

"That's bullshit and you know it," he says. "The federal government is coming down here to interfere in our affairs and they're just looking for a fall guy. I know how your departments work; I've seen more than enough of it on TV. And didn't the FBI just have a massive scandal where some of its own agents were found to have been working for a foreign enemy? I saw it on the news. The president was talking about it. Complete reorganization, he said. If this is how you go about doing your jobs then no wonder it all fell apart." He glares at me with pointed eyes.

"Dad, calm down." Judy turns to me. "I need to know what's going on, right now."

"We're just here to ask a couple of questions," I say. "We're trying to establish when the wall between the kitchen and the living room was built. Once we do that, we'll have a better idea of who could've had access and might have put your sister in there."

"You're talking about the wall where she was found." Judy draws in a deep breath dropping her head, like all the strength is gone out of her. "I can't believe you would think we had anything to do with this. You, of all people, know how important Jessica was to me. I was devastated when she disappeared. Are you telling me all those afternoons we spent together, all those weekends that we talked about her about what would happen if she came back, even planning trips to go find her...you're telling me after all of that, you think my father had something to do with it?"

I can practically feel the pent-up rage in Judy, radiating out from her in waves. It's something I felt a little bit of yesterday, but apparently our presence here has brought it out fully.

I'm not sure we're going to get anywhere with either of them. And I realize now that the news still might be too raw for them to be able to look at this in any way other than emotionally.

"Judy, I'm really sorry. I'm not saying your father had anything to do with this, I'm just trying to find the truth. I never had the chance to know Jessica personally, but I knew her through you. And I know how important she was to you, which is why I want to do everything I can to find out who did this."

"Oh, this is just a load of bullshit. She's just angling to get a big win," Ashford says, attempting to make his way down the steps still using his cane.

Judy glares at me then huffs and goes to her father. "Dad, no, you stay up here. You know you're not good on steps when you've been drinking."

"Girl, I've been walking up and down steps without your help for fifty years. I think I can—"

Just as he says it, his cane slips on the top step and he loses his balance, tumbling down. All three of us rush to him at once. His brandy bottle clatters on the ground next to him, the amber liquid pouring out onto the gravel.

"Dad!" Judy reaches him first and helps him into a sitting position, but he just swats her away once he's up. As Anna and I get close he waves his cane in our direction, his grip on it still firm.

"Don't you come any closer. You're not welcome here. I won't have people accusing me of murder walking on my property. You are free to leave at your convenience."

"Dad, are you all right?" Judy asks.

"Just, leave me. I can do it," he says, getting himself up and climbing the steps again.

I can see leaving is the best course of action right now. Maybe I'll be able to talk with Judy again later, but tempers

118 • ALEX SIGMORE

are running too hot and our presence here is only making the situation worse.

Judy manages to get him back up the steps despite his protestations. Once he's up and I'm sure he's not going to fall again I motion to Anna that we should head back to the car. When I reach my driver side door, I look back and see Judy is still watching us from the porch. Her father has disappeared back inside but she's glaring at me, giving me a steely-eyed look. I know that look. It means that what little trust still remained between us has now been broken. Whatever I was going to get out of Judy by being her friend, has now disappeared like a puff of smoke. Which is only going to make things harder.

I give her a resigned look and get back into the car. Anna sits beside me, her gaze neutral as she stares out the front windshield.

As we pull away, she speaks for the first time. "You did the best you could, it's a tense and volatile situation. Sometimes people react irrationally. Perhaps when tempers calm."

I scoff. "Yeah, that could have gone better."

"Maybe, maybe not. Even if Judy hadn't been there, her father would've told her about our visit eventually anyway. More than likely, her response would've been the same in the end."

"I was just hoping that I could do this without hurting Judy any further. She's been through enough."

"I can't disagree with you there. Jake Ashford is...a lot."

The way she says it makes me want to chuckle. "That's putting it mildly." I sigh. "His combativeness tells me that he either had the wall installed himself, or he knows who did it and when. But getting that information out of him is going to be nearly impossible. Which means we need to find another avenue of investigation."

"Is he still on the suspect list?" Anna asks.

"Definitely. If he has a temper like that around us, just

imagine what it's like for his kids. We'll also probably need to talk to any known associates, especially from around the time Jessica disappeared. But, it's been so long, I don't know if any of them would even remember his behavior from that long ago."

"You're hoping to find a specific incident that could explain… What? A psychotic break?"

I turn the car back onto the main road and head back into Fernview. "You're the psychologist, is that plausible?"

She's silent for a moment. "It's not out of the realm of possibility, but it's unlikely that Jake Ashford would've had a psychotic break, killed his daughter, then gone back to life as normal. I believe you have the right idea, looking for any other incidents around that time that would line up with the disappearance. But we should also be looking for other, long-lasting effects that would still persist to this day."

I turn to her. "Like drinking?"

"That *could* be a symptom. Then again, it could just be a coping mechanism upon learning that his daughter was dead."

She's right. I can't forget that until this week, as far as anyone knew, Jessica had run away fifteen years ago. I have to remember that not everyone has been as jaded by this job as I have. Where I will automatically go to the worst-case scenario, a lot of other people will hold out hope. Hope beyond what is reasonable. It's only human to want to believe that somehow everything is going to be okay. That we will see our loved ones again and that the horrors of our past are all nothing but a bad dream.

"Okay. New plan. We find out as much as we can about that house, and Jake Ashford before doing anything else."

"How do we do that?" Anna asks.

"Records."

Chapter Fifteen

SINCE IT's obvious we're not going to get anything from Jake
Ashford, our next stop is going to be the town permit office.
Unfortunately, they're already closed for the evening, which
means we're at a dead-end until tomorrow. But I plan on
being there as soon as they open, so we can get a look at the
public permit records for the house. They should tell us when
the wall was built, who the contractor was, and how long the
construction took—assuming whoever built the wall actually
applied for the appropriate permits. If the wall was built
specifically to hide the body, then it's possible it was done
without the proper permitting, in which case we'll have no
choice but to return to Ashford with a new strategy. My gut
tells me that Jessica was placed in that wall when it was originally constructed. That makes the most sense; if someone was
planning to do it, that would have been the best and easiest
opportunity.

It's probably a good thing the office is closed because by
the time we get back to the hotel and I drop Anna back at her
car, my eyes are going blurry. She agrees to meet me first thing
in the morning to keep working on the case. I like working
with her, and I'd much rather deal with her than Hodge. She

tries to get me to dinner again, but I'm too exhausted. It's been a really long day, and I need to decompress. But as soon as I'm back in my room, I realize all I've done is given myself a chance to think about Zara. What kind of undercover assignment is she working on? What sort of danger is she in? And why didn't she give me a heads-up? Probably because she knew I would worry, and I'm willing to bet she thought she could pull it off before I noticed her absence. She and I are going to have a long talk when she gets back—though I have to admit it feels a little weird being on the other side of that conversation. Usually, I'm the one trying to keep things from her so *she* won't worry.

With some effort, I turn my attention back to Jessica Ashford, and I go over the files Anna brought me again. Included in them are the original missing person's report from nineteen-ninety-eight. It states that Jessica went missing on the evening of April twenty-fifth, and hadn't been seen since. No contact with family or friends as of one month after the disappearance. After that, there are no further updates. The file hadn't been closed, but it had been signed off by a Detective Palmer who believed she had run away. It was his belief she would eventually return home to her family.

If only he'd known how right he would be.

As I'm reading back through Hodge's notes, my stomach rumbles. I probably should have taken Anna up on dinner because now I'm starving. There are a couple of places to eat around here, some I know from having visited them as a kid, but I don't feel like venturing out. The odds I'll run into someone I know are better than average and the last thing I want to do is be pulled into another discussion about my profession or what I was like as a kid. So instead, I head down to the lobby and spring for a pack of crackers and a tin of nuts.

I get through about half of each before my eyes completely glaze over and I'm forced into bed. I shoot Liam a good night text and settle in, hoping for a restful night's sleep. But my dreams are punctuated with conflicting images of people and places from my childhood, all revolving around that house and the wall that currently stands there. Every time I try to get away from the house, I end up right back in front of it, staring at that fucking wall. It's like I can't escape it.

When my phone wakes me up I feel like I've barely slept an hour, even though I probably got almost a full night. As I'm getting ready my phone buzzes again. I figure it's probably Liam checking on me, but when I check the caller ID I see I missed a call from Fernview Police. Concerned, I call the number back immediately.

"Fernview Police Department, is this an emergency?"

"Good morning," I say. "No. This is Emily Slate. I just received a call from there?"

"Oh, Emily, yes," the officer says. "Just a minute. Captain Reyes wanted to speak with you. I'll put you through to his line."

A second later the phone clicks. "Reyes."

"Captain, it's Agent Slate. Did you just call me?"

"I did, I hope I didn't wake you."

"No, I was just getting ready. I want to be over at the permit office when they open at nine." I head back into the bathroom with the phone balanced between my ear and shoulder. I can get ready and talk at the same time.

"Then you've made some progress. I wanted to get in touch because I know Detective Hodge was supposed to assist you these past few days, but we've literally been putting out fires all over town."

I'm in the middle of putting deodorant on, but I pause. "Wait, there was more than one fire?"

"Three, in fact. One looks like it was caused by an open flame too close to the house—fire pit that hadn't been properly secured. The other two we're still looking into. But that's why I wanted to call. I can make Hodge available if you need him, but if you can do without him for another day or so it would be helpful."

"Actually, Dr. Forest and I have been making some good progress already. If you don't mind, I'd like to continue working with her."

"Dr. Forest?" he asks. "Oh, I didn't realize she was still assisting you. I thought that had only been on Sunday when you needed help with the neighbors."

I give him a brief rundown of what we learned yesterday from the Carvers, and then our unfortunate encounter with Jake Ashford. "I believe she's an asset. She has a unique way of looking at things."

"Well, if you think she can help and her schedule is clear, be my guest," he says. "But I want to bring Hodge back on this as soon as we have these other issues wrapped up. Technically it's still his case, even though you're the one working it."

I roll my eyes; glad he can't see. "No, I understand."

"Good. Keep me updated, and good work so far. Glad to know we can eliminate the Carvers as suspects. That was some legwork driving all the way down there. I doubt any of my guys would have gone to the trouble."

And that's your problem, I think, but don't say aloud. The last thing I want to do is antagonize Reyes. "It was a nice drive," I tell him.

As soon as I'm off the phone I finish getting ready quick then head back to the hotel lobby. I grab a banana and a muffin, along with whatever brew they have in the breakfast area before I head back out. Despite never having visited the town permit office before, I know exactly where it is. Fernview has a small downtown, and everything is grouped, meaning all the municipal buildings are within a block of each other. Finding a convenient place to park, I tear through my meager breakfast, watching the doors of the permit office as if by concentration alone I could make them unlock.

At ten minutes before nine, Anna knocks on my passenger

window and I unlock the doors to let her in. I didn't even see her walk up. "Cold front coming through," she says, once she's inside. She's still in jeans today, but her black coat is much longer and looks warmer than the one she had yesterday. "Is it always this cold here in January?"

"From what I can remember, yeah. It has something to do with the wind coming off the Appalachian Mountains. I'm not really sure how it works. But I always recall the first two months of the year being frigid."

"I'll need to invest in some warmer clothes, I think."

"Aren't you used to this, coming from Boston?" I ask.

"I didn't think I'd need them," she replies. "I got rid of most of my really heavy stuff. Seems kind of stupid now, but I thought central Virginia weather would be more like Florida."

"That's the beauty of this place," I say. "You get Maine in the winter, Florida in the summer. It's always one extreme or another."

As we're chatting, a woman climbs the steps to the permit office, unlocking the front door and making her way inside. "That's our cue," I say and we both step out into the windy morning. I pull my own coat tighter as we mount the steps. The florescent lights above us are just flickering to life when we step inside.

"Oh," the woman we saw enter says, holding her hand to her chest. She's standing on the far side of the room, close to the light switches. "You startled me. Usually I don't see anyone until at least lunchtime."

"We didn't mean to frighten you," Anna says. "We are eager to look through some records."

The woman laughs. "I believe that's the first time I've ever heard anyone say that, and *I* work here." She settles in behind the main desk in the lobby. "What sort of records are you looking for?"

"Construction permits, specifically, residential ones," I tell her. "We're looking to see if anyone filed permits at four-nineteen Heritage Road, here in Fernview."

"Do you know when?" the woman asks, already typing on her computer.

I exchange a quick glance with Anna. "Anywhere from two-thousand-four until two-thousand-fifteen." That covers the entire time the Ashfords would have lived in the house.

The woman peers closer to the screen. "This may be a little more difficult than you were expecting. We're in the process of digitizing everything, but we've only made it back as far as twenty-ten. I can show you those records now, but everything before that will be in the stacks in the basement."

"Let's start with the online records," I say. "Maybe we'll get lucky."

"Allrighty," the woman says. "I'm Bea, by the way. Unfortunately I'm the only person the town sees to pay to work in this office, which is why we're so behind in getting all the records scanned in." She motions to a pile of banker boxes behind the desk. "Those are today's project and will probably take me most of the day." She types while she speaks, her age obviously not slowing her down. If anything, I'd describe her as feisty.

"We appreciate all your help," Anna says. "It looks like a large and thankless job."

"I wish someone would tell that to the town council," she replies. "Okay. No permits filed for that address after twenty-ten." With two taps the screen goes blank. She opens the drawer next to her, pulling out a large set of keys on a ring as big as an orange and stands. "Downstairs we go."

Before she heads down the hall, she returns to the front door and locks it. "I don't mean to alarm you, but since it's only me here, I can't leave the place open with no one watching the front. Which is technically against the fire code, but what am I supposed to do? I'm just one person."

"We don't mind," I say. "You don't look like the kidnapping type."

This produces another laugh from Bea. "C'mon." She motions as we follow her down the narrow hallway to where we make a turn down a set of steps. The floor below is shallow, and my head almost touches the ceiling. If Liam were here, he'd have to duck. "This building was built sometime in the eighteen-hundreds and yet the council thought it would make a good place to store records." In front of us is a caged door, separating us from the rows and rows of documents behind it. Bea unlocks the door with the first key she finds in the middle of the ring and swings the door open for us. "If you need to photocopy anything, just bring it back upstairs, you can use the big copier we have in the back office. It's large enough for blueprints if necessary."

"Thank you," I say, stepping in. "Any clue where we should start?"

"Everything is organized by district and each district is in a different quarter of the town. Northwest, northeast, etc. Quarter, district, street. At least, that's how it's *supposed* to be. You wouldn't believe how many times I find documents in the wrong place. It's like people don't know how to put things back where they found them, so now I do it. No offense."

"This reminds me of the evidence locker at the police station," Anna says.

"I didn't realize you were with the police," Bea says.

"We're not...technically," I tell her. "I'm with the FBI and Dr. Forest here is a consulting psychologist."

"Oh, that makes me feel a little better. At least you know what you're getting into here."

I glare at the rows and rows of documents. "Yes, we do."

Chapter Sixteen

DESPITE BEA'S claims that everything "should" be organized by district, Anna and I quickly find that's not the case. It only seems like half of everything is where it should be, which means it takes us the entire morning and early into the afternoon before I finally find the right set of files. My stomach is rumbling from too little food and too much caffeine, but I'm not leaving here until we have what we need.

"This looks like it might be it," I call to her from across the stacks. She pokes her head around into my aisle.

"Really? Thank goodness. And you have to do this sort of thing all the time?" she asks.

I get up off the floor, grabbing the file and bringing it into better light. "More than I'd like. A lot of the time my job involves wading through piles and piles of useless information, looking for that one nugget I need."

"I can't stand it when things aren't organized," she says. "I know where everything is in my office at all times...or at least, I think I do. But there is real science that shows a clean work area helps clear our own mental clutter, allowing us to focus on our primary tasks."

"Yeah, I hate a mess too," I say, though I think back to my

bedroom with all of my childhood photos still in random piles. I'll take care of that when I get back.

The box is marked with my house's neighborhood, from 1990 until 2010, which should be what we're looking for. I set the box on the table, opening it up to find it stuffed with documents. I start handing piles to Anna, who skims over them. "These look like permits for some of your old neighbors. Here's one for Ms. Holloway—the widening of a door and the addition of a ramp to her back entrance."

"Does it say who the builder was?"

"Griffin Construction…looks like a local company."

I pull out a few more documents, flipping through them. None of them are for my house. I have to face the possibility that whoever built the wall never wanted anyone to know what they were doing. If that's the case, then it could have been anyone.

"Oh…Emily, look," Anna says, pointing at the box. Right below my hand a piece of paper is sticking out with my old address on it. I pull out the work order and find it's the first in a series of documents, all relating to the renovation of the house.

"I think this is it," I say, pulling the rest of the documents out and spreading them all out on the table. "It says here the construction was at the request of the homeowner, dated May, two thousand eight."

"Then Ashford really did have the work done," Anna says.

"And that's almost ten years to the month after Jessica went missing." Already my mind is buzzing with coincidences upon coincidences. I add this one to the list.

We spend a few more minutes reading over all the documents. It seems the permit was filed in May, but the construction wasn't completed until June, giving someone a full month to get Jessica in that wall. In addition to the wall, other, smaller items were completed at the same time: moving a water line, changing out some of the electrical, and a few other, cosmetic changes. But most of it centered on this wall.

"Where does this leave us?" Anna asks.

I look up at the top corner of the permit. "It seems Ashford also used Griffin Construction for the work. I wonder if back then this company was the one all the neighbors recommended to each other."

"That would make sense. People generally trust the word of someone they know up to ten times more than if information came from a stranger. If one person in the neighborhood had a good experience with Griffin, it's not out of the realm of possibility they recommended them to anyone else who wanted work. And we already know Jake Ashford isn't shy about getting into other people's business," she says, matter-of-factly.

"We need to talk with whoever runs this company," I say. "They should be able to tell us who the site foreman was, and how many different people worked on the project. That will expand our suspect pool, but at this point I don't see we have a choice."

"Even though Ashford hired someone to build the wall?" Anna asks.

I put everything else back in the box except for the files relating to the house. "One way or another, we'll need to eliminate everyone else as possible suspects before I can approach him again. You saw how volatile he was; if there's even a chance someone else could have had a hand in this, we need to find it before heading back there."

Once we've packed everything back up, we head back upstairs with the files. Bea assists us in copying everything, making the work go fast, for which I'm grateful. Within minutes we're back outside and headed to my car. But something has been bothering me and I've been putting it off, even though I should have brought it up first thing this morning.

"Did you not tell Reyes you were continuing to assist me on the case?" I ask as soon as we reach my car.

"Was I supposed to?" Anna asks. "If I'm bothering you—"

"No, it's not that," I say. "I just spoke to him this morning and he was surprised to hear you were still assisting."

She quirks her mouth. "That's probably because he's used to me sitting in that office all day, going over whatever they bring me. Reyes is competent, but he often forgets that I'm not just a glorified secretary. Once he asked me to bring him a coffee."

I raise my eyebrows. "Did you?"

"I brought him the can of grounds from the station's kitchen. He didn't ask again after that."

I chuckle, getting in. "I bet he didn't."

"Does this mean I'm still on the case?" she asks, leaning down and looking through the open passenger door, but not getting in the car yet.

"I'm happy to have you here as long as you have the time," I say. "It makes going through stuff like that a lot less tedious." I nod toward the permit office.

"Great," she says, getting into the passenger side. "What's next?"

I pull out my phone, doing a quick search to find Griffin Construction. "I want to talk to whoever runs this company. They should have their own records; things they wouldn't have filed. At least, I hope they still do."

"Lunch on the way?" Anna asks.

My stomach rumbles again at the mention of food. "Definitely." But as I look at my search results, I frown. "Damn. Looks like they went out of business a few years ago."

"But they were local, right? Maybe whoever ran the company still lives here."

"Let's hope so," I say. I find the company's webpage, announcing their closure. All the other links are dead, but the header across the top shows two men, side by side. Under them it reads: Connor and Mac Griffin. "Okay, new plan. First lunch, then we'll need to head back to the station and see if we can't find if either of these men still lives here."

"Great," Anna says. "I know the perfect place for lunch."

AFTER A QUICK LUNCH AT A DINER I HADN'T BEEN TO IN AT least fifteen years, Anna and I head back to the station. The diner was exactly the same from what I could remember. I think Mom might have taken me there a few times. I recalled the brown wainscoting that was on every wall, but nothing else. Anna, for the most part, sat silent for the meal, seeming just to enjoy the food. I found myself in the strange position of being the one that had to steer the conversation; but she seemed just as happy sitting in silence as she did when we were discussing the case. She's a strange sort of person, not like Zara at all who would have been chatting away the entire time. But she emits this ethereal sense of calmness that only a therapist can, I suppose. Regardless, I find her presence comforting.

Back at the station, we manage to look up both Connor and Mac Griffin using the DMV database. Mac's license expired in 2016, making me think he probably moved to another state. However, Connor's is still active, and gives his current address on the east side of town.

As we're making our way back out of the station, we see Hodge getting out of his car, headed our way. His face contorts when he sees Anna. "What are you doing here?"

"Didn't the chief tell you? She's assisting me on the case," I say.

"Assisting—doing what?" His face looks like he's smelled something bad.

"I'm providing my professional and practical experience in helping Emily track down Jessica's killer," Anna says, proudly.

"But this is my case," Hodge says.

"Reyes told me you were busy with the fires. Have you already wrapped those cases up?" I ask.

He shakes his head. "No, it looks like they're going to be more complex than we thought. As far as we can tell, at least two of those fires were set on purpose. We may be looking at an arsonist working in the area. I don't have to tell you this isn't the best timing."

"Sounds like you have your hands full." I try not to sound patronizing, but I'm finding it a little difficult after Hodge's whining.

"It's nothing I can't handle, but obviously the Ashford case has to go on the back burner while we investigate who is setting these fires. So I guess it's a good thing that you're here."

I nod. "I guess it is."

He doesn't say anything else, only gives us a resigned look before heading into the station.

"You think he resents us for working on this case without him?" Anna asks.

"I don't really care. As far as I'm concerned this is our case now. And I would really like to wrap it up before Hodge decides he can't sit on the sidelines any longer." We head back to my car, but I notice Anna giving me a strange sort of look. "What?"

"You don't like working with local police officers, do you?"

I sigh. "I never set out to be that way. When I first started working with the Bureau, I had hoped that I'd be able to work hand-in-hand with the LEOs to solve cases. But it seems like more often, especially recently, I've just been butting heads with every department I encounter. Thankfully Fernview isn't nearly as combative as some of the others, but I've had some real bad incidents lately. Just a few months ago I had to arrest a local police chief for obstruction and conspiracy in relation to a case I was working. He's still awaiting trial."

"I guess that's why you like working with me," she says. "Since I'm not technically on the force."

She may have something there. I hadn't really thought about it until just now. In fact, I still thought I was being neutral while dealing with the Fernview Police. But I'm thinking now that Anna might be right. Maybe I've been allowing my own prejudices to get in the way. That's not something I ever wanted; I had hoped I would never act like all the other typical FBI agents.

"You're right, I need to be better about this. I guess after butting heads with local departments for so long I've started to expect that they're not out to cooperate."

"It makes sense," Anna says. "I know you're probably sick of me saying things like this, but I can't help but look at this through a psychological perspective. Your relationship with the local departments is always going to be a reflection of your experience. If you have a bunch of bad experiences, you're going to expect bad experiences in the future."

"I guess that's true. From here on out I'm relying on you to keep me straight. Don't let me get down into the mud with these guys. That's not what I got into this job to do."

She gives me a sly look. "Some of these guys can be dicks. So…no promises."

WE PULL UP TO CONNOR GRIFFIN'S HOUSE A LITTLE AFTER two-thirty. From the front it looks like a normal home, but as we were turning the corner to approach, I spotted his back-yard littered with both equipment and materials, some of which may be left over from the construction business and Griffin had nowhere else to store it. The house itself is unas-suming, without a lot of frills. I just hope Connor Griffin kept his company's records and didn't destroy them when he went under. They're going to be our only resource to who might've had access to that house when that wall was built.

Anna and I make our way up to the front walk, but the door opens before we can reach it. Before us stands a man in his mid-fifties, his hair entirely gray and dark brown eyes. Strangely enough, he's leaning on a cane much like the one Jake Ashford uses. It's even on the same side. All at once, alarm bells are going off in my head. Did he know we were coming? Though he greets us with a smile, I can see it doesn't quite reach his eyes. He's suspicious of us too.

"Connor Griffin?" I ask.

"Good afternoon," he says. "How can I help you?"

I pull out my badge. "I'm Agent Emily Slate, with the FBI. This is Dr. Forest. We're investigating the murder of a young woman who was discovered in between the walls of a house."

He takes a step back, his eyes wide. "In the walls of a *house?*" he asks. "I'm assuming you're here because my company built the house." He's not showing any tells that make me think he already knew about Jessica, but I'll need to keep a close eye. If he already did know about her, he could have been preparing for this day for a long time. I think back to her ID, that was still in her pocket.

"Not quite. We have construction records that show your company was the one that built the wall. The house was built in the sixties. We were hoping you might be able to provide us with some more information about the construction."

He leans heavily on his cane. Unlike Jake Ashford, he's not wobbling on it from being drunk. "Oh." He hesitates a minute as if he's making a decision to allow us access or not. Finally, he looks away. "Come on in."

I glance over to Anna to see if she is feeling any apprehension about Mr. Griffin, but her face is neutral. I also have to remember Anna is not an investigator and doesn't find herself in dangerous situations and thus may not know what to look for. I, on the other hand, am cautious. We can't be too careful. And given that we still don't have a solid suspect, Mr. Griffin could be just as responsible for Jessica as anyone.

Griffin holds the door open for us and we step into the small living room. It's modest, and it's clear the man lives alone. Everything in the house is set up for one. No couch, just a La-z-boy, with a small side table sitting off to the right. On top of the table sits a beer that's warming, beside an empty microwavable dinner tray. Most of the room focuses on the large TV. Even though I already know the answer, I ask anyway. "Just you here?"

"I lost my other house in the divorce; it went to my ex-wife. There didn't seem to be a need to furnish the place with stuff I can't use."

"We saw you had a brother who was in the business with you," Anna says.

"Yeah, Mac moved down to Miami. Said he was sick of the cold and wanted to work on his tan." He gives us a sideways grin. "But really he just wanted to go down there to gawk at women." He circles the room, clearly uncomfortable that we have nowhere to sit. "I'm sorry to hear about the girl, I'm assuming this was recent?"

"Her body was found just a few days ago. But she had been in the wall for some time," I say.

"All right. Let's see what we can find. Do you have the address?"

"Four-Nineteen Heritage Road. Here in Fernview."

"Got it." He heads down the hallway, not indicating if we should follow or not. I doubt he'd try to run even if he wanted to—that cane isn't going to allow him to get very far.

"Mind if I ask what happened?" I say behind him, both to let him know we're coming with him and out of genuine curiosity.

"Construction accident. Spinal injury, which then ballooned into medical bills I couldn't afford, hence the business. And it seems like my wife was only happy in our marriage when she could buy what she wanted. She didn't like spending all our money on medical bills. Took the kids and moved to Richmond. I still see them, though. I drive up there every month for a long weekend."

"I'm sorry to hear that," I say. "Didn't you have insurance?"

"I did, but the company ruled it was outside their coverage. I tried suing them, but I could only afford so much in lawyer fees and by then I had almost six grand in medical bills."

"That's terrible," Anna says.

I was suspicious at first, but after hearing his story, Connor Griffin doesn't strike me as the kind of person who would kill a woman and stuff her into a wall. I don't see any motive—unless he's just a stone-cold killer and the sob story is nothing but a ruse.

"Here we go," Griffin says as we enter the back bedroom. It's full of boxes, most of them labeled *files* with a small desk in the middle. I look over at Anna and her face falls—probably at the prospect of spending even more time going through a bunch of records.

"Heritage…that's off Hemlock, right?" Griffin asks.

"Colonial, but it runs parallel to Hemlock," I reply.

He snaps his finger with his free hand. "That's right. I don't get out around town much anymore. I draw disability so my income is limited. Doesn't allow for much other than groceries and gas these days." He goes about searching through the boxes, pushing one aside, then the next one. "Here."

"Here what?" I ask.

"It should be in here, if we really did the work," he says, pulling out a box with one hand.

"Wow, that was fast," Anna replies.

"If there is one thing I appreciate, it's organization," he

says with a smile. "I was in charge of it the entire time we ran the company. If you'd have left it up to my brother none of this stuff would be in any kind of order. Hell, he probably would have shredded all of it."

He sets the box down and slowly lowers himself to the seat before rifling through it. "Yep. Here it is. Son of a—we really did install that wall." He scans over the first few documents before handing them to me as he inspects a few others. "I actually do remember this one now. I thought it was odd because the homeowners wanted to close off this passway."

"Why is that odd?" Anna asks.

"In an era when everyone else is going for 'open concept', knocking down walls—sometimes when they shouldn't be—people putting more of them up sticks with you. See here?" He unrolls a large blueprint of the entire first floor of the home. "It ruins the entire flow of the house. It cuts off the living room, making it into a dead zone."

"Did you work on this project yourself?" I ask.

He shakes his head. "No, looks like Carlos Guiterrez was the lead on this one. I signed off on it though. And I recall doing the inspection once the wall was up and finished. Carlos told me his guys got the wall up quicker than even he'd expected. He'd come in one morning and the whole thing had been finished when he wasn't there." He flips another page. "Yeah, here, look. My notes: *Final wall inspection, CG indicates done ahead of sched.*"

I exchange a look with Anna. "We need everyone's contact information that worked on that project," I tell him. "Including Carlos."

Chapter Seventeen

"WE'RE TIED HERE eighty-two to sixty with the Blazers in possession of the ball. Harmon has it, drops back and goes for the three-pointer—and makes it! Eighty-five to sixty as the Wolfhounds recover the ball, heading back down the court. Jamal Davis looks to—"

"Hey, can you see if there's anything else on?" I ask, taking a swig of my beer.

The bartender looks up from cleaning his glass. "Sure, this thing's over anyway, ain't it?" He grabs the remote, flipping through the channels. "What are you in the mood for?"

I check my watch. Seven-oh-five. It should be on by now. "Check the news. I've been on the job all day."

He chuckles. "Not many people like me to turn it *to* the news," he says, flipping it over to Fernview's only local station – WBGJ. The pretty newscaster's face takes up most of the screen, but she's talking about flooding somewhere in Brazil. Damn. I begin tapping my foot. There should be *something* on it today.

C'mon, c'mon, I think, taking another swig of my beer. Glancing around, there's no one near me, other than the bartender. The place is dead tonight, cold weather's probably keeping lots of folks home. But this has been a very eventful day for me. The first in a long time. Ever since I learned that FBI agent was in town.

It was pure dumb luck they found Jessica. Though I can't say I'm surprised. If I'd really wanted to hide her, I would have driven out to Glendale and thrown her body in one of those endless caves they have out there. Those things go on forever. But that wouldn't have been very poetic, now would it?

"And in local news, police are concerned about a rash of fires that seem to all have struck in the same day." I have to keep the smile off my lips as I turn my attention back to the TV with glee. "Authorities say they've had to call in additional support from Lynchburg and even as far as Roanoke to help manage what police are calling a serial arsonist."

The image flips over to Captain Reyes, esteemed officer of the Fernview Police. "We know for a fact two of these fires were related and we're still examining the third. We ask the public to be on the watch for anyone setting uncontrolled fires, and to make sure all your home fire suppression equipment is up to date. Three families lost their homes today."

"Captain, do you have any leads on who could be responsible?" the interviewer asks.

"At this time we're still pursuing the evidence," he replies.

"That means they don't know shit," the bartender says, turning back to me and placing the clean glass up on the shelf before grabbing another. "They've got no clue who could have done this. I know the Tomlinsons—they've had to go down to the Y—lost everything."

"That's terrible," I say, taking another swig of my beer so he won't see me smile. "Are they okay?"

He shrugs. "Well, everything they owned was in that fire, but thankfully they weren't home. "

"That's good to hear."

He nods to my empty bottle. "You want another?"

"Sure." I slide the bottle over to him and he dumps it in the trash before popping the cap on another natty light and sending it my way. I catch it with one hand.

"Who do you think could have done such a thing?" he asks, looking back as the interviewer is wrapping up. She's standing in front of the Parker place, which was the second place I hit today. There's not even a support beam left standing. There wouldn't be—not with the accelerant I used. That fire would have burned hotter than fifteen-hundred degrees. Nothing would have survived that, not even human remains.

I shake my head, doing my best to show sympathy. "I have no idea." I knew by staging the first fire to look like an accident from the home's fire pit that I would give myself a little more time, and I was right. While everyone was engaged with putting out that fire—thinking it was nothing more than a freak accident, I was able to get over to the other two houses and take care of them before anyone was the wiser. I've been planning for this day for almost fifteen years now, hoping I'd never have to move forward with it. But as soon as I found out Jessica's body had been discovered in that house on Heritage, I knew I didn't have a choice. I had to get rid of the others. And that was before I knew the FBI was even involved.

I scoff. The FBI. Nothing more than another useless bureaucracy. But the fact they called her in sends a little surge through my groin. It means they're taking this seriously. As they should be. I can't wait to see what she does—how she reacts when she realizes Jessica wasn't alone. And I'm more than ready for her or anyone else who thinks they can come after me.

"Whoa there, settle down," the bartender says as I drain the entire bottle in one swig.

"Can't, I gotta be back home. Good to see ya, Charlie."

He eyes me like he's not sure I'm okay to drive. "Yeah, you too." I leave him still cleaning out his glass. I only stumble once to my car, my bad leg still bothering me, but I make it without anyone seeing. Were the fires overkill? Maybe. I mean, they probably wouldn't have found the others for a few weeks at least—not unless they put the pieces together. But I couldn't take the chance. The discovery of Jessica's body set everything in motion. I can still remember that night—I remember how soft and pliable she was. The thought sends a wave of pleasure through me as I get into my car. Little did I know that experience would open up a whole new world for me. And I was patient—never rushed the process and was rewarded for it.

Secretly, I think I wanted her to be found. If for no other reason than to give this little community something to hem and haw over—something they'd never seen before. Now the cops are fighting me on all sides, and they don't even know it. I laugh aloud as I pull out of the parking lot onto the main road, headed back home.

But as I'm feeling the effects of the beer, I decide to take a detour. I head downtown instead, into the glowing lights of what few multi-story buildings Fernview has. This town is pathetic, and its people are pathetic. That's why I like it. They have no idea what kind of person lives among them, goes to their community meetings, helps out with church functions, passes out candy on Halloween. But now they finally have their first glimpse. This town has finally seen the horror that is among them, and that's going to change everything.

I pull into the lot across from the police station and shut the engine off. Normally I'd just go home, but this is no normal day. My buzz starts to wear off after about twenty minutes and I begin to reconsider sitting here, goading them before I catch sight of the FBI agent leaving the station, heading for her car. She doesn't look like anything special, and she sure as hell doesn't notice me. Why would she? She already looks defeated, like she has no chance at figuring out who put poor Jessica in that wall.

"What's the matter, Agent Slate?" I ask as she gets in her car and drives off. "Hit another dead end?" I've changed my mind. I'm *glad* the FBI agent is here. She's making this a lot more exciting. If it was just Reyes I'd be bored, and I'd feel like all my preparation was for nothing. But knowing the FBI is here, working the case, makes it real.

I chuckle again as I start my car and head back out of downtown, toward home. I wonder if she'll ever figure out there were three other bodies in those homes I torched. She probably hasn't even connected the fires to me yet. We'll just have to see how smart she is, which means I'll need to keep an eye on her, but that shouldn't be a problem. Not with my connections.

When I pull into my driveway, all the lights in the house are off. It takes me a minute to get out, and I feel that familiar twinge of pain in my leg. I hobble up to the door and let myself in, grabbing my walking cane from the umbrella stand, glad to finally have it to lean on. I let out an exhausted breath. Normally I'd hit the hay, but it has been an exciting day. I need something to calm me down first.

I head down the hallway, turning into the bedroom where I keep everything I don't use on a daily basis. It's organized enough that I can walk around without tripping over anything, but not so much that anyone would consider me a neat freak. Not that I'd allow anyone in here anyway. I go to the closet, and pull back the rug on the floor, revealing the small cutout I'd built into the floor all those years ago. Inside sits the metal box, which I retrieve. It's been a few months since I've taken a look, but tonight's a special night, and I want to remember it.

Opening the box is always a thrill, and this evening is no different. Inside are four different trinkets. A scrunchie, a locket, a bracelet, and a pair of lacey underwear. Each one priceless. I lean down and I find I can almost still smell them. Memories flood my brain and I unbuckle my belt.

It's been a good day. I deserve a good night.

Chapter Eighteen

"GOOD MORNING!" Anna says as I walk into the police station. We left Connor Griffin's place yesterday with a slew of information and decided to split the names, working well into the night investigating his employees. We'd made some headway, but eventually I had to call it. I can't pull all-nighters anymore and still be good the following morning. I need at least three or four hours. I spoke with Liam this morning and there's still no news on Zara, which I think is starting to create an ulcer somewhere. I haven't had much of an appetite, either. I've never worried about anyone like this, not even Matt. But I'm wondering if this is what everyone else felt all the time when I was undercover?

"Morning," I say. "I hope you weren't here too late."

She sets a packet of papers down in front of me. "No, I went home soon after you did. Sleep is an important metabolic function. But that's not the good news."

I arch my eyebrow. "The suspense is killing me."

"Your ill attempt at humor notwithstanding, I have something you're going to want to see. It's the full autopsy report on Jessica Ashford. It came through overnight."

"Really?" I ask, grabbing the stack of papers. "Finally. Have you read it?"

She nods. "I just finished skimming it. Dr. Wallace is very thorough."

"She better be, considering it's been six days since she was discovered," I say, flipping through page after page of medical jargon.

"Consider the body. This was no normal autopsy. It's not like she was some fresh body off the street, having died only a few hours before. Chemical breakdown makes everything harder."

"It says here they're estimating the time of death over twenty years ago. That would have put it not long after she disappeared." I scan the pages some more. "Subject's bone growth and density is consistent with what we would see from a semi-developed teen. When she died, the subject was more than likely no older than seventeen years." I look up. "Which means she died a long time before that wall was built."

"Which means someone had to store her for all that time," Anna says.

I keep reading. "Microscopic crystallization of the under-lying cellular structure lends itself to the conclusion that the subject's body had been subjected to below-zero temperatures for an extended period of time. This could range anywhere from a few months to years." I pause, thinking. "So someone killed her not long after she disappeared, then stored her body in a freezer until they put her in the wall."

"It's very strange," Anna says.

I take the files over to an empty desk and take a seat, going over every word from the coroner. There's no doubt about it; the evidence shows Jessica was killed a long time ago, longer than I'd originally thought. I'd just assumed she'd been killed closer to when the wall was built, and it had been more of a convenience to put her there than anything else. But now I'm not so sure.

"What are you thinking?" Anna asks, taking a seat at the desk across from me.

"I should ask you that question," I say. "What would you call a killer who keeps a young girl's body frozen before finally hiding it in the house her own family moves into?"

She thinks for a few minutes. "I can see two possibilities. Either we're dealing with someone who made a mistake and is looking to repent, or this is someone who is looking to make the Ashfords suffer."

"Can you elaborate?" I ask. I'm having similar thoughts, but I'd like her perspective, just to see where she's coming from.

"It's possible Jessica's death was an accident."

I flip back through the files. "It says death was likely caused from a contusion on the skull, where it's cracked."

"People fall and hit their heads every day. It's not uncommon. In that case, our 'killer' may be nothing more than an innocent bystander who didn't want to be implicated in a murder investigation. He could have witnessed the accident, took care to preserve her, and then, in an act of contrition, decided to reunite her with her family when they moved into that house."

"From your tone I gather you're not fond of this theory."

She shakes her head. "It requires a few variables. First, the 'killer' must feel responsible for Jessica's death, without it actually being his fault. Also, typically, people don't preserve bodies on ice for almost a decade. Which would suggest a mental imbalance of some kind. And if we're to consider a mentally unbalanced person, then we're much more likely to lean toward option two."

"Which is?"

"He killed her without cause and decided to preserve her body until the time came when he could exact his revenge on either Jake or Judy Ashford. However, it wouldn't have been a public revenge, not at first. He would have needed to be content with the fact that Jessica might never be found. The revenge would have been in his mind only."

"Except," I say, closing the file again. "Now the secret is out. Or, it will be as soon as the media gets hold of it."

"Right, which could act as a catalyst of sorts. If the killer is still alive, it's possible this discovery could have kicked off a series of events to which we don't know the scope or outcome."

I lean back in my chair. "I hadn't considered that. So you're saying you think it's possible this killer may start operating again?"

"I can't speculate—it's impossible to know what he will or won't do. But I do know as far as he's concerned, his world has changed now. People know his secret, even if they don't know who he is. He could become volatile and begin lashing out or decide to begin taking new victims. This is about where my expertise ends."

I swing the chair back and forth, lost in thought. "Hang on a second." I flip open the files again, running through them one more time. "I thought so. The coroner thinks she was sexually assaulted. Hairline fractures around the pelvic area with no evidence of regrowth. It probably happened right before...or even right after she died."

Anna shudders. "Sorry," she says, recovering. "I'm not really used to any of this."

"Pray that day never comes," I say, turning back to the report. "So more than likely she was assaulted. Maybe we'll get lucky and there will be something left of a DNA sample from her remains. Though, given the amount of time that's passed, I doubt that's likely."

She takes a deep breath, looking off in the distance. "Back to the Griffin Employees?"

"Look, Anna," I say, standing. "I really appreciate your help. But this is all way beyond the scope of your responsibilities with the town. Why don't you leave the rest of this to me? That way you can get back to your normal routine."

When she looks up at me I see a fire burning in her eyes like I've never seen from her before. Gone is the calm and even-tempered woman. "I'm not about to quit. Not now, and not until we find this bastard. If you don't want me working with you on this anymore, I'll keep going alone."

"That's not what I meant," I tell her. "But this job—what we see takes a toll on us. If you're not prepared for it, it can eat you from the inside."

"And you think I'm not mentally strong enough, is that it?" she asks, hurt in her voice.

"I just…you don't have to do this. I do."

She shakes her head. "You know that's not true. Hodge will never let you forget this is his case. You could go back home to D.C. right now if you really wanted to. But you don't. Because you want to see this thing through. Just like I do."

She's got me there. I thought maybe this was all becoming too much for her. But I see now I've underestimated her determination. "Okay, then. We keep going."

"Together?" she asks. I nod. "Good."

"But if you're right, and the discovery of Jessica's body is acting like a catalyst for our killer, we might not have the leisure of time anymore. He could be planning something right now for all we know. We need to root him out, assuming he's still even alive."

"What do we do?"

"Keep working on Griffin's employees. We need to establish alibis for them when that wall was built. It's not going to be ironclad, but it will be a start. Anyone who can't give you something rock solid like they were out of the country, keep them on the list. And bonus if they lived in Fernview in the late nineties."

"What are you going to do?"

"What the original investigators should have done the first time," I say, grabbing my coat and heading for the door. "Find out what really happened to Jessica Ashford."

~

ONE OF THE GOOD THINGS ABOUT A SMALL TOWN IS ANYTHING you need is reasonably easy to find. Leaving the station, I head for the town library that sits closest to my old high school. I used to spend a lot of time there as a teen, usually because I didn't have much else better to do. Little did I know I'd need it one day for a murder investigation. I tend to agree with Anna, I think we're dealing with a real sick bastard here, one who gets off on the idea that Jessica was stored in the same house where her family lived.

He just didn't count on the house as also belonging to an FBI agent.

I pull up to the library and head inside, all the familiar sights and smells hitting me all at once. The place has been repainted, but otherwise it's the exact same as I remember it. But the best part is the smell of the books that permeates the air. There's nothing quite like the smell of old books.

"Hello," the young man behind the desk says as I approach. "Can I help you find something?"

"I'm looking for yearbooks from Fernview High, from 1995 to 2000."

"Sure, they'll be down in the reference section, over there to the left. Bottom row. You can't miss them. Are you an alumni?" he asks.

"Something like that," I say. "Thanks." I head down to the reference section and find row after row of yearbooks, all lined up by year. Thank God; I'm not sure how many more broken filing systems I can search through before my mind explodes.

I run my fingers along the books until I find the one I'm looking for: 1997. I pull it out and start flipping through the pages. I find Jessica's picture about halfway through, but that's not what I'm looking for. Instead I scan the rest of the pages, looking to see where else she was active. She was in volleyball, it seems, as well as a few after-school clubs. And in each of the social pictures, the same girl is always beside her, smiling. But I don't recognize her, not at first. It takes me a few minutes of looking back through Jessica's grade to find the girl.

"There you are…Mindy Coolidge." The name is familiar at once, and it all comes back to me. Mindy was one of those cool kids that I only knew about peripherally. She was headed out right as soon as I was coming in. I remember one particular school assembly where she was due to make a speech about the virtues of not doing drugs or alcohol or something like that, and instead she turned it into a speech about all the health benefits of different types of narcotic substances, complete with citations and evidence to back it all up. I remember the entire staff was furious, cutting her off halfway through, but it made her a school celebrity. I also remember sitting there that day, thinking I'd never be cool enough to do something like that.

Wow, I wonder where Mindy Coolidge is now.

I flip back through and look for any other common people who surround Jessica in the pictures, but Mindy is the only one that's consistently there. Strange, I didn't see anything about the cops interviewing her when Jessica disappeared. I wonder if they even did. At that age, friends are everything, and if anyone knew what was going on with Jess, it was probably Mindy.

"Find what you needed?" the kid asks as I head back out.

"I did. Listen, you wouldn't happen to know a Mindy Coolidge, would you?" It's worth a shot. In a town this small, the odds he at least knows the name is better than not.

"Oh, you mean the lady that does all the hair? Over at Cool Cuts?" he asks.

Cool Cuts? "Umm…that could be her, yes."

"Sure, that place is just off Barringer Road, in the strip mall. You can't miss it."

I knock once on his wooden desk. "Thanks."

Chapter Nineteen

JUST LIKE THE KID SAID, *Cool Cuts* is smack dead in the middle of the small strip mall. When I was a kid this place held a bank, a collectible coin shop, a tattoo parlor and I think a small counter diner. All of those are gone now, replaced with a thrift store on one side, and a laundromat on the other. Cool Cuts splits them, taking up two of the units that have been combined into one. The parking lot is empty except for one car parked in front of the thrift store and another parked in front of my destination. Inside Cool Cuts sits a woman sitting in one of the three chairs, spinning as she plays on her phone. As soon as she sees me her eyes go wide and she puts the phone away, getting up and sweeping away hair from around the chair she'd been sitting in.

"Hi there," she says with faux enthusiasm as I walk in. "Here for a trim?" I recognize her immediately as an older version of the girl I saw in the yearbook.

"Actually no," I say and hold out my badge. "I'm Emily Slate, with the FBI." Mindy's face turns into a frown as she approaches to look at the badge. I notice deep lines have made their way into her features, leaving her looking older and more tired than she probably is. Though her hair is as bright blonde as it was when she was a teenager, without a hint of gray anywhere.

"The FBI?" she asks.

"You're Mindy Coolidge, right?" I ask.

"Mindy Coldwater. I haven't been Coolidge for about a decade or more now." She points to a framed picture of her and another woman shaking hands sitting close to the cash register. "My business partner and wife. Jenna Coldwater. We kept part of my name for the business, though. Better than Cold Cuts." This elicits a nervous laugh from her.

I *knew* I recognized that name. "You both went to Fernview High, didn't you?"

She pulls her brows together. "Yeah, we did. How did you know that? Oh, well, you're FBI, I guess if anyone would…" She's staring at me, and I realize she probably recognizes me from somewhere deep in her brain.

"I went to Fernview High too, but I was a few years behind you."

"You did?" she asks. "Slate?" She taps her lips a minute. "Oh! You were the one whose mother—" She clasps her hand over her mouth, a mortified look on her face.

"It's all right," I say. "But yeah, that's me."

"Wow, so you really work for the FBI? Like…in Richmond or…"

"I'm in D.C. now." Her eyes grow even wider.

"Good for you." It's a pleasant enough comment, but I can feel the undercurrent of jealousy in her words. I can't really blame her. If I were stuck cutting hair in the same town I grew up in and found out someone four years younger than me worked at the FBI I'd probably have a hard time containing my emotions too. Not that I think she's petty; it's just human nature.

"I'm wondering if you can help me with a case I'm working. It's concerning Jessica Ashford."

Something in her face changes and for a second I think I

might have lost her. She turns away from me, going back over to the station where she was sitting before. She begins arranging some of her tools. "Jess? What's…going on? Did someone find out where she went?"

"In a manner of speaking," I say. "I'm sorry to be the one to tell you, but her body was found a few days ago."

"Her…body?"

"Yes, she's dead."

Mindy closes her eyes, and I can practically see the wave of pain wash over her. She sinks into the chair, dropping her head into her hands, overcome with emotion. She doesn't move, but I hear sobs coming from her. It's so sudden and so powerful I can't help but feel like crying myself. But I hold still, allowing Mindy to feel her feelings.

We stay like that for a good five minutes. I keep my distance, giving her the space she needs and Mindy just lets it all out. Finally, she looks up. "Where?"

"Here. In Fernview. They found her…in the wall of a local home."

"A *wall?*" she cries out and the tears fall even harder. The reaction is more than I would have expected—like I had delivered fatal news about a close family member. "Oh my god." Mindy and Jessica were closer than I'd originally assumed. I'm no good in these situations; Zara is always the one who is better at comforting people. I can never tell if someone just wants to be left alone or if they really want me to try and soothe them. There's no hard and fast rule for everyone, so I just end up standing there, like an idiot.

"I'm sorry," she says after a few minutes. "I didn't mean—I always knew she was…it just never made sense."

"The fact the cops ruled her disappearance as a runaway?"

"Yeah," she says, dabbing at her eyes with a tissue from the station. "Jess wasn't the kind of person who just 'ran away'. Not like that. Not without telling anyone. Do you know who did it?"

I shake my head. "That's why I'm here. I wanted to see if you could tell me what you knew about her, especially around the time she disappeared. Did the cops ever speak with you?"

She blinks a few times, wiping her eyes. Her mascara has run down her cheeks. "I tried to get my parents to let me go down to the station and make a statement, but they said I didn't need to be making the police's job harder for them by making up stories. My parents and I never had a good relationship. Still don't." Her eyes flash to the picture of her and her wife again.

"Would you be willing to tell me?" I ask.

She sniffs a few times, then nods. "But I need a drink or something. I can't—not here." She goes over and pulls on the little chain connected to the neon OPEN sign. It goes out as she flips off the lights. "It was a slow day anyway."

I follow her back out of the salon after she grabs her purse and her keys and locks up, making sure everything is off. "There's a little bar around the corner, Charlie's. Do you know it?"

I nod. "I remember."

"I'll meet you there." She heads for her car, pulling out her cell phone. I'm sure to call her wife to let her know what's going on.

Mindy isn't quite what I expected. I always saw girls like her as ending up moving to New York or L.A. and becoming models or actors, not running a small salon in their hometown. But I'm grateful she's willing to speak with me.

A few minutes later I pull into Charlie's parking lot. The place is relatively empty on a Wednesday afternoon. Mindy pulls in right beside me a minute later. She's managed to compose herself and fix her makeup. "Thanks," she says as she gets out. "I just can't talk about Jess—especially not without a little pick-me-up."

"It's no problem." I follow her into the bar. Even though I've probably passed this place a thousand times, I've never been inside before.

"Hey, Charlie," Mindy calls out, waving to the bartender.

"Mindy," he replies, then gives me a furtive nod.

"I need a Jack and Coke," she says, sliding up to the bar. She turns to me. "You?"

"Just water for me," I reply. "I'm on the clock." Charlie returns with our drinks quickly, then disappears into the back somewhere. "You come here a lot?"

She grabs the straw and tosses it in the nearby trashcan, then tips the glass and drinks the entire thing all at once. When she sets it back down there's nothing left in the glass but ice. "Yeah," she says, breathless. "All the locals come here at some point. It's the town's unofficial meeting hall."

I take in the rest of the bar. It's cozy and welcoming, and there are pictures of the town's history plastered all over the wall. In addition to the high tops close to the bar, there are a couple of other tables on the far side of the room, next to the large windows that let in a lot of light, giving the place a lived-in, yet rustic feel. The shelves behind the bar are stocked with every type of liquor anyone could want and it looks like they have a couple local brews on tap. I can see how a place like this would be a hub of conversation here in Fernview.

"C-can you tell me if she suffered?" Mindy asks, playing with the ice cubes in her drink, not looking at me.

I decide deflecting is probably the best strategy. I knew Jessica and Mindy were friends, but Mindy's reaction tells me there was something deeper there, and I don't want to be cruel. "We're still gathering evidence," I finally say.

She nods and I see a few more tears escape her eyes. "We were going to leave this place together; did you know that?" She's talking more to herself now than me, getting lost in her memories. But I sit next to her, my water untouched. I'm here to listen. "We had a plan. Once we graduated, we were going to take my car, drive out to Malibu. Get discovered by some movie producer." She looks up and her eyes are wet again. "Stupid, huh?"

I shake my head. "Not at all. There's nothing wrong with having a dream. I wanted to leave Fernview too."

She nods. "I'm glad you made it out." She sniffs, then wipes her nose on her sleeve. "Don't get me wrong, I love my life here with Jenna. She's a lot smarter than I am. Takes care of the business side of stuff. I just cut hair." She tips the glass again and gets what little water has melted in the bottom. "If Jessica hadn't left…I probably wouldn't have ever met Jenna."

"So that's what you thought? That Jessica left town?"

"It's what everyone said," she replies. "But I never believed it."

"Did you ever speak to Judy after everything happened?" I ask.

She shakes her head a few times. "Not really. She was a lot younger than us; we always saw her as the annoying little sister type whenever I would go see Jess at her house. But after a while I had to quit—her Dad was too much to bear at school and at that house. Also, I didn't like the way he looked at me."

Something pulls at my memory. "Wait, her dad at school?" I ask, confused.

"Yeah, he was the principal, remember?"

This is news to me. "Not when I was there, he wasn't. It was Mr. Powell."

"Oh," she replies. "I know he was the principal during my last year—when Jess…" She trails off. "Maybe the school board fired him; he was always so mean to everyone. I remember one time I was complaining about some math class, and he stuck his head into Jess's room and told me not to bother with math, that I wasn't cut out for jobs that required it."

I lean on the bar. "I've been hearing that a lot about the man."

She turns to me. "You don't think he had anything to do with it, do you?" she asks.

"Why would you say that?"

"I just know he was pissed about the guy Jess had been talking to online right before—"

"Wait," I say. "What guy?"

She shrugs. "She wouldn't tell me. She pretended like it was some big secret. Like she couldn't tell me, her best friend!" She huffs. "I think…I think Jess knew I had feelings for her. Things were different then; you just didn't come out and say it. And I was still so young and confused. All I knew was that I didn't want to lose her; I didn't want my life to be without her. I think some part of her knew that, so she didn't like to talk to me about guys she was seeing."

"But she was seeing someone," I say. There was nothing in the report about this.

"She said they had an 'online' relationship." She chuckles, but it's mirthless. "You know, back when *that* was taboo."

"But…that was the late nineties. She couldn't have been using a dating site. They didn't exist yet."

Mindy shakes her head. "No, it was all through AOL. Remember those days?" She looks at me a minute. "You're probably too young. But I know they met up a couple of times at least."

"So he was local," I say. "And you have no idea who it was?"

She shakes her head. "Sorry."

"What about the night she disappeared?" I ask. "Did you talk to her?"

"It was a Saturday. We had volleyball practice that morning and I remember she seemed distracted by something. We were in the gym, and she kept looking in the direction of the offices the entire time. I remember being irritated that she wasn't focusing on practice. I even said something mean to her, but none of it seemed to faze her."

"Okay," I say. "What happened after that?"

"Once practice was over, I tried talking to her in the locker room, but she said she had a lot to do and she needed to get home. That was the last time I ever saw her." The bartender emerges from the back, but stays at the other end of the bar, giving us some privacy. Mindy shakes her empty glass at him, and he comes down with a fresh one, retreating just as quietly.

I take a deep breath and finally take a drink of my water as Mindy goes to work on Jack and Coke number two. Jessica's *online* boyfriend could be anyone. Am I going to have to talk to every guy who attended the school while Jessica was there to try and find this guy?

"I'm assuming she was nervous because she knew whatever she had to tell her dad wouldn't go over very well," Mindy says absently.

"He didn't like the guy," I say.

Mindy nods. "He didn't like *any* guy. Which made my stupid brain think that maybe there could have been something between us. He wouldn't have objected to me, right? But I know I was just making excuses back then, coming up with reasons to force things to work. He never would have accepted me, not that it matters. All I do know is apparently they had some massive fight the night she disappeared."

Everything else in the bar seems to disappear as I train all of my focus on Mindy. "Tell me everything you know about that."

"I only heard about it from Judy a few weeks after the funeral," she says. "She came up, asking me if I had heard from Jess, thinking maybe she was still keeping in touch with me after running away. She told me Jess and her father had a huge screaming match, and she ran out of the house. Judy was in the back bedroom and heard everything."

"Did Judy ever tell the cops about the screaming match?" I ask.

Mindy shakes her head. "I don't know."

"And you think it was about this guy?"

She shrugs. "Who knows? It could have been about anything. I mean, my parents were bad, but they weren't *that* bad."

"She never confided in you what she needed to talk to him about?" I ask. It seems strange, especially if the girls were as close as Mindy has insinuated.

"No, but then again she started acting weird once she got with that guy she was talking to. We didn't talk or hang out as much once he came into the picture."

I pull out my phone, making a few notes. "How long was their relationship?"

"Maybe a few weeks?" Mindy says. "Not long at all. But then again, in teenage time, a few weeks is an eternity." She drains the rest of her glass.

"I really appreciate you taking the time with me today," I tell her. "And I'm sorry you had to learn about Jessica this way."

"It's not your fault, you're just doing your job," she says, shaking her glass for Charlie.

I decide I can't leave her here without knowing she'll be okay. I put my hand on her shoulder. "Do you need me to call anyone for you?"

She looks up, a weak smile on her lips. "Jenna will be here after she gets done with her other job. Don't worry, she'll take care of me. Thanks though. I just need some time to… process." I nod and slip off my stool. Mindy has been a treasure trove of information. At least now I have a better idea of where to begin looking.

As I'm heading for the door, I feel a tug on my jacket. I look back to see Mindy hanging on to me, half off her stool. "Hey," she says. "Get that son of a bitch."

I place my hand on hers. "I will."

Chapter Twenty

"THIS IS AGENT KANE," the woman on the other end of the phone says.

"Agent Kane, this is Emily…Slate," I say, feeling apprehensive though I don't know why. Anna sits across from me, the two of us having met back up after my conversation with Mindy. I gave her the full rundown of what Mindy told me, and the two of us came up with a gameplan of how to proceed from here.

"Agent Slate," Kane says, surprise in her voice. "I didn't expect to hear from you, is everything all right?"

"It is," I say, though I'm gritting my teeth. "I'm sorry to bother you. Usually this is something I'd bother Zara with, but I've been told she's working undercover. Liam says you came from analysis too."

"Oh," she replies. "Yes, but that was a long time ago. I transferred out years ago."

"Still, I'm wondering if you can answer a tech question for me."

There's a pause on the other end. I know I'm going out on a limb here, but I need information and I need it quick. And given my options I at least have *met* Agent Kane. I worked with her on my last case and found her to be a competent agent, along with her partner. "I may be a little rusty, but sure, go ahead."

"I'm looking into what is essentially a cold case from 1998. Our victim was apparently harboring an online relationship with a person of interest. My question is, if they were using America Online back then, is there any way to retrieve their message conversations?"

"Hmm," she says. "I'm assuming this was using AIM, the in-program messaging service and not emails?"

"I think so," I say.

"Unfortunately, those wouldn't be stored anywhere except on the original computers that were participants in the conversation. Back then companies didn't save and backup everything that happened on their servers. AOL in particular was adamant about privacy. If the messages were through an online chatroom, it's possible they could be recovered. But if they were just using direct messaging from one person to another, their computers would have saved an archive of those conversations, but it wouldn't have been stored anywhere else."

Damn. "Doesn't sound to me like you're rusty at all," I say, though I'm a little deflated. I was really hoping there would be some way to retrieve the messages.

"Well, some things you just don't forget I guess."

"What about finding out the identity of the other person?" I ask. "Would that be possible?"

"Do you have their username?"

I let out a frustrated breath. "No."

"Then it's the same problem. AOL does keep a record of its users, but without the unique name, it's impossible to know who you're looking for. Again, that information would be stored on the recipient's original computer."

I sit back and notice Anna studying my face. I turn away. "Well, thanks anyway. It was worth a shot."

"Agent Slate, hang on," she says. "Is it possible the family of your victim may still have the computer they used?"

I pull my mouth into a frown. "It was twenty years ago."

"I know, but you'd be surprised. A lot of people never throw their computers away, even ones that are ancient. Some people are too afraid that someone will extract their data while others are just lazy. It might be worth checking out."

"That's good advice, thanks," I say.

"You're welcome," she says. "I'm glad you felt you could trust me with this. Zara tells me it takes you some time to warm up to people."

I shoot another glance at Anna. She's turned her attention to the closest window, watching something outside. "Guilty as charged."

"Well, if you need anything else, I'd be happy to help. At least until Agent Foley gets back."

"Thanks," I say, really meaning it. "If you hear anything from her, will you let me know?"

"Absolutely," she says.

"I take it's both good and bad news," Anna says once I get off the phone.

"You could say that." I stand and walk around the conference table to look out the window myself. Reyes and Hodge are still pre-occupied with these fires, which they have now all definitely connected to one person. They think the firebug set the first one to make it look like an accident to give him cover to set the other two. All three used a similar accelerant. But it seems like the houses were targeted randomly. If I weren't already working on this Ashford case, I'd be neck-deep in that investigation, trying to figure out what was going on.

"Where do we go from here?" she asks, drawing my attention back to the present.

"My friend at the FBI said that the only way those messages might still exist is if Ashford still has the computer Jessica used to send them. And what are the odds of that?"

Anna shrugs. "Fifty-fifty?"

I chuckle. "I like your optimism. So our options are to go after Ashford again and see if he's got this computer, or confront him directly about what he and Jessica argued about that night."

"Or speak to every boy that went to Fernview High between 1996 and 2000," she deadpans.

"Yeah, or that. That'll be a dead-end though. If our killer was a fellow student, he's not going to admit to having a relationship with her right before she died. He'll just deny it and be lost in a sea of potential suitors. And then we'll have wasted all that time for nothing."

"Do you think you can get a warrant for the computer?"

I think it over. "Maybe. But we'll have to bring Hodge in, seeing as the two of us are technically just consultants. I can't go to a local judge on his behalf—he'll have to be the one to do it."

"Seems like that would be easier than trying to talk to Ashford again." She's turning side to side in the chair but is laser-focused on me. "Wouldn't it?"

But I'm not thinking about Jake Ashford. I'm thinking about Judy. She never mentioned her sister and her dad had a fight—even back when we were kids. She always told me she never knew what happened, that she heard Jessica leave and hadn't thought any more of it. Either she was lying back then, or Mindy is embellishing things now, for what reason I don't know. Maybe because Jake Ashford is just that much of an asshole, and she needed to invent a reason to hate him even more.

"Emily?" Anna asks.

"Yeah," I say. "You're probably right." I check my phone for the time. Somehow, another day has slipped by with little progress. "Let's go over what you found."

"Okay," she says, pulling out a file folder from her side bag which sits on the floor. "I'm glad you asked. I started with the man Griffin mentioned, Carlos Gutierrez. It took a while to track him down, and I had to get some assistance from one of the other officers, but we found him living in Houston, with his family."

"Did he have any memory of the project?"

She shakes her head. "Unfortunately, he was involved in an accident of his own a few years back. His wife told me he was struck by a falling metal pipe on site. Even though he had on a hard hat, it broke through and impacted his skull. He's been in a wheelchair since 2014."

"That's terrible," I say. "Still, it doesn't exonerate him. He could have had something to do with it before the accident."

She nods. "I kept him on the list. Griffin's records also showed four other guys on that job. Two of them still live here in town, one lives in Maryland and the last one passed away two years ago."

I arch an eyebrow. "Work related?"

"Let's just say I'm glad I didn't go into construction."

"Doesn't that seem odd to you?" I ask. "One death, and another life-altering injury? On guys who were on the same worksite?"

She pauses. "You think it was intentional?"

I take a deep breath, trying to wrap my mind around all the details. "At this point I don't know what to think. Who are the two who still live in Fernview?"

She looks over her notes. "Freddie Blevins and Diego Cordova."

I rub my temples. "Okay, let's start with them. We'll do a deep dive into their lives, see what comes up. If we can't find anything, we'll go speak to them."

She stacks her papers together, placing them back in the folder. "And here I thought helping you would get me *out* of the office."

"Sorry to disappoint," I say.

"Oh, I'm not disappointed," she replies. "I just hope this all leads to something."

"You and me both."

Loose ends, loose ends.

I've been sitting in my car, staring at the house for what seems like hours. But really, it's only been about forty-five minutes. Just long enough to wait for most of neighbors' lights to go out.

He's predictable. Always has been.

When I woke up this morning, I realized that the fires weren't enough. If I'm going to keep my secret—and therefore my status in this community—then I must make sure everything is ironclad. I can't leave anything to chance. Does that mean that things are going to get a little bit messier? Absolutely. But it will be worth it.

I check right. No signs of life. The streets are quiet, and most people have already gone to bed. I check left. The main road that connects to this one is empty. No one out tonight, why would they be? It's a school night after all.

I open my door and ease myself out of my car, careful of my leg. I've been resting it up all day, to give myself the strength but I need to get through this evening. I close my door, but not all the way so it doesn't latch. I already disabled the lights inside the cabin, so they don't come on when I open and close the doors anyway. This will just make getting away easier. Not that I'll need to, because I already have all of this planned out.

I make my way across the street, just like I'm your average Joe out for an evening stroll. If anyone looks outside, they'll just see a man with his hands in his pockets walking along the sidewalk. When I move into a dark spot in between the street-lights, I take a left and head back along the driveway, around

166 • ALEX SIGMORE

to the back of the house. There are no lights back here, but my eyes have adjusted to the dark and I can see everything just fine. The back door is locked, but I knew it would be. I crouch down and pull a key set out of my pocket and go to work on the deadbolt.

I wouldn't be doing this if the FBI wasn't in town. The cops have no idea that this man could implicate me. But *she* might figure it out. I've been doing a little research on Agent Slate; it seems like she's a more than competent agent. And she's had quite a few wins under her belt. Not someone I want to underestimate. Which means now there will be another death on her head. Of course, she won't know that until it's too late. But she's something of a rogue element, and I can't predict exactly what she's going to do, so I have to cover all of my bases.

I have to be smarter than her. I have to make sure that no one can find out what really happened.

The deadbolt clicks and I'm able to turn the lock. The door swings in on a dark kitchen. There are no lights on anywhere that I can see. Good. The house is quiet, but of course it would be. He lives here alone. No family, no pets, nothing. He's kind of like me that way.

As I make my way through the house my bad leg twinges. Crouching down on it wasn't a good idea; I'm just not as young as I used to be. But I can't stop now just because of a little pain. I need to get through this, even though it's not going to be easy.

Down the hall I spot a stream of light coming underneath one of the doors. It seems he's still up after all. And he happens to already be in the room I need to get into. Well, he's making this easier than I expected.

I'm careful to stick to the walls going down the hall so I don't announce my presence with a creak in the floorboards. Fortunately, luck smiles on me and I make it to the door without a sound. Of course it does, why wouldn't it? This is what needs to happen. Fate is on my side.

In one swift movement, I open the door. He's sitting on the other side of the desk reading something. He glances up, bewildered for a split second. His eyes go wide as soon as he sees me and even though it's been a few years, I can tell he recognizes me immediately.

"What are you—"

He moves to grab his cane, but before he can get to it I'm around the desk and have him in a chokehold. He swats at me, his weak arms doing everything they can to get me let go, but I only hold on tighter. I can feel the fight starting to go out of him. He's a crippled, feeble man, with too many days behind him and not enough ahead. He manages to grab hold of his cane and tries to use it as a weapon, but I wrench it out of his hand and throw it on the ground, all while continuing to tighten my grip around his neck. Finally, after what seems like ten minutes, he produces a small gurgling sound before his entire body goes limp. I hold on for a minute more, just to make sure, but when I let go he slumps forward, his face landing on the newspaper he was reading. His entire face is purple. I check his pulse, then double-check to make sure he's not breathing.

The deed is done, part one complete. This frees me up for part two.

I look around the room, boxes and boxes of records stacked one on top of another. It takes me a few minutes, but I find the box I'm looking for. But when I open it and go through all the records, the ones I need aren't there. While it's possible he could've misplaced them, I've never known him to be a disorganized man.

Suddenly, bile rises in my throat. Is it possible?

I scan the room for anything else that could be out of place. Everything else is right where it's supposed to be. I grab a few more boxes opening them up to make sure the files are where they're supposed to be. Nothing else is out of order, I don't understand. There is no way he would've known to pull the files, not unless...

I open up his desk drawers, tossing aside stray pens, notepads, even an old cassette. Finally, I find it in the side drawer. A business card.

Her business card. Slate.

She's already been here; she's beaten me to it.

Chapter Twenty-One

BY THE TIME we left the station last night it was close to midnight. Anna and I spent all evening researching the two suspects from Griffin Construction, making little progress. Despite finding nothing connecting them to Jessica Ashford, we headed out to interview both of them anyway. Neither could remember the job in question, even though we had the documentation stating they were on the job that day. But given their breadth of work, I'm not surprised. I didn't have any reason to believe they were lying, but at the same time I can't eliminate them from the suspect pool because they had full access. Both seemed surprised and even shocked when we told them why we were there. And on top of that, I can't find a motive for any of the workers. None had prior interactions with Ashford or his daughter and neither even recalled meeting the man, which is significant. So far everyone who has met Ashford has no trouble remembering him.

I have to hand it to Anna though; the woman can research. She showed no signs of slowing down as we poured through resource after resource before finally exhausting them all. She also showed no sign she wanted to quit, which makes me think she either doesn't have anyone at home waiting for her, or she's looking for reasons to stay at work. Though, given her profession, I'd suspect it's the latter. She reminds me of me, especially when I first started working at the Bureau. Some days I'd spend sixteen hours at the office, much to the chagrin of my superiors.

I don't think we have any other choice; we're going to need a warrant for Ashford's home. If by some miracle he does still have that computer, we need it. It could be our only way of finding out who Jessica was talking to. That person could very well have been the last person to see her alive.

"Here," Anna says as I walk into the station the following morning. She's already at the front, waiting for me, coffee in one hand and a scone in the other.

"Where did you get a scone?" I ask.

"There's a place close to my place," she replies. "It's blueberry."

"Thanks." I take a bite, having skipped breakfast again. "Wow, this is really good."

"Best in town," she says. "I always have one or two or five before I start on my sessions. They help keep me calm."

I shoot her a look. "You? Need help staying calm?"

"I'm a very nervous person by nature," she says, shooting me an embarrassed smile and I realize she's serious.

"Then why go into psychology?" I ask.

"Would you believe it was the best form of self-therapy I could think of?" she asks.

"Are you telling me you became a therapist to give yourself therapy?" We head down the main hallway, toward Reyes' office.

"In a manner of speaking. But isn't that what everyone does? They choose the profession they feel like they need to explore? I'd be willing to bet being an FBI agent satisfies some deep need within you. Something you may not have even recognized about yourself. Perhaps a need for justice, or the desire to help those who can't help themselves."

"I mean, I guess," I say, my mouth half full of scone.

As we enter Reyes' office he looks up, then waves us off. "Whatever this is, it can wait, I've got a thousand things that need taking care of first."

"The fires?" I ask.

"Word came in overnight that human remains were found at one of the sites. The forensic teams are going back out to the first two to make sure we didn't miss something at the other properties." He picks up the phone to make a call.

"Human remains?" I ask. "I didn't know any of the families lost someone in the fire."

"Nan, get me Dryden, over at the pathologist's office," he says, then turns to me. "They didn't. These were someone else. Apparently, someone was inside the house that didn't belong there."

"The arsonist?" Anna asks.

He shakes his head. "No, this was at the first property, so we know it wasn't the arsonist." He pauses. "Yeah, Paul. This is Captain R—yeah, I know…"

As he speaks I can't help the gears in my head turning. I motion for Anna to follow me out of his earshot. "Three fires all in one day. And now a body is found in one of them."

"That suggests the fires were set to cover something up, not just for the fire's sake," she says.

"Have you had a lot of experience with arsonists?"

"In practice only," she replies. "I haven't worked on a case yet involving one." She turns to look at Reyes. "Though, considering this, maybe now I will."

"I've worked a few arson cases—one that was particularly gruesome—but it's been my experience nine times out of ten the fire serves a purpose beyond destruction. I think you're right, that our arsonist is looking to hide a secret."

Her eyes go wide. "What kind of secret?"

"I have a hunch," I say just as Captain Reyes hangs up. I head back over to his desk. "Captain, do you have a list of all the missing persons out of Fernview in say the last twenty years?"

He glares up at me like I'm crazy. "No, Agent Slate, I don't keep something like that here in my top desk drawer."

"I think it may relate to your fires," I reply.

He's clearly frazzled, but motions to the door anyway. "Talk to Tate. I'm sure he can get you a list. Now if you please, I've got about a dozen more calls to make."

Anna and I head back out to the bullpen, finding Owen Tate working at his desk. He looks up as soon as we approach. "Lost already?"

"Cut the shit," I tell him. "I need a list of all the people reported missing from Fernview starting in 1998."

He practically barks out laughing. "So? Go find it yourself. I've got an actual case to work on here, we're dealing with more than just some dead girl."

"Some dead *girl*?" I say, loudly. I can already feel my blood rising.

He purses his lips, sitting back. "Now w—"

Before I can say anything, Anna steps in front of me, getting right down on his level. "Listen to me, you homunculus. This is not just some *girl*. This was a living, breathing person who was sexually assaulted, murdered, and bagged up like old trash to be disposed of. You will not disrespect her again. Otherwise I will find you mentally incapable of empathy, and thus a danger to yourself and others on the job. And yes, I will make that my official recommendation."

His eyes are wide. "You…"

"Allow me to stop you there. I *can*. Now get us that list."

Tate looks around at the other officers who are staring at the three of us, mumbles something under his breath, then gets up, heading for some of the cabinets on the far side of the room. When he comes back, he's got a folder in his hand. "If you need help with your misplaced anger, I'd be happy to schedule you some time," Anna adds.

He hands the folder over without another word, then goes back to his desk.

Anna gives me a triumphant smile, then leads us away from the bullpen, back to the conference room. I have to admit, my respect for her has gone up a few notches. "Homunculus?"

"In this instance, it means tiny man," she says, handing me the folder.

"Nicely done," I tell her, then open the folder. Inside are single-page reports for sixty-seven people. "This is less than I expected."

"Small town," Anna says.

I nod, then spread all of the sheets out on the conference table. "What are the names of the families who lost houses yesterday?"

Anna leaves for a moment, then returns with a situation report for EOD yesterday. "Hale, Parker and Tomlinson."

I scan over the pages. "Look." I grab one near the middle. "Cameron Hale, went missing in 2011." I look a little further. "And here, Sasha Parker, missing in 2007." I find the final name near the end. "And Regina Tomlinson, missing since 2016. What do you want to bet the remains they found belong to one of these women?"

"You're saying...the arsonist is the same person who killed Jessica Ashford?"

"That's exactly what I'm saying. He didn't just stop with her, he kept on murdering and hiding bodies. Each in the homes of their families."

"But...how?" Anna asks.

"I don't know," I grab the three relevant reports and head back down to Reyes' office. He's on the phone, then glances up at me with an annoyed look.

"Just make sure they're thorough. Fire Chief said it burned close to fifteen-hundred degrees. If there's something left, it's going to be small," he says. "Yeah, okay, keep me updated." He hangs up the phone. "Now what?"

I lay the three missing person's reports in front of him. He furrows his brow, but when he scans the names of the missing women he grimaces. "Is this right?"

"I think we're all chasing the same person here, Captain," I say. "Your firebug is our killer, and he's cleaning house. Literally."

"Christ," Reyes mutters. "How many more are there?"

I hold up my hand. "How many more fires have you had? It's clear he's destroying evidence, going back and cleaning up his mess. I was wrong; he didn't expect us to find Jessica. And when we did, it set off a series of events none of us could predict. I guarantee you find remains from all three of these women in those homes, if there's anything left to find."

"That's what the chief was just saying." He's staring at the missing person's reports. "The fire was hot enough to turn bone into ash. The fact that anything was left at the Hale house was pure luck." He picks up the picture of Cameron Hale. "Missing at sixteen years old."

"If he kept to the pattern," I say. "Then she probably died shortly after she went missing. They all probably did."

He shakes his head like he can't believe it. "This was not the quiet little town I was hoping for when I moved here."

"That goes for both of us," Anna says. "Captain, if Emily is right, this man is very dangerous. There's no telling what he might do, especially to maintain his anonymity. If anyone else has any inkling he might be responsible, their lives could be in danger."

"Have you made any progress on an identity?" he asks.

"That's why we came in this morning," I reply. "To ask you to get a search warrant for Jake Ashford's home. We figured it was easier than asking Detective Hodge."

"A warrant for what? You think he's the killer?"

"For an old computer he may or may not have," I reply.

"We found out Jessica was talking to someone online before she disappeared. It's our only lead at this point. Everything else has fizzled out." If the killer really is the same person who set the fires, that pretty much exonerates Carlos Gutierrez and the other injured man. As well as the worker who lives in Texas, assuming we can prove he was there when the fires were set.

"Okay," he says. "Judge Meredith owes me a favor; I think I can get this across pretty—"

"Captain," a sergeant says, sticking his head in the office.

"What now?" Reyes asks, exasperation coloring his cheeks.

"Just got a call. Neighbor just found a body."

Chapter Twenty-Two

WE'RE STANDING outside Connor Griffin's home, watching as the lights from the emergency units reflect off the house's white siding. These things always seem to take so long.

"It looks different today, don't you think?" Anna asks. "The house?"

"What?" I find I'm having trouble concentrating. We were just at this house yesterday, speaking with Mr. Griffin, and today he's dead. One of his neighbors saw that his back door was open and came over to check on him. They found him in the back room, where he stored all his records. The same room where he brought us.

"It feels different too." Anna is staring up in the house, but she seems lost in thought. The place is surrounded by emergency vehicles, and an ambulance sits off to the side its back doors open, waiting for the body. Unfortunately, there will be no reviving him, he was DOA.

"I guess I don't get what you mean."

She furrows her brow. "The house just seems...lifeless. I don't know how to explain it, maybe it has something to do with homes being more vessels than just static structures. They hold our lives, our experiences, and our memories. And when a life is extinguished, it almost seems like the spirit of the house was extinguished along with it." She glances over at me and pinches her features. "Sorry, I get a little philosophical sometimes. It must be the stress."

"No, I get it. But this means that you are right, and we have a serious problem. I don't think it's a stretch to assume the person who killed Connor Griffin was the same one who killed Jessica Ashford. The killer knows we're on his trail."

As we're speaking, Captain Reyes exits the house, headed straight for us. He holds up a small white card in an evidence bag. "Your business card was found at the crime scene."

I nod. "That's because we came to see Mr. Griffin yesterday. His company was responsible for building the wall in my old house. We were trying to get some records from him of any employees who may have had access to the house when the wall was built."

"And? Did he give it to you?" Captain Reyes seems more belligerent than normal. I know he feels the weight of this case pressing down on him, especially now that even more bodies are piling up.

"He did. We were looking into his employees, but if I'm right and the same person who set the fires killed Jessica, then we can probably eliminate most of them as suspects. One of them is disabled, another is dead. The two we spoke with have no motive, but we're not taking them off the list yet. This has to all be the work of the same person. Jessica, the fires, and now Griffin."

"Ashford?" he asks.

"I can't be sure. It's not looking likely, but I don't want to eliminate him just yet. We need to find out if he still owns that computer. It could be the only link that we have."

Reyes sighs, looking back at the house. "I have to tell you Agent Slate; I don't like this. This demonstrates an escalation that I'm not comfortable with. Who knows what else this guy could do?"

"That's why we need to find him, as soon as possible. Do you think you can get that warrant today?"

"I'll get right on it. In the meantime, if you're going in there, make sure you have the proper equipment on." He heads off pulling his phone out of his pocket to make a call.

I turn to Anna. "You can stay out here if you want, but I need to look around. I need to see if anything is different from yesterday. Just to be sure."

She gives me a determined look, and I realize I'm being too easy on her. "No, I can handle it. Plus, I was in there too, it never hurts to have a second pair of eyes."

I nod. "Okay, then."

We head to the front of the house, and I grab a pair of gloves and some booties for my shoes, slipping them on before going inside. This part of the house right inside the door looks the same as it did yesterday. La-Z-Boy, side table, TV. Though there's no microwave dish on the table, nor is there an open beer bottle. As we make our way through the back of the house, I don't see any differences, until we get to the kitchen. The forensic technicians have marked areas that need investigation was small yellow placards. One of them stands close, writing something on an iPad.

"Is this where he got in?" I asked.

The tech nods. "Looks like he broke the lock or jimmied it. We're still investigating. No fingerprints though, probably wore gloves."

He wouldn't have been in a hurry; he would've wanted to make sure no one heard or saw him. I follow the path that I think he took through the kitchen, into the long hallway in the back. An officer stands at the furthest door, which was the same one where Griffin let us look at all his records. All the other doors are open, but the rooms are empty of people and nothing looks disturbed. Which only reinforces my theory that this was no random break-in or burglary. It's all connected. I check behind me to see Anna still has that steely determination on her face. I don't want to patronize her by telling her to prepare herself, though I hope she's ready.

I show the officer my badge quickly and he nods, allowing us to step into the room.

Compared to yesterday, I can't believe this is the same room. There are boxes and boxes of overturned records, and papers are scattered all over the floor, so many that the floor itself isn't even visible. The whole room has been trashed.

In the middle sits Griffin's desk, and the man himself is splayed out on it. His face is purple and bloated and it's clear to me that he died from asphyxiation. Hodge stands off to the side, watching us. When I look up, he looks away, back at Griffin's body. Another forensic technician is attempting to dust for prints, but it doesn't look like he's having much luck.

"Surprised you showed up," Hodge says. "I would've included everything in my report."

"Sometimes you just have to see it for yourself," I say. "Strangled?"

"Looks like it," he turns to the side and coughs once, covering his mouth. "Neighbor found him just like this. We have to wait until they finish the forensics before we can move him. Found your business card though, right there on top of his desk."

"Reyes already showed me. We left it with him yesterday in the event he remembered anything we might have missed." I check on Anna and find her staring at Griffin, as if she's frozen to the spot.

"That means he saw it too," she says.

"What?" Hodge and I ask at the same time.

"The killer. He knows you're working the case, Emily." Her voice comes across haunted, like she's trying to predict my future. I'm not even sure she's doing it on purpose, but I have to suppress a chill from running down my back.

"That's okay," I finally say. "It's nothing I haven't faced before."

"What was your conversation with Griffin about?" Hodge asks.

"We wanted the files relating to the construction of the wall in the Heritage house. His company was responsible."

"And? Did he give them to you?" he asks.

I nod. "Just the ones relating to that property." If somebody were to tell me a tornado came through here, I'd believe them. An entire lifetime of organization destroyed in a few short minutes. "If the person who killed Griffin is who we think they are, they must've been looking for those files too."

Hodge tilts his head at me. "Then I guess it's a good thing you got to them before he did."

I don't like the implication in his words, but I let them roll off my back. I'm not about to get into a confrontation with Hodge, especially not right now. Anna has finally taken a few steps forward, examining Griffin. From the way her face is pinched I can tell it's taking a lot of her concentration to show that she's not upset. Seeing a dead body, especially in this condition, is never easy. Couple that with the fact that we spoke with him yesterday, and he seemed fine, tends to make it difficult for the human brain to resolve something like this. As I'm sure she's all too aware. Instead of saying anything, I just let her take all the time she needs.

"I want to get a look at those files as soon as possible," Hodge says, apparently oblivious as to how this might be affecting her.

"They're back in my hotel room. I'll get you copies," I tell him.

He shakes his head. "No, I want the originals. I'm officially taking over all aspects of this case."

Anna looks up for the first time. "You can't."

"I can. We believe the same person who set the fires is the one who more than likely killed Jessica Ashford, *and* Connor Griffin, which means that all this now falls under my purview."

"We'd come to the same conclusion," I say. "I guess this means you don't need me anymore?"

"If you'd like to stay on and help, you are more than welcome to. But it seems to me, that you really haven't made much progress at all. You've just run into a bunch of dead ends."

"We've been working our asses off, and now you think you can come in here and take control of everything?" Anna says. Her cheeks flush and I see that same emotion that came out against Officer Tate rear its head again, only this time it's not restrained.

"Do I have to remind you that you are a *consultant?*" Hodge says. "You're not an investigator, you're not even on the force. I'm not even sure what you're doing here."

"She's here because she's insightful, passionate, and determined to get to the truth," I say. "Which is more than I can say for you, especially when you thought this was nothing more than a cold case. How much effort did you really put in on Jessica Ashford before I got here?"

He dodges my question. "It's not a cold case anymore," Hodge says. "And I don't really care what you think about it. This clearly falls under local jurisdiction, so unless you want to file a formal protest, I'll be taking over."

I work my jaw, trying not to blow up. I think that's just what he wants. And I'm not going to give him the satisfaction. "Fine. You're right. This is a local issue, and your case to do with as you please." I motion to Anna that we should go. We make our way back out of the house and back to my car.

"Can he really do that?" She asks.

"Yes. And Reyes will probably back him up." I start the car.

"Then what do we do?"

"We'll need to move fast if we're going to beat him to it," I say. I don't trust Hodge not to look for the easiest explanation. He may have the authority to take over the case, but that doesn't mean we can't keep following what threads we still have.

"Beat him to it?" she asks. "But we don't have the warrant yet."

I pull away from the scene, watching Reyes in my rear-view mirror still talking on the phone. "Nope. We'll just have to try to convince Ashford to help us without it."

Chapter Twenty-Three

Sloppy.

I know it. But it can't be helped, not at this stage. I need to be fast—that FBI agent is too close—much too close on my heels. I can't believe she already got to Griffin. How could she have figured that out so quickly? I've been keeping an eye on the man for years; just in the event I ever needed to enact the final protocol. I was perfectly content to let Connor Griffin live out his days in that miserable little house of his, driving off to see his daughter every month, then coming back to an empty home, nothing but microwavable meals to greet him in his desolation.

Not that I ever had anything personal against Griffin; he never crossed me—at least not like some of the others had. He was a decent guy, I guess. But that wasn't enough to save him. Not when he could ID me. Maybe he didn't even realize he could, but eventually it would have come out.

And now that woman has the records I need.

Slate. Her name is Slate. I can't forget that. She thinks she's clever; but I'm about to show her how behind she really is. She's not going to pull one over my eyes, not after I've spent so much time preparing for this.

But first I need to get those records. I remember thinking it was better for me that Griffin kept everything on paper; nothing online. That's good. My understanding of the internet begins and ends with Windows. If files needed hacking I'd have to hire outside help. And had that been the case I would have ended up with another body. There can't be any loose ends now.

Like I said, sloppy. Not anymore. I need to make sure this is clean.

Should I have taken her business card? Maybe. I left that room in a wreck. They wouldn't have missed it. But I don't need it. I already have all her information. And it's not like I'm going to call her up, not unless I get stupid.

Damn, I'm getting distracted again. I can't afford that. Not right now.

I pull up to the hotel, parking around the back. It was easy enough to find out where she was staying; all I needed to do was check the parking lots of the hotels around town last night. Her car might not be something flashy, but it's easy enough to pick out in an uncrowded parking lot. And I remember it from the other night when it was parked at the police station. Thankfully she's not here right now, though. No, I'm sure she's working hard on the case, going over the evidence, trying to figure out how to track me down.

And all the while she has no idea where I am.

I head back around to the front and enter like any other guest. The man at the front desk barely looks up but I don't stop to talk to him. He's not my target. He doesn't say anything, and I glance down the hallway looking for the person I did come to see. But it's empty. I wince, then head to the elevator and take it up to the second floor. I'd prefer the stairs, but my leg is killing me and I'm doing good just to stay upright.

On the second floor I find my quarry: right there in the middle of the hall. I approach slowly and check around to make sure no one else is close. As I reach the laundry cart, a young woman with curly red hair pulled back in a loose pony-tail steps out. For a second she's startled, but puts on a fake smile anyway, as I'm sure her boss has instructed her to do.

"Oh, hi there—" she begins until recognition forms in her eyes. Her brows draw, showing her confusion. "Hey…Mr.—"

"Hey there, Kristin," I say, my voice soft and friendly. "How have you been?"

"Fine, I guess," she says. "What are *you* doing here?"

I feign embarrassment. "I probably shouldn't be telling you this, but it's a little upsetting. I was here with—a lady friend last night and I'm afraid I left my watch in my room. You didn't happen to see it, did you?"

A sly smile comes over her face. "Really? *You?*"

"What?" I ask, playing along. "I can't have a good time every now and again?"

"Yeah, of course," she says, tucking a stray hair behind her ear. "It's just…weird…thinking of you as just a normal guy, I guess."

I let out a belly laugh that's only halfway forced. *Oh, if you only knew just how special I really am.* "I can see that. Anyway, I know you've been working here ever since graduation, so I was hoping you could help me out. To be honest I was trying to get out of here this morning without you seeing me."

"Yeah, I didn't see you when I came in. What room were you in?"

I make a motion above us. "Up in four-sixteen. Did you see it in there?" I know it's far too early for her to have made it to the fourth floor already.

"I haven't had a chance to check yet, but when I make it up there, I can let you know."

I pinch my features together. "Well, that's the thing. I have to head out of town this morning, and if it's not there I'd like to know. I'm not going to be able to rest until I know where it is. It was a present from someone very close to me."

"Oh," she says, looking back at the room. "Well, I still need to finish up this floor first. If I were to go up there I'd have to take the cart and—"

"Would you mind if I just took a look?" I ask. "I was just in there this morning."

She screws up her face. "Well…I mean I'm not supposed to…"

"Here," I say, reaching into my jacket pocket. "Let me make it worth your while." I produce a small bag full of pretty clean hash. "It's the stuff I use. Nice and mellow."

Her eyes go wide. "Really?"

I toss her the baggie and she opens it, taking a whiff. "Nice." She stashes the bag under her apron. "Okay, here's the master. Bring it right back, okay? I'm almost done with this room."

"No problem," I say, taking the keycard from her. "Thanks. I'll be just a few minutes." She gives me another tepid smile and I head back to the elevator, allowing it to take me to the third floor.

This was the floor that I saw the elevator stopped on last night when the FBI agent got in. And there are twenty-four rooms on this level. As I step out, I realize I don't have time to search all twenty-four. But I'm willing to bet the FBI doesn't want housekeeping coming in and out of her room. I scan the hallway for any hang tags asking for privacy.

I approach the first one and tap on the door a few times. "Housekeeping," I say, in a light voice.

"We don't want any, can't you read the sign?" a man's voice comes from inside. I move on to the next one and decide to change up my tactic.

"Concierge." I know this hotel isn't fancy enough to have a concierge, but if someone does actually open the door I fit that description better than someone who just brings towels.

"What?" a female voice asks on the other side of the door and I watch the peephole go dark.

"Just checking on our guests, ma'am," I say. "Is there anything you need? Anything we can help you with?"

She pauses. "No…no thank you." She moves away from the peephole again. Boy, the stories I could write about the people in this place. What are they getting themselves into? I check two more rooms before I come to the first one where someone doesn't respond. Ironically, it's room three-sixteen, right below the room I "supposedly" stayed in last night.

Using the keycard, I open the door to a dark room. "Hello? Anyone home? We're just doing a wellness check on the occupant of his room." There's no response and I flip on the lights, to an empty room. As soon as I see the dark blazer and the black suitcase I know I've hit pay dirt. This is her room.

Quickly I allow myself in and begin examining her things, pulling a pair of gloves on before I get started. Her clothes are all still in her suitcase…obviously Emily Slate isn't one of those people who likes to "unpack" when they go somewhere. She's probably used to living out of a suitcase all the time. Always traveling, always bringing justice to the people. I chuckle, moving on, looking through what little remains in the room. No laptop, and no files from Griffin. Damn. That means she has them with her in her vehicle. That's going to make things much more complicated.

I check the bathroom, just to make sure, and only find a smattering of toiletries. Though there is a small simple-looking ring on the counter. Hmm. Perhaps…no. I should wait. But then again…this woman thinks she's smarter than I am. That she can beat me at my own game.

I take the ring, pocketing it.

Just as I reach the door, I pause. Slate isn't stupid. Nor is she careless. Would she keep the files on her? Or would she want them where no one else could get to them? If they are here, she wouldn't just leave those files out, in the event house-keeping did come in the room by mistake.

188 · ALEX SIGMORE

I check between the mattress and the bedsprings, but there's nothing there. I look behind the nightstand…again nothing. I think I've perhaps misjudged her, except when I feel around on top of the shelf in the closet. At the very back my fingers graze something, and I reach out, pulling the packet down.

It's the files from Griffin. The ones that can be traced back to me. I *knew* she wasn't smarter than I was. But she is a challenge, I'll give her that.

I tuck the files into the back of my pants and pull my jacket back over them before leaving the room again. I might as well have just conquered Mount Everest. And when Emily Slate comes back to her hotel room tonight, she's in for a surprise. I wish I could be there to watch when she realizes they're gone. I'm sure she'll notice the ring too; and then she'll know it was no accident. She'll know *I* was there, that I beat her. Now, with these in my possession there is only one more loose end to take care of. Not that he could ever ID me, but a smart enough person could put it together—given enough time. If I eliminate him, then the sequence will be complete. Full circle.

It's poetic in a way—I've been waiting all these years, watching…and now I finally get to take the last measure. But of course this means…well, too bad for poor Kristin.

I take the elevator back down to the second floor. It hasn't been more than nine minutes. It took a little longer than I'd anticipated, given how many people had DO NOT DISTURB signs on the doors, but nothing I couldn't handle.

Kristin is beside her cart which has moved down to the next room already. She's glaring at me with what might be suspicious eyes. Not a problem.

"Thank you, my dear," I say, holding out the card for her.

"Did you find it?" she asks.

I pull my sleeve back to show the watch I've had on all along. "It fell back behind the bed. Sorry it took me so long, I had to move it out from the wall and move it back. But no harm done. I really appreciate you letting me look. I won't be back in town for another week."

"Well…" she says. "I guess as long as you found it, no harm done."

"Hey, you got a few minutes to take the edge off?" I motion to the weed I saw her stash in her apron. "I could use a quick one before I have to get on the road."

She glances to the room, then back to me, probably thinking she'll never get another opportunity to take a smoke with someone who used to scold her for being late to class.

"Five minutes," she says. Kristin never was a bad kid, she just never had ambition. She came into this world without a purpose and will leave the exact same way. Her grades were always mediocre to bad and she could always be found out behind the football bleachers with the other burnouts. It was how I knew this contingency plan would work if necessary.

She locks the cleaning cart in the room she's working in and leads me to the nearest back exit. My truck isn't parked too far away. As soon as we're outside she pulls out the bag. "Got any papers?"

She's opening the bag, her attention focused on it and she doesn't see me coming. Within a second I have a hand over her mouth and my other arm wrapped around her neck, choking off her air supply. She's a tiny thing, and it doesn't take long. I check the surrounding area, but there's nothing but woods behind the hotel and there's no one back here anyway. Still, I move quick and get her into the bed of my truck, then cover her up with the blue tarp I have in the back.

Poor girl. And just think, if Agent Emily Slate hadn't left those documents in there for me to steal, she could still be cleaning the hotel rooms right now. But I knew coming here this was a possibility. I'll have to dispose of her body quickly—though I doubt management will care. Kristin is the kind of girl you expect to just walk off the job one day and never come back. They'll hire a replacement in no time.

Before I get back in the truck, I take a second to lean up against the side. My leg is throbbing, and I need to head back home and rest before I finish things up, otherwise I'm not going to be able to walk. I'll deal with Kristin, then tomorrow…tomorrow I finish my work.

For now, I have everything I've come for.

Chapter Twenty-Four

"WHAT DO YOU MEAN STOLEN?" Liam asks. I'm standing outside my hotel room while Officer Tate and another officer fill out a robbery report. One of the same forensic technicians that was at Connor Griffin's house is inside as well, gathering any evidence that might have been left behind.

"I mean, he gained access to my room, and stole the construction documents." I pause a beat. "And my ring."

"What ring?" Liam asks.

I haven't told him about it because I think some part of me still feels guilty for carrying it around. But at my heart I'm a sentimental person. I may not have worn my wedding ring because it made me a bigger target on the job, but that didn't mean I didn't keep it with me at all times. Even after everything I found out about Matt and the Organization, I continued to keep it close. But more recently I've been leaving it behind and not carrying it with me. Ever since coming back to Fernview I've left it in the hotel. Somewhere in the back of my mind I know I'm trying to divest myself from it—but it's not something I can just quit doing cold turkey. And now it's gone. *He* has it.

"My wedding ring," I say miserably. "I...still carry it. Or...I did."

There's silence on the other side. I know this probably hurts him, but we're still early in our relationship. I haven't told him everything yet. And it's going to take me a long time before I'm able to open up about all of it. "Emily...I'm so sorry."

I wince. Classic Liam. I expect him to lash out, to complain that I'm holding a torch for a man that betrayed me, or to accuse me of not being able to move on. But instead, he's supportive, just like always. I have to swallow to keep the tears from rising in my eyes. "Thank you."

"You think it was him? The man who killed Jessica Ashford?" he asks.

"I know it was," I reply. "We've hit the hornet's nest out here. As soon as we found Jessica Ashford all of these things began happening. These fires, then Connor Griffin's murder, and now this. He's cleaning house. And there's no telling who else is in his crosshairs."

"Why would he take your ring? I get the files, but...was it valuable?"

I shake my head even though he can't see me. "Not particularly. Just to me. Maybe he just wanted me to know it was him. I dunno. He's playing a game with me now—and I can't deny he knows who I am and that I'm on his trail. Which means this has gone from bad to worse."

"Em," Liam says and I can already hear it in his voice before he says it. "Maybe it's time to let Wallace know what you're doing. That way he can provide support if—"

"If I do that I'm just asking for trouble," I say. "Plus, I'm still off the clock. I'm not working as an FBI agent right now. Just as a concerned citizen."

"And if you end up shooting someone?" Liam asks. He knows the regulations as well as I do. There are certain stipulations an FBI agent is granted when working as an officer. But as a civilian we're not always provided all those same protections.

"We'll cross that bridge when we come to it." Tate is shooting me dirty looks. "Listen, I gotta go. I need to track this asshole down."

"Em, let the cops there do their job," Liam replies. "And don't get in over your head. If I have to I'll come down there myself."

"I'll be fine," I say, then pause, holding the line a minute longer. "No word from Zara?"

His voice softens. "Nothing yet."

That pit in my stomach grows. I don't like that she's been out of contact so long. "Okay. Thanks. I'll talk to you soon."

"Okay," he says. "Be careful."

"Thanks," I say. "Bye." I linger a moment longer, waiting for him to hang up. The truth is I'm unnerved, though I'd never let Liam know that. This man found out where I was staying and broke into my hotel room and magically there don't seem to be any witnesses. Who *is* this guy?

I slip my phone in my pocket and approach Tate. "Anything?"

"We'll let you know how the investigation proceeds once I'm finished here," he says brusquely. "Did you give anyone else the key to your room?"

"I'm not a moron," I tell him. "No one comes in and out of my room on the road but me and any other officers with me. Unless the hotel gave someone access. Have you spoken with them?"

He nods. "The manager doesn't have a clue. And housekeeping said they don't access rooms with the tag on the door."

"Well, someone got in here," I tell him. I catch him smirk before he wipes it from his face. "What?"

"Nothing," he replies, then goes to talk to the other officer.

I head over to the forensics technician, but I can already

see she hasn't come up with anything from the look on her face. "There are literally hundreds of fingerprints," she says. "It's going to take weeks to go through them all."

"Yeah, I'm not doing that," Tate replies. "Talk about a waste of time."

I hate that I agree with him. Whoever was in here wasn't stupid enough to leave his fingerprints anyway. But how did he manage to access the room? There's no forced entry and the window doesn't open, which means he had to have a keycard. There's no other explanation.

I head out of the room down to the elevator bank, but I'm too impatient to wait. Instead, I take the stairs back down to the first level. But as soon as I'm out of the stairwell my phone trills.

"Slate," I say without breaking my stride.

"It's Hodge. I just got the news. The files are missing?"

"Stolen, from my room," I say.

He makes an annoyed grunt on the other end. It sounds a bit like a warthog. "You never should have let them out of your possession," he says.

"Do you keep all your case files on your person at all times?" I snap, catching sight of the front desk.

"I want you to know I've spoken with Captain Reyes. He wanted me to communicate that while we have appreciated your assistance on this case, you have been officially removed from the investigation. You're to halt any further actions regarding Jessica Ashford."

I stop. "Hodge. This bastard just broke into *my* room. I'm not tucking tail and going home; not until I get my property back."

"The Fernview Police will handle that matter," he says. "We'll mail your property back to you if we recover it. But as far as this case is concerned, your services are no longer needed."

"Hodge, don't do this," I tell him. "Whoever this guy is, he's still a step ahead. You need my help."

"No, Agent Slate, I think you've done enough," he says before finally hanging up.

"*Dammit*," I say. The man at the front desk sees me coming and his eyes widen. I pull out my badge as I approach the desk. "Who has a master keycard?"

He glances at the badge, then back at me, blinking profusely. "Um…well the maintenance staff, the housekeeping…we keep one here at the desk. But honestly, anyone with access to our system can code one. But they'd have to know how."

"And how many people know the system?" I ask.

"I don't know. Maybe a dozen or two?"

"Does the system log every time a master key is created?" I ask.

He nods.

"Good. Search for any master keys or additional keys to three-sixteen created since I checked in." He types the information into his computer, biting on his lower lip as he does it.

"Sorry, it takes a minute. Okay, here we go." He runs his finger down the screen. "I don't see any additional master keys or secondary cards keyed to that room since Saturday." He looks back up.

"How many master keys in circulation right now?"

He types again and it takes an agonizingly long time for the information to populate. "Looks like at least fifteen."

"*Fifteen?*"

"Well," he says, his voice becoming a little higher. "Master keys get lost, or broken. Someone will take one home by accident. My housekeeping girl left with one today when she just up and quit. That's why we tell guests to place any valuables in the in-room safe."

I glare at him and he shrinks back from the desk a little.

"Wait, your housekeeper quit today? When? What happened?"

He glances to the side. "I'm not really in a position—"

"*Tell me,*" I say, more forcefully.

"All I know is she locked her cart in one of the rooms and is gone. I tried calling, but it goes straight to voicemail."

"Is her car missing?" I ask.

"She rode the bus here for her shifts," he replies.

"And she has a master keycard?" I ask.

"It wasn't on the cart when we inspected it," he replies. Why would a housekeeper want my files? Unless she broke into my room specifically for the ring and took the files as what…insurance? No, that doesn't make sense. Still, I need to talk to this girl.

"Where can I find her?" I ask.

"Listen, I wouldn't even bother," he says. "Kristin wasn't known for being the most reliable employee. We only hired her because it's so hard to find anyone willing to do this job."

"Last name, address and phone number." He sighs again and searches through his computer, then relays the relevant information to me. "Thank you. And get me a list of everyone who made a master key or who has used one in the past two days," I tell him. "I want names and phone numbers for those people as well."

"T-that'll take some time. I have my other work that—"

"Are you refusing to assist the FBI with a robbery that occurred on *your* premises? Under *your* watch?" I ask, my words coming out harsh and angry. I *am* angry. I'm angrier than I want to admit about losing that ring.

"No, of course not," he says, regaining some of his composure. "A list. I'll start working on that right away."

"Thank you," I say. I turn and head back to the elevators, checking my phone. It's already past ten p.m. I'm unlikely to get anything else done tonight. Still, I'm feeling anxious. Despite common sense pointing to it being the housekeeper, I know it was *him*. I don't like that he was in my room, going through my stuff. I have half a mind to take everything in my suitcase and wash it. Who knows what he might have touched.

As I head back down the hall, I see Tate and the other officer approaching. "Ms. Slate," he says, his condescending tone unmistakable. "We've completed our initial assessment and taken our report. We'll be in touch if we find the person who did this."

"Cut the shit, Tate," I say and I catch that smirk again. I know for a fact they're not going to investigate this case any further. I need to find Kristin Pruitt.

He hands me a copy of the report. "Have a nice evening, Ms. Slate." He and the other officer head off and I'm left with the technician who is just finishing up. She's packing up her bag as I enter the room again.

"You were at Connor Griffin's house earlier, weren't you?" I ask.

She nods. "It's been a long day."

"Well, thanks for coming out anyway. I know it's a long shot."

She grins as she lifts her bag. "No problem. And don't let Tate get to you. He's like that with everyone. Just one of those people who is constantly miserable. Half the time he's down at the bar, drunk off his ass and yammering away to anyone who will listen."

I slump down on the bed. "Sounds about right."

She gives me another nod. "Good night, Agent."

"Night," I say. Once she's left and I'm alone again, I can't help but feel like the room is no longer secure. If he could get in once, he could get in again. I should probably move rooms, but I don't want to give him the satisfaction of knowing he got to me. He's obviously been watching me. But for how long?

I check my phone, looking at the address for Kristin. If I recall it isn't too far from here. I call her number, despite the late hour, but like the clerk said, it goes straight to voice mail.

Instead I hop up, grab my coat and I'm back downstairs and in my car before Tate and the other officer have even pulled out of the hotel parking lot.

The entire time I'm headed to see Ms. Pruitt I'm trying to figure out what her connection could be to the killer. Is she an accomplice? A relative? Or did she really have nothing to do with it?

When I reach her apartment complex I realize I'm not in the best part of town. Still, that's never stopped me before. Pruitt's apartment is on the floor below ground, where the property slopes down in the back. I take the dark stairs down, careful of my surroundings until I come to her door. I give it a hard bang a few times, but keep my eye on the corner, just in case someone decides to jump off the balcony and make a run off into the woods.

But there's no answer on the other side. I bang a few more times before I finally hear rustling. Eventually a young woman with dark bags under her eyes answers the door. Her skin is mottled and ashy, and it looks like she hasn't had a shower in a week. "Ms. Pruitt?" I ask.

She shakes her head. "Nah, she ain't here. I'm Rhi."

"Roomate?" I ask. She nods. "Have you seen Kristin this evening?" I ask.

"Who wants to know?" I show her my badge and she sobers a little. "Oh. Nah, I haven't seen her since she came in last night. But sometimes she stays out pretty late."

Of course. I should have guessed she wouldn't be here. "What can you tell me about her?" I ask.

"Kris? Um, not much. She keeps to herself. Quiet. Pays rent on time. That's about it."

I let out a long sigh. This is going nowhere. The odds I'm going to get the full truth out of Rhi are low, at best. Still, I pull my card out and hand it to her. "If you hear from her, tell her to call me. It's important. She might be in danger."

"Danger?" Rhi asks, taking the card.

"She may be with someone we consider very dangerous," I tell her.

"Oh," Rhi says, looking at the card. "Yeah, okay, I'll tell her."

"Thanks," I say, then leave the young girl. I'm starting to get that bad feeling again—like maybe Kristin didn't run off after all. If the killer came to the hotel to steal my stuff, Kristin might have gotten in the way, or been at the wrong place at the wrong time. I don't like to admit it, but I think we could be looking at another possible victim here, even though it doesn't fit the killer's pattern. He's off-book now, cleaning house. Which means he might be taking more risks, more deviations. We saw how easily he dispatched Connor Griffin.

When I get back to my hotel room, I still feel that same invasion of privacy. I take the desk chair and prop it up under the door, despite already having thrown the deadbolt and the security bar. I don't need to be taking any more chances than necessary. And despite all these precautions, I still probably won't be able to sleep. I had hoped to meet with Ashford this evening, but when I came back to freshen up and found my room had been ransacked all that went out the window. And now we might have another missing girl. I just can't catch a break here.

I'll have to confront Ashford first thing in the morning if there's even a chance of finding this man. By making this personal and thinking he's going to get to me, he's made a big mistake. And he's underestimated me if he thinks I won't use everything I have to come after him.

Chapter Twenty-Five

WHEN I PULL up to Jake Ashford's property the sun is just breaking the tops of the mountains in the distance, bathing the landscape in an orange-yellow glow. The entire drive out here the sky was lit up in early morning purples and pinks and now is just turning the bright clear blue that I remember here as a kid. Sometimes the air could be so crisp and clean it's like it was made brand new each day. It's barely seven thirty and I doubt I slept more than an hour last night, but I needed to get out here before Hodge or anyone else realizes I'm not going back to D.C.

I get out of my car and am halfway to the front door when it opens, revealing Judy in a thick robe. I stop short.

"Emily," she says, hugging herself. "Here to accuse my father of murder again?"

"I'm sorry, Judy," I say. "I should have handled that better. No, I'm here because I need your help."

"*My* help?" she asks, an air of incredulousness about her.

"Well, your father's," I say.

"My father isn't feeling well," she says. "And he certainly doesn't want to speak with you. After what he told me you did, I don't blame him."

I wince. "Judy, I was only doing my job. I have to investigate everyone who lived in that house, no matter who they are. You have to admit, your dad can be overly combative sometimes. I can't just ignore that."

Her face turns into a scowl. "So that means what? He killed Jess? Just because he's got anger issues doesn't mean—"

"No, I agree, it doesn't mean that," I say. "Which was why I never accused him of anything. All we did was ask a few questions. That's all. It doesn't help me if we don't find the right person, but the only way I can do that is by asking people who lived there. That includes you, too."

"You think I had something to do with it?" she asks.

I shake my head. "I remember how broken up you were after Jess disappeared. You think I've forgotten but I remember all those conversations we had. That's what drew us together, my mother and your sister, right? That's why we got close, because we both understood each other's pain. There's no way you could have ever had anything to do with it. That thought never crossed my mind."

She sighs, then seems to deflate a little. "So then what do you want?"

"Do you remember, right before she disappeared, her talking to some guy?"

Judy bristles. "She was always talking to guys. She was popular. So what?"

"This was one guy in particular. She would have been talking with him a lot online."

She brings her brows together in concentration. "Maybe? I remember she was online a lot. Because back then we only had one phone line and every time she got on the computer it tied up the phone for everyone else. I tried complaining to dad that she was hogging the lines, but he just told me it was first come, first serve. I should have been quicker if I wanted to use it first."

"That's a nice thing to tell a fourteen-year-old," I say.

Her visage breaks and she cracks a small smile. "Yeah. A real understanding guy, my dad. He was always doing that kind of crap. Pitting us against each other, to the point where I really began to resent Jess. I think that's why it hit me so hard when she was gone. I felt like part of it was my fault for always trying to compete with her, despite being three years younger."

"I remember all the guilt you had. You've been carrying that for a while, huh?" I ask.

She shrugs. "I've spent a lot of time in therapy."

I step forward, carefully. "Judy…that night Jess disappeared. Did something…happen?"

It's subtle, but I notice she hugs herself tighter. "Happen?" she asks and I can already see it in her eyes.

"A fight? Between her and your dad?" I ask.

"How did you—"

"I spoke with Mindy Coolidge—Coldwater. She said that you told her about it, back when it happened. You never said anything to me about it. All those years and you never mentioned it."

She pinches her features and wipes a tear from her eye before it can fall. "I told Mindy because I was still young and stupid," she says, finally. "But I figured out pretty quick that their fight had been all my fault, something which Dad *never* let me forget."

"Your fault? How?"

"That night, Jess came into my room. She said she needed my help—that I needed to back her up on something. I'd been so mad at her that night, and I can't even remember why now. It was about something stupid; something Dad told me she'd done that had just upset me so bad. So I blew her off; I told her whatever she needed to do she could do without me. Then, about ten minutes later, I hear her and Dad going at it in the living room. Next thing I know, she's gone." She pulls back a sob. "The worst part was, when she left, I was *glad*. I was too stupid to realize I'd never see her again, or that was even a possibility. I figured she'd be back home in another hour."

"Jude," I say, sympathy enveloping the word.

She shakes her head, like she's trying to forget all of it. "Can't change it now. Can't do anything about it."

"But you know that wasn't you, don't you?" I ask. "That was your dad, poisoning the two of you against each other."

"That's what my therapist says too. Still, doesn't make it all go away, does it?"

I can't help but think back to Matt. "No. It doesn't."

She sniffs a few times, then wipes her eyes again. "Hell of a thing."

"Judy, I'm going to find him. I'm close. Is there any chance your dad still has that computer that she would have used back then?"

"Are you kidding?" I can already hear the disbelief in her voice. "Dad's a packrat. He never throws anything away. Especially not old, obsolete computers. He always says he can do something with it one day. Like he's going to take it apart and build himself a new one." She rolls her eyes, even though they're tinged red.

"You really think he still has it?" I ask. I'm usually not one to put a lot into hope, but this is a step in the right direction.

"I'm sure he does, it's just a matter of finding it." Vapor escapes her breath as she holds herself tighter. "Would you like to come in for some coffee? I just made it fresh."

"What about your dad?"

"He's upstairs asleep," she says. "Another late-night bender. He won't wake up until noon."

I smile. "Then I'd love one."

An hour later Judy and I are rummaging around in her father's basement looking for the computer, after having a nice long talk over some coffee and scones. I'm glad to see the years haven't hardened her like they have her father. Deep down, she's the same Judy I used to know; the same one I left behind when I went off to D.C. I regret that now; I shouldn't have cut ties with everyone just because I wanted to get out of Fernview. But at the time I figured the only way I could truly get away was a clean break. That meant from everyone and everything.

"God, there is so much *junk* down here. What am I supposed to do with all this when he's gone?" Judy asks. She's changed into jeans and a sweatshirt, both of which are covered in dirt and dust, much like my own clothes.

"When my father passed I had all these heirlooms he'd left," I say. "I ended up giving a lot of them away, because I didn't know what half of them were, and I could only fit so much stuff in my home at the time. Then when Matt died I just got sick of all of it, and sold everything. Started over with just the bare minimum. I've got maybe two boxes of old pictures and things from my childhood. That's it."

"That must be pretty liberating," she says, lifting a plastic snow sled out of the way.

"I guess. Sometimes I feel like I might have gotten rid of something important, but at the same time I don't have to deal with all that stuff, which is nice."

"I bet," she says.

I stop moving stuff for a minute and watch Judy. I've been so focused on Jessica's case, I've lost the thread of why I came to Fernview in the first place. Well—at least the reason I convinced myself to come here, anyway. Can I trust her, though? Now that we've cleared the air, we've fallen back into the same relationship we left; like the years haven't even passed us by. This was the whole reason I came here, wasn't it? To find out the truth behind those letters?

"The real reason I came back was because I received a letter in the mail a few months ago, then another just a few days ago," I say, watching for her reaction. She doesn't stop moving things out of the way.

"A letter?" she asks.

"From my mother."

Judy stops and looks at me, confusion on her face. "What?"

"Yeah, that's what I said too. I had the handwriting analyzed. It came back inconclusive."

"I don't understand. Was it an old letter that she scheduled to have delivered to you?"

I shake my head. "It referenced a recent case I'd been on. She said she saw me on TV."

"What the hell?" Judy asks.

"I know someone is trying to get under my skin, but what I don't know is why or who. I figured I could do some investigating while I was here; see if I could dig up anything on Mom. Things I might not have known."

She goes back to moving things around. "Have you found anything yet?"

"I've been a little occupied," I say with a smile. "I tried tracking down some of her old friends, but didn't get very far. You never heard anything…weird about her, did you?"

"Weird? How do you mean?" Judy picks up an old monkey stuffed animal that's missing an arm and tosses it to the side.

"I don't know. I just feel like…I don't know much about Mom's past. She never really talked about it with us. I think Dad knew something, but not all of it. He always told me when I was little that it hurt her to talk about her life before us. I used to think he told me that just so I'd stop asking, but I'm wondering now if maybe there wasn't something to that."

"You could always ask my mother," Judy says. "They knew each other, didn't they?"

"Did they?" I ask. "I didn't know."

"I think so," Judy says. "I remember Mom being pretty upset when you mother died. I was still young; Jess watched me when she went to the funeral."

"Your mom was at my mom's funeral?" I ask. "I never knew that."

Judy shrugs. "It was a long time ago. We were what, eleven?"

"Twelve," I correct her.

"It's hard to remember back that far sometimes," she says. "Especially about something so painful." I remember now why Judy and I got along so well. We understood each other's pain so intimately. No one else at our school had lost someone close like we had.

Immediately my eyes begin to well up. "I should have called."

"Hmm?" she asks, looking up, then sees my distress. "What's wrong?"

"I never should have just cut you off. I should have kept in contact," I say.

"Hey." She comes over and rubs my shoulders. "It's a two-way street. I didn't call either. I think I was just irked that you left for this amazing new life. My therapist says I have something of a jealous streak that I have to watch."

"You didn't deserve that. Not after everything we went through together."

"Neither did you." She gives my shoulder another rub. "But we can do better now, right? And from what you told me, you've been through the wringer lately."

I chuckle, "Yeah. I guess I have."

"Well, I'm here for you. Whenever you need me."

"Thank you," I say. Judy backs up and almost trips over a small pile. She saves herself, but half the pile collapses, revealing an old woven laptop case.

"Oh," she says. "Wait, that's right. It was a laptop, not a

desktop. I'd forgotten! Dad bought the laptop because he thought it would be better to be portable." She grabs the bag, unzipping it. Inside is a very boxy laptop, held down by a strap. "Yep, here it is."

"I can't believe it's actually here," I say.

"Yeah, but what are the odds you'll even be able to turn it on? I mean look at it. It's a dinosaur."

I pick it up; it's dramatically heavier than I expected. Like lugging around a brick. "As long as the information is on there, we'll find a way to get it. Do you mind if I take this for a few days? I promise to get it back to you."

She waves me off. "If it can help you find Jess, then, have it. Dad won't miss it. I'm not even sure he comes down here anymore."

I take the laptop and lug it upstairs. "Thank you. And thanks for your help."

Judy gives me a big smile. "You're very welcome."

Chapter Twenty-Six

As I'm driving back from the Ashford place, my phone buzzes in my pocket. I glance over at the laptop, hoping it's not Hodge or Reyes hounding me to get out of town already. It's a free country—I can stay wherever I want. But I'm sure they have to know I won't just give this up. The nerve of Reyes—asking for my help then getting Hodge to dismiss me...though now I wonder if Reyes even knows. All I have is Hodge's word that it came down from Reyes to let me go. It's possible—

My phone buzzes again and I grab it, trying to keep my focus. "Slate."

"Emily? You're not at your hotel. What's going on?"

"Anna," I say. "I'm sorry, so much has been going on. Someone broke into my hotel room last night and stole the construction documents."

"What?" she says. "Are you okay?"

"I wasn't there. It happened while we were at the Griffin place." I give her the full rundown of everything that's happened since last night, including my dismissal from Hodge and finding the laptop this morning.

"How can I help?" she asks.

"Can I come to your place to set this thing up? I need to coordinate with D.C. to get anything useful off it. My…friend who normally handles these kinds of things is out of the office. I'm thinking this is going to take a while to find any useful information."

"Ummm…sure," Anna says. "I can be back there in a few minutes. Just…ah, crap. Just don't be mad, okay?"

That makes me pause. "Mad? About what?"

"You'll see when you get here," she says, then shoots over the address.

Wait a second. I recognize this part of town. It takes me another fifteen minutes to get to that side of the town, and I end up going past a large wooden gate, until I find myself driving in the middle of a golf course. This is Windemere, the "fancy" neighborhood in Fernview. Complete with its own Country Club and eighteen-hole golf course. Mom and Dad used to drive us up here at Christmas to look at all the rich people's decorations.

What is Anna in her beat-up old van doing living up in the nicest neighborhood in Fernview?

I follow the directions on my GPS until I reach the only townhome development in the neighborhood. It's a small set of units that are on a small hill overlooking a valley and a couple of the holes of the golf course. There's also another gate. For *townhomes*. When get up to it, I have to press the call button.

"Name?" a voice says on the other end.

"Special Agent Emily Slate with the FBI," I say, deadpan.

"Yes ma'am, one second please," the voice replies, a little more animated. A second later the gates open, and I find Anna's unit. She's got five parking spaces out front, one of which is taken up by the beat-up old minivan. There's also a Lexus in the next spot belonging to her.

As I get out, carrying the heavy-ass laptop, I'm trying to figure out what her game is. Why all the pretense? But before I can fully appreciate the gravity of the situation, Anna comes bounding out of the townhome, coming down the steps and meeting me halfway. She's dressed in similar clothes from the other day, though she's got on a long, plush coat that comes all the way down to her ankles. "Emily, I'm sorry. If I'd known you'd be coming here I would have told you sooner, it's just…" She looks back at her place like she's embarrassed by it.

"You haven't told anyone where you live, have you?" I ask.

She shakes her head.

"And your fledgling business?"

"That's exactly as I described it. I have two clients right now. Per week."

I lean around her, and I can already see the luxury furnishings inside the door she left open. "Not enough to pay for all this I assume. Unless they're both movie stars."

She averts her eyes, shaking her head at the same time. Up here the wind is worse than it was at Ashford's, and it whips past us, blowing her hair so that it almost covers all her face.

"Look, let's get inside," I say and she nods, leading me back. I've never been in these homes before, but the foyer is all marble, despite it being a townhome. It's like a smaller version of a mansion—everything is pristine, clean and looks more expensive than my car. Above us a glass chandelier hangs from the thirty-foot ceiling that reaches up all three floors.

"I can explain," Anna says.

"You know what? It's none of my business," I tell her. "This is your personal life. Where can I set this thing up?"

Her shoulders drop as she pulls the hair out of her face. "I just…I didn't want—"

"Anna," I say. "It's fine. You don't owe me an explanation."

She lets out a breath. "Okay," she says and leads me through the main foyer beside some impressive-looking stairs. To my right is a large dining room which then connects to a kitchen and living area in the back. Everything is some variation of either black or white. "Here, you can set it up right here." She points to a breakfast banquet that's attached to the back of the prep area in the kitchen. Almost like anyone sitting here would be at the chef's table if this were a fancy restaurant.

"Hey, Ans." Just as I take a seat I look up to see a bare-chested man with nothing but a towel on come halfway down the stairs. His dark eyes are penetrating, and his hair is still wet. A trim beard covers a chiseled jaw.

"Holy abs," I whisper.

"Shoo!" Anna says, waving at him. "I told you to stay upstairs!"

"I can't find the body wash." He takes a look at me then winks.

"It's behind the regular soap, in the hall closet." She turns to me, her face beet red, matching her hair. "I'm so sorry. Give me just a minute."

I stifle a laugh. "No, take your time."

She runs to the stairs and almost runs into the man, admonishing him under her breath the entire way, until she's practically pushing him back up the stairs without another look in my direction.

Wow. I didn't see *that* coming. It takes me a second to focus again. I need to figure out if I can get anything off this laptop. I didn't want to go back to my hotel, not with its shitty security. Not to mention I'm still waiting for that list of names from the front desk. I really hope the manager didn't tell me he could just get me that list to get me off his case. Maybe once I get this thing squared away Anna will be willing to help me track down the housekeeper.

Right now, I need to get this thing up and running.

Inside the case are a bunch of cables, along with the actual laptop itself. I pull the machine out and I don't even bother pressing the power button. The screen is much smaller than I expected; I forgot just how primitive these things were. Back then they seemed like the pinnacle of technology. I grab the power cord and plug it in, finding the nearest outlet. I switch the unit on and for a second I think it's beyond saving. But after about thirty seconds I hear a humming sound and a large blue "D" comes up on the screen. Above me I hear someone stomping around and muffled voices, but I try to keep my attention on the computer. Finally, I see the Windows 98 logo and I groan. This is going to take forever.

By the time Anna comes back downstairs, I'm still staring at the same screen, waiting for the main menu to pop up.

"Sorry about that," she says. "He's my...um, houseguest."

"Uh huh," I say. "Do you know anything about computers?"

"I know how to turn them on. And I know how to take them to the store when I push the button and nothing happens. That's about it."

"Damn," I say.

"Is that really the computer Jessica Ashford used?" she asks.

"According to Judy, it is," I say. The screen flickers, then the main windows page comes up. I try moving my finger on the trackpad but the cursor is painfully slow to respond. It's about two seconds behind me, making navigating using the trackpad nearly impossible. "Ugh, I really wish Zara was here. She could get in and out of this thing in five seconds."

"Have you heard anything about her yet?" Anna asks, her face pinched in worry as she takes a seat across from me.

"No." I don't look at her as I say it. I can't let my brain open up to all the reasons I haven't heard anything yet. Instead, I pull out my phone dial the only person I know who can help me with this at the moment.

"This is Agent Kane," she answers on the other end.

"Kane, it's Slate," I say.

"Emily. I'm sorry, I haven't heard anything about Agent Foley yet."

I wince. "That's okay. I'm actually calling because I need some computer help."

"Oh," she says, her voice more animated. "Sure, what can I do?" I give her a quick rundown of the situation and what I'm dealing with.

"If I were there I could just clone the hard drive and we'd be able to pull every bit of data off it," she says. "But since you're down there and I'm up here, we're going to have to do this the hard way. Unless you want to drive the unit back tonight?"

"Can't do it, we're on a tight schedule here. Things are quickly evolving, and we need to get this guy off the streets," I say.

"Can you get the computer connected to the internet?" she asks.

"I doubt it has Wi-Fi if that's what you're thinking."

"No. Not on a unit that old. You'll need a T1 cable and an ethernet port to start. Do you know where you can make a hard connection?"

Right, I remember those. I dig through the other cables in the laptop case. There's a gray T1 cable at the bottom. I turn to Anna. "I don't guess you have an ethernet jack in this house."

"We can check the multimedia cabinet," she says.

"Kane, hang on," I tell her. I follow Anna around the kitchen to what looks like a pantry cabinet, but when she opens it, it's full of computer equipment. Some of it I recognize as security devices, and others look like an entertainment hub. Anna searches the various black boxes and outlets until she finds what we're looking for, on the back of a silver box hooked up to four other devices.

"Will this work?" she asks. I plug in the cable and thankfully it's long enough to run back through the kitchen all the way to the table where the computer sits.

"Okay, it's connected, but we had to route it through one of her security devices."

"That's not a problem," she says. "Give me the name of the unit and your address." A few minutes later she comes back on the line and proceeds to give me a complicated set of instructions to follow to ID the computer and connect to the internet through the ethernet line. It's crude, but twenty minutes later she's able to confirm the connection on her end and even take remote control of the computer from her side.

"This is going to take a few hours to copy due to the speed of the connection," she says. "But once I have the data, I should be able to find what you're looking for relatively quickly."

"So I just leave it? Like this?" I ask.

"Yep. Leave the rest to me."

"Thanks, Kane. I really appreciate this."

"You got it, I'll give you a call back when I find something."

I hang up and turn back to Anna. "Okay. As long as we don't touch it, we should be good."

"No problem," Anna says. "That looks way too intimidating for me, anyway."

"So now what?" Anna asks.

"I still need to track down the housekeeper. Odds are she's the one who got in my room and stole those files. There must be something in there that points to our killer; something we missed when we first went over them."

"Are you thinking it's one of the workers?" Anna asks.

"I don't know. We know for sure it couldn't be two of them. The two we interviewed though, I didn't get anything from them that would indicate they had any interest in Jessica Ashford. We're missing something here, I just don't know what it is."

"What about the other victims?" Anna asks. "Maybe they're connected to one of them instead?"

"That's not a bad theory," I say. But in order to find out it would help to have the original files. The same ones I left back in the conference room when we'd learned Griffin had been killed. It had always been my intention to come back to them and continue my research, little did I know I'd be banned from working on the case.

"If we could get a look at the missing person's files and do some research, I might be able to find the common thread between all four victims. But without them…" I hold up my hands. There's no way I can get back into the station without Hodge finding out, and perhaps Reyes too, if he really is on Hodge's side.

"I could get them," Anna says. I look up. "The files. Who's to say I'm not in there consulting on another case?"

"But if Reyes finds out you illegally took files from the station, he could charge you. You could even do time."

"To find the answers we need, I think it's worth the risk." She gets up and grabs her coat. "The same ones Tate gave us, right?"

I nod. "I'm sure Hodge has taken everything we were working on. But honestly, Anna, you don't have to do this."

"I do. If for no other reason than I like you. The killer knows who you are, and that you're on his heels. You could be in danger too, and I doubt Hodge is going to care very much. We need to find him."

I'm touched by her compassion. "What about your… guest?" I ask.

"Oh, he'll be fine. He knows to stay upstairs. I'll be back as soon as I can."

He knows to stay upstairs? What is he, a trained dog? "Okay," I say, unsure.

She shoots me a sly grin as she heads out. "Be right back."

Chapter Twenty-Seven

Two hours after Anna headed out with no word has left me antsy. I've been waiting on a call from agent Kane, but haven't heard anything yet from her either. Still, the computer is running, and as far as I can tell, everything looks good on this end. I just hope she's getting what she needs.

Every now and again I'll hear a thump from upstairs. I have no idea what that man is doing up there, and my curiosity has almost won out more than once. It seems Dr. Anna Forest is keeping a few more secrets than she let on. Personally, I think it's kind of funny. There's this whole other side of her that she doesn't let anyone else see. Part of me really wants to go up there and ask him who he is, what he's doing here, and what his relation to Anna is. But again, just like the townhome, it's none of my business.

In the meantime, I keep going back to the victims. Our killer is obviously trying to cover up his tracks. But why wait until now? Is it just that he's afraid of being found out? Why didn't he do this years ago? I have to assume it's because Jessica's body was discovered, and now he's in a panic.

Maybe panic isn't the right word. Maybe he's been waiting for this. I might have this wrong, but there's something about this guy…the very fact that he or his accomplice broke into my hotel room to steal those documents and my ring doesn't sound like someone who is panicking. A panicked mind wouldn't have been able to track me down, and surgically get into that room. No, this is something else. I just don't know what yet.

My phone buzzes and I glanced at the caller ID. I'm expecting agent Kane, but instead it's Anna who's calling.

"Hello?"

"Emily, it's me," she says, her voice hushed.

"Are you okay? What's going on?" I thought she was going to retrieve the files from the police station and then come back here.

"I can't get out of here; Reyes has everyone on alert. There are cops everywhere. If I try to leave, someone will see me, I know it. But I thought I could snap you a few pictures, at least that way you'd still be able to read the files."

I shake my head even though she can't see me. "No, that will take too long. Can you take a look at the files without anyone seeing what you're doing?"

"Well, I'm in the utility closet if that answers your question."

I smile at the thought of her hunkered down inside a tiny closet in the police station with a bunch of files wrapped in her arms, all while attempting to call me to clandestinely give me this information. It's quite comical, though I don't share that with her. "Okay, scan through the files and see if there's anything that stands out to you. We're looking for any commonalities between Jessica Ashford and the other three victims that we suspect were in the other houses that were lit on fire."

"Oh, that's something else," Anna says. "I happened to pass the coroner's report that came back on that first house fire. I grabbed it too. It looks like the remains belonged to Erin Parker, who went missing 2007."

"The first house—the one Reyes thought was an accident —it belonged to the Parker family, didn't it?" I ask.

"Yep. So it looks like your theory holds water."

"Okay, then I think we can definitely say that the person who set those fires is our killer. They were looking to cover up those bodies. Except it looks like in their haste to do that, they might have let us right back to them."

I hear rustling on the other side of the line as Anna flips through papers. "This is gonna take me a minute, says there are a lot of pages here."

"Just skim the reports," I say. "Look for commonalities in hair color, eye color, where they went to school, any extracurricular activities they may have shared. This guy picked them from somewhere, we just need to find out where."

"Okay, she says. "It looks like they were all similar in age. Erin Parker was sixteen, Cameron Hale was seventeen and the Tomlinson girl was also sixteen. Jessica Ashford was seventeen too, wasn't she?"

"She was. There anything else that connects them?"

"Nothing is jumping out at me. Wouldn't Hodge have looked at all of this already?"

"Yeah, but I don't trust Hodge to make the connection. This might be his case, but he'll want to make a quick collar." I rub my temples. What am I missing?

"If Jessica Ashford was talking to a boy about her age when she was taken, then he wouldn't have been a peer to any of these other girls," Anna says. I stop rubbing and focus. She's right. These deaths span almost twenty years; he would have been a lot older than the other girls, even if he was Jessica's age back in 1998.

"That's a good point. So it's someone who is watching teenage girls—someone who may have access to them."

"Like a coach? Or a teacher?" Anna suggests.

"Wait a second," I say. "Jake Ashford was the principal at Fernview High back in the late nineties."

"He was?" she asks.

"Yeah, but he retired after Jessica went missing. I came in just as he was leaving."

"But I thought you said Jake Ashford didn't do it," Anna says.

"Maybe I was wrong. Maybe something *did* happen with Ashford, and it drove him mad. Losing a daughter like that—you're the psychologist, could an incident of that nature push him into re-creating the event with other girls about his daughter's age?"

"To what end?" she asks.

"I don't know. Maybe he was trying to make amends. Or maybe he was replaying things with each of them, in an effort to keep her memory alive? You tell me."

She's quiet on the other end of the phone for a minute. "Without subjecting him to a full evaluation I'm not really in a position to speculate. From what I recall on his initial interviews with Hodge after Jessica was found, he didn't strike me as the kind of person who would suffer that kind of psychotic break." She pauses again, lowering her voice. "Then again, it has been known to happen. But like I said, it's hard to speculate until I can evaluate him further.

"Damn," I say. "Is there *anything* else? Something that maybe seems…innocuous?"

"The Hale file…" she begins. "It references another case here in the back. But that's another file; I'd have to go into records to grab it."

"Do that, even if it's something tiny I want to know about it," I tell her.

I can already hear her frustration on the other end. "Okay, but you gotta give me a few minutes. I'm not exactly the most popular person around here at the moment."

I smile. "I believe in you, Dr. Forest." She doesn't say anything else before hanging up and I wonder if maybe I've tried a little too hard. I can do that sometimes. But as I'm busy doubting myself, I hear that thump upstairs again.

"Okay, that's it," I say to myself. I can't stand this anymore. I have to know, even if it isn't any of my business.

I make my way up the stairs to the second level, which is just as opulent as the first. I'd like to know where Anna is hiding her money. Wherever it is, she's putting it to good use. There are a series of bedrooms up here, and the doors to each one are closed. I hear the thump again, which comes from behind the furthest one. Part of me knows I should go back downstairs and keep to myself, but the stronger part of me tells me to open that door and find out just what the hell is going on here.

As I'm reaching for the door, my phone buzzes again. *"Shit,"* I say and scramble back downstairs, suddenly more embarrassed than I have any right to be. "Did you get the file?"

"Yeah, got it right here," she says. "Are you okay? You sound out of breath."

"Fine," I say. "What's the file on?"

"Traffic accident," she says as I hear more pages flipping. "A Reginald Hale was in a car accident—hang on. It wasn't an accident. Another party claimed Hale cut him off and caused him to run his car into a ditch. And it looks like Hale had a history of speeding tickets and traffic violations. Hale made a complaint that the other driver made the whole thing up, but it doesn't look like anyone ever followed up with either of them."

I sigh. "In other words, it has nothing to do with the girl's disappearance."

"Well, maybe," she says. "The report was filed six days before Cameron Hale disappeared."

I'm back in the chair, but I sit up. "Six days?"

"Yep. Do you think it could be related?"

"Who was the other party?" I ask.

"Umm...Brodie Tyler...a local teacher at Fernview High." My eyes go wide. There's no way that's a coincidence.

"A teacher? Does it say who the officer who took the report was?" I ask.

She chuckles on the other end. "Yep. Your favorite person."

"Not Tate."

"Sorry," she says, though she doesn't really sound it.

"It's not much, but I think maybe we should talk to Tate, see what he can tell us about the accident. He might remember something about the report. It's a long shot, but I think it's worth investigating."

Anna is silent on the other end for a minute. "Anna, you still there?"

"I just poked my head out, looking for him. Tate's not here anywhere."

I get up, pacing around her kitchen. "He must have the night off."

"Which means he can be anywhere."

I think back to my earlier conversation with Judy. "Wait, I have an idea. Get out of there; I need you to meet me somewhere."

"Gladly," she says. "Just tell me where."

Chapter Twenty-Eight

WHEN I PULL up to Charlie's bar, Anna is already there, waiting in her beat-up minivan. I can only think of that vehicle as comical now. We both get out at the same time and she rushes over with her phone in her hand. "Here, I took some pictures of that traffic report, and a few from the other files anyway. I thought we might need them."

"Good thinking. According to Judy, Owen Tate is usually here when he's not at work."

She nods. "Yeah, he's got a reputation all right. I should have guessed."

As we start making our way to the door, I pull her aside for about a moment. "I hope it's okay that I left the computer there at your place with your...friend."

Her cheeks go red again. "Oh, yeah that should be fine, no problem at all."

I want to head for the door, but I just can't help myself. I turn to her again, my hand back on her shoulder. "Okay, I know I'm being nosy, but what's the deal there? It's been driving me nuts."

"It's nothing...bad, if that's what you're thinking. We

just…we just have an arrangement. I've been doing sort of a study."

"A study?" My eyebrow arches.

"Yes, on dominant and submissive relationships. It relates to my work as a therapist, but don't worry he's not a patient or anything. This is just an experiment I'm performing on my own."

I can't help but smile. "Well good for you, you'll have to let me know the outcome of your…study."

"So far the results have been very, um, illuminating."

Now I am so glad I didn't go into that room upstairs. Who knows what I might have found behind that door.

We head back into Charlie's for the second time in two days. The same bartender is at the bar, hunched over and writing what looks like expense reports. The place looks empty, given it's only around four in the afternoon. The only patron sits on the third stool, Owen Tate, right where we expected to find him. He's bent over a frosty mug of beer, taking slow sips.

"Officer Tate," I say. "Enjoying your day off?"

He looks over his shoulder at me, a grimace on his face. "What the hell do you want?"

"I have a couple of questions about an old traffic stop of yours, from a few years back."

"Traffic stop? This doesn't have to do with that robbery last night, does it? I told you; I'd let you know if I came up with anything."

"Then let me ask, have you tracked down the missing housekeeper yet?"

"The missing who?" he asks.

"I didn't think so." I shoot a knowing look to Anna.

He groans. "Can't you just leave me alone?"

"I think both of us would like nothing better," Anna says. "The only problem is this traffic case may relate to this killer everyone is so keen to find."

"What are you talking about?" he growls.

I nod to Anna. "Show him the pictures."

She pulls out her phone and scrolls to the pictures of the accident report. "Remember this? It was your report, wasn't it?"

He blinks a few times as he tries to get a good look at the tiny writing on her phone. "This was like six years ago. How do you expect me to remember anything from this?"

"According to the report, this Brodie Tyler complained that Reginald Hale cut him off in traffic, causing his car to go into a ditch," I say, watching Tate carefully.

He shrugs. "Yeah, so?"

"But Reginald Hale's argument was that Tyler ran a red light and almost rammed into him. That him going in the ditch was his own fault and that he was being a reckless driver."

Tate waves me off. "Reggie was notorious for traffic violations. Everyone in the department knew it. I think he had at least ten parking tickets and maybe two moving violations before this. This was the one that lost him his license for six months."

I cock my head at him. "Oh, so you do remember it?"

Tate takes another swig of his beer. "It's not like it was a big deal. With Reggie's history, I figured it was open and shut. Tyler didn't have any priors—not even a speeding ticket."

"But you never followed up?"

"Look, I don't know how it works in the FBI, but I have a stack of cases on my desk *this high* at any given moment. I don't have time to follow up with everyone." He holds his hand flat at his eye level to emphasize his point.

"Even though Reggie Hale complained that he wasn't the instigator this time?"

Finally, Tate turns to me. "What do you want from me? What do I have to tell you to get you to go away?"

"Does the name Cameron Hale sound familiar to you?" I ask.

For a second his face blanches. "Missing girl," he says. "Twenty-fifteen?"

I shake my head slowly. "Twenty-sixteen. Six days after this report was filed."

"That's not possible," Tate says.

"There was even a reference to it in the back of Cameron's missing file. *Someone* made the connection. Were Reggie and Cameron related?" Anna asks.

Tate nods. "She was his niece."

"Didn't it seem odd to you, that she went missing just six days after this traffic altercation?" I ask.

"We didn't think she was missing," Tate says, more emphatically. His beer sits forgotten, on the bar. "We thought she was a runaway."

"Do you still think that?" I ask. "The Hale house was one of the ones that burned two days ago."

Red splotches have crept across his cheeks. A sure sign of inebriation. "Yeah, but that's the house of Jim and Catherine Hale, not Reggie."

"Cameron's parents."

"Right. I'm not even sure Reggie still lives in Fernview, to be honest. I haven't seen or heard from him in years."

"But when Cameron went missing, he did still live here, didn't he?"

Tate turns back to his beer. "Yeah, he did." The three of us stand there in silence, for a moment as we contemplate the reality of the situation. "So, what? You think Cameron's disappearance was somehow related to Reggie's accident?"

"I think it's very possible. How much do you know about this Brodie Tyler?"

Tate shrugs again. "What's there to say about Brodie? He grew up here, everyone knows him. He's pretty active in the community, he's even here a lot of nights. He and I were friends growing up."

"He's a teacher, isn't he?" Anna asks.

"Yeah, he's been teaching science and engineering over the high school for as long as I can remember."

"At Fernview High? I never had him as a teacher." I say.

"I think there might've been a few years when he taught Latin, or something else. I don't really know; I don't keep up with the goings-on at the local high school."

I think back to my days at Fernview. I don't remember Mr. Tyler, but the school was rather large. Fernview only has one high school for all its students, and it's easy to only see a person once during the whole year, if you didn't have the same schedule as they did. It's possible he could have slipped by me, and I just never paid attention. Of course, it's not like I was an investigator back then. I was just trying to get through each day without getting my ass kicked by some of the other girls.

"Do you know if Brodie Tyler ever had any altercations with Jake Ashford?" I ask.

"I don't know if I would call it an altercation. But Brodie has told me on more than one occasion, that Ashford only got that principal job because he bullied some of the school board members into it. Brodie always thought that he deserved the job instead. They were both teachers coming up."

I shoot a look at Anna. "And Brodie told you this?"

"It's no secret," Tate says. "Plus, with the way Ashford is, you get a lot of people in here complaining about him. Not so much anymore, but back in those days, the man was a bear to everyone. It didn't matter who you were."

This means that Brodie Tyler was directly involved with family members of at least two of the missing girls. And being a high school teacher would've meant he would have easy access to the other victims. "How much do you know about Tyler? Does he have a short fuse?"

Tate chuckles. "Brodie? No, he ain't like that. Everything that happens that man just rolls off his back. Sure, he'll complain now and again, but he does it all in good humor. I've never even seen him get mad at anyone. Everybody likes the guy."

I motion to Anna to follow me over to the other side of the bar. "What do you think? I know I keep hitting you with these hypotheticals, but we're dealing with a chameleon here. Someone who has blended into this community, and Brodie Tyler sounds like just the person we could be looking for."

"I haven't been here very long, so I haven't had the pleasure of meeting Mr. Tyler, or hearing anything about him," Anna says. "It's certainly possible that he could be the person you're looking for, but I can't speculate on his mental state."

Still, the fact that Brodie Tyler could have had Reginald Hale and Jake Ashford as enemies is too much of a coincidence to ignore. It's nothing solid, but it's something. I need to find Brodie Tyler.

"I'm not saying he's our guy, but I definitely think he's worth speaking to."

"I can't disagree with you there," Anna says. "Like you said, every avenue, right?"

We head back over to Tate. "Thank you for all your cooperation, officer. You've been very helpful."

"Wait a second, you don't really think Brodie had anything to do with this, do you?"

Before I can answer him, my phone rings. I give Tate a not so sweet smile before excusing myself outside to answer.

"Agent Slate, this is Kane. I managed to finish cloning the hard drive. You said you are looking for Instant Messenger data?"

Finally, we're getting somewhere. "Yes, specifically from around April of nineteen-ninety-eight. The conversation would have been between our victim and an unknown person who she might have confided in."

"I haven't had time to get into the messages yet; there are a lot here around that time period. But the username of the person who the account was registered to was j-a-s-h-8-1. Remember when usernames were short and sweet?"

"That's gotta be her. Jessica Ashford. Who's the other party?"

"I don't have a name. All I have is their Instant Messenger username. It's b-r-o-t-y-5-5-3."

My heart almost skips a beat. BroTy553.

Brodie Tyler.

Chapter Twenty-Nine

WITH THE CONFIRMATION from Agent Kane, I don't think there's any doubt anymore that Brodie Tyler is our man. I gave Anna a quick rundown of the situation then ran back into Charlie's, telling Tate to call Reyes and put an APB out on Brodie Tyler.

"Did he say he'd do it?" Anna asks as soon as I come back out from Charlie's.

"He wasn't very enthused," I say. "I don't know if he's taking me seriously or not." Not to mention he's already three sheets to the wind. But at least he won't be able to say we didn't try to warn him. I'll need to call Reyes myself.

"His friendship with Tyler may have prevented him from thinking clearly on this matter," she says.

I nod. "I need to get over to see Jake Ashford, his life could be in danger. If he can identify Brodie in any way, shape, or form, then he could be next on the list." And if Judy is still staying with him, then she could be in the crosshairs too. The only thing I can't figure out is why Brodie would've killed Connor Griffin. What was on those construction documents that could've connected them to him? It makes me hope this all isn't just one big coincidence. As it is, the evidence against

Tyler is pretty flimsy. Even if Tate does call it in, Reyes may not take him seriously.

"Are you going over there right now?" Anna asks.

I head to my car, looking over my shoulder to respond. "I don't think I can wait. I want to make sure someone's watching them if Tyler shows up."

"Then I'm coming too," Anna says.

I shake my head. "No way. You're a civilian, and I'm not putting your life in danger. You've been more than helpful enough already."

"So you're benching me to? I thought only Reyes did that." I can see the hurt on her face, but it can't be helped. If Brodie Tyler really is planning to go after Jake Ashford, I don't need to put Anna in any additional danger. I return and give her a soft smile, placing a supportive hand on her shoulder. "It's not like that. You've done a great job, but this is potentially a very dangerous situation, and I don't want to put you in between a serial killer and Jake Ashford."

"Aren't you technically a civilian too? In this instance, at least?"

I nod. "A civilian with a loaded Glock nine and trained in hand-to-hand combat. Trust me, I can take care of myself. But I can't ensure Jake and Judy Ashford's safety while I'm worrying about you. At least not until Reyes gets us some backup."

"He's not going to be happy that you're still on the case," she says.

"I don't care. I'm not leaving Jake Ashford out to dry just because Captain Reyes or Detective Hodge don't want me here anymore. They're going to need to take this seriously." I head back to my car.

She screws up her face. "How are you gonna make them do that?"

"Question Jake Ashford about Brodie Tyler. See if he can backup Tate's story. He would know better than anyone else if there is an issue between them, or ever was. It will also help if I need to confront Brodie Tyler. But like you said, I'm just a civilian in this case, more than likely Hodge would be the one to go after him."

"Okay," she sighs. "I guess all I can do is wish you luck."

I nod. "When you get back to your place, you can disconnect the computer. Kane already has everything she needs. And don't worry, my plan is to get Jake Ashford into an interrogation room, maybe then you can pull a psychological profile on him."

She smiles. "I'll be sure to be ready."

I hop inside. If Brodie Tyler is planning on going after Jake Ashford, I want to be there when it happens. Whether I'm actually on the case are not. As I'm driving out to the Ashford place, my phone rings again. "Slate."

"Emily, it's Agent Kane again. I've been going through some of these messages between the two parties. Some of this is…disturbing."

"Disturbing?" I ask. "What do you mean?"

"As far as I can tell, it looks like he was attempting to groom her. The messages start out innocent enough, and there are a lot of them. But as they go on and on, he starts to assert a more dominant personality over her, getting her to do what he wants her to, and using her father's antagonism to drive a wedge between."

"Can you give me an example?"

"Sure." She clears her throat. "*JAsh81: are you sure we need to go this far? Sometimes my dad isn't so bad.*

BroTy553: you know this is what needs to happen. Have you already forgotten how he embarrassed you the other day? That incident in the bathroom?

JAsh81: no, I haven't forgotten.

BroTy553: your father doesn't care about you. He doesn't care about anyone, other than himself. You of all people should know this. The fact that I have to tell you, says a lot. Maybe you're not ready for this. You may just not be mature enough yet.

JAsh81: no, I can do it. You're right, he's a monster. He needs to pay."

"So he was trying to get her to turn against her father," I say thinking out loud. "To what end?"

"From what I can tell, they were planning on running away together. She was going to go live with him, until they could get out of town, and head West."

I grip the wheel harder. "Then how did she end up inside a wall? Something must've gone wrong. And why would Tyler have gone after all these other women?"

"I don't know," she says. "I just read the messages."

There's no doubt in my mind anymore. Tyler was the man Jessica was talking to right before she died; he was probably the very last person to see her alive. But I still need to figure out how he connects to Griffin. "Agent Kane, can you do one other thing for me? I hate to ask."

"Sure, name it. It's the least I can do with Zara being out of town."

"Can you do a background check on a Brodie Tyler living here in Fernview? I need to know if there's a connection between him and Griffin Construction."

"Not a problem," she says. "I've got some time this evening if I can get back to you?"

"Sure. And if you find out anything else, let me know as soon as you find it."

"Will do."

I hang up and press the accelerator a little harder. If Tyler groomed Jessica, did he try grooming the other girls too? It's hard to say, but I could be looking at the birth of a sociopath here. Now I wish I *had* brought Anna along; she'd at least be able to give me her professional opinion.

It takes me another ten minutes to get out to Jake Ashford's place, and when I pull up, I see that Judy's car is still in the gravel lot in front of the house. I guess she's just decided to stay here while they figure out all the funeral arrangements for Jessica's body. It's late afternoon, and the sun is already beginning to dip behind the tree line. But there are no lights on in the house. A chill runs up my spine, and I pull out my phone calling the station directly.

"Fernview Police Department, is this an emergency?"

"This is Special Agent Emily Slate," I say. "I need to speak to Captain Reyes."

"He's in the middle of a conference right now, can I have him call you back?" The officer on the other end of the line says.

"What about Detective Hodge? Is he available?"

"He's in the conference with Captain Reyes," she responds.

They're meeting about the case—I'm sure of it. "I need you to put me through to them immediately. This is an emergency."

There's a pause on the other end. "Just one moment." She sighs as she puts me on hold.

As I'm waiting, listening to the music, I cut my engine and turn the lights off. But when I do, the door opens and two figures step out. Judy is in front, a terrified look on her face. And behind her, a large man with his arm wrapped around her neck. They're both staring right at me. With his free hand the man motions for me to get out of the car. Even in the low light I can see the tears streaming down Judy's cheeks.

I step out of the vehicle, keeping the phone to my ear and silently willing Reyes to pick up. "Brodie Tyler, I presume."

A devilish quick grin spreads across his face. "Agent Slate, it's a pleasure to finally meet you. Now lose the phone, or I snap her neck."

Chapter Thirty

"YOU'RE JUST IN TIME, Agent Slate. We've been waiting for you," Brodie Tyler calls out. I toss my phone over on the grass, though I didn't hang up. Hopefully if Reyes ever gets on the line, he'll still be able to hear something. In the same movement I slip my service weapon out of the center console of my car, stepping out so Tyler can get a good look at me.

"Tyler, this is over," I say, using the door as cover and aiming my weapon at him. "Let Judy go."

His eyes flash and he tightens his grip, positioning himself behind Judy even more. She only covers about eighty percent of him, but he's got her in such a hold that the smallest movement could snap her neck. The man is built like a linebacker —all muscle and probably tops out around six-three. He's got dirty-blonde hair and a moustache to match. There's something unassuming about him; I can see how he easily disarms people. There's like an aura around him that just makes seem trustworthy. He's a big guy, but he comes across as one of those men who is harmless.

So much for stereotypes.

"Agent Slate, you're not a stupid person," Tyler says. "Right now I'm exerting about six pounds of pressure on

Judy's neck. In less than a second I can increase that tenfold. She'd be dead before she hit the porch. I'm not standing down. You are."

"What did you mean when you said you were waiting for me?" I ask, trying to figure out how to get Judy away from him.

"Toss it or she dies," he replies, obviously not stupid enough to get drawn into a discussion while I still have it. Judy is pleading with me with just her eyes. I remember that look from when we were kids. It was the same look she'd give me when she just wanted me to listen and understand.

Fuck. I toss the weapon.

He chuckles. "And here I thought you were smart. You probably could have killed me and just lost poor Judy here. But that's sentimentality for you." He looks past me. "I'm surprised to see you're alone. I thought for sure you'd bring the cavalry. But this works to my advantage. Once you're out of the way, I can go right back to life as normal."

"You mean living in the community you've been terrorizing for twenty years?" I ask. I'm still using the door as a barrier, though I don't see a weapon on him. He doesn't need one.

"*Terrorizing?*" he says, the word cutting across his teeth. "I'm sure you're familiar with Newton's second law of motion? For every action there is an equal and opposite reaction? That's all that's happening here. People make choices and those choices have consequences. The sad truth is most people aren't willing to face those consequences."

There's only one way I'm going to be able to help Judy. I need to get close. Extracting myself from behind my car, I take a few slow steps toward them. "Tell me, what crime could Jake Ashford commit that would cause you to murder his daughter? Did he kill your child and I'm just not aware of it?"

He sneers. "Jake Ashford is a bona fide asshole. The very definition of the word. Thankfully at least one of his daughters didn't follow in his footsteps." He pulls Judy closer, and she cries out. "Did she?" She's not going to last long like this —I need to get to her.

"He's—he's already hurt Dad," Judy whimpers. "I tried to stop him—"

"Hush, my dear," Tyler says, tightening his grip on her. Judy gasps for breath and I have no doubt he's cutting off her windpipe.

"Let's talk," I say, my eyes shooting to Judy again. "Explain this to me. I don't get it."

His grip loosens and he cocks his head at me. "Really? I thought for sure you would have figured it all out by now. The locals called you in to track me down, after all."

I shake my head. "Finding Jessica's body was an accident by the current homeowners. They were doing renovations in their house."

He frowns. "No, I was told she was found by the police, and they called in the FBI once they identified her."

I mock suppress a laugh. "Not at all. That used to be *my* house when I was little. They called me because they thought my parents might be suspects. I'm not even here in an official capacity. Technically, I'm still on vacation."

He goes red in the face. "You're on *vacation?*"

I nod. "It looks like you've been getting some bad information." I imagine Tyler must have been listening to Tate's drunken rantings over at Charlie's. I guess it's a good thing Tate is a sloppy drunk—can't keep his facts straight. "We didn't even know there were other bodies—at least not until you burned those homes."

He stares at me like he can't believe it. "This entire time, I thought they brought you in because they had some idea of who they were dealing with. But they never knew, did they?" he asks.

I shake my head. "They had no idea. They don't even

know your name. I just figured it out myself. You know, between my massage and pedicure."

"Very cute, Agent Slate," he says, dismissing me. "I can't believe this entire time—then all I did was lead them straight to me."

"Well," I say, tilting my head to one side. "You pointed them in that direction. I have to say though, stealing those files and my ring wasn't very smart. Unless you were purposely trying to antagonize me."

"I thought…" He screws up his face. "You had to know that I wasn't just going to sit around and let you win."

"So you had a friend of yours break into my room?"

He barks out a laugh. "Hardly." And in that moment, I see the killer beneath. The one who took the lives of all those girls. He did it and he feels no remorse. Suddenly I understand.

"She let you in, but you couldn't leave a witness…"

"See, you figured it out after all," he replies with a wicked grin. Kristin Pruitt wasn't an accomplice; she was another victim. *Damn.* I can beat myself up later for not seeing it sooner, but right now I need to focus on Judy.

"A lot better than those local cops, huh? They aren't very smart, are they? Otherwise, how could you have managed to get away with all of this for so long?"

"I'm careful, for one." The look on his face tells me he's proud of himself, though the knowledge that Reyes didn't bring in the FBI to chase him down has hurt him. He thought he was more important than that—even if they didn't know exactly who he was. He may think he's different than other people like him, but he's not. In the end, they're all narcissists. But I can use that.

"And the amount of time between your victims—you're patient too. Most people I meet like you can't help themselves. They escalate, each victim coming sooner than the last. But you…you've managed to stretch them out over a long period of time."

"It's a small town," he says, though he seems lost in thought. I can see that his grip on Judy has loosened even further. "People would notice if it happened too often."

"You were able to operate undetected all this time. But I still don't understand—why kill Jessica? What did she do?"

That brings him back to the present and I see I've made a miscalculation as his grip on Judy tightens. "What did she *do*? That little bitch—I never should have trusted her. She turned out to be just like her father."

I hold a hand up and slowly approach closer. "I understand you're upset, but I need you to explain it to me."

"What's wrong?" he growls. "I thought you were clever."

I shake my head. "I know you were in close contact—that the two of you were conspiring against Mr. Ashford. He'd hurt the both of you, and you found each other—and your revenge."

"You're damn right he did," Tyler says. "He did the worst thing someone can do to a person—disrespect them. That's bad enough when you do it to fully-grown adults, but to do it over and over again to impressionable children…" He puts his lips beside Judy's ear. "Isn't that right, my dear? Growing up with a father like that must have been unbearable."

"That makes Ashford the monster, not you," I say, locking my gaze with Judy's. Tears fall freely now, streaming down her face. I'm sure all she can think of is how these will be her last moments on earth.

"Don't insult my intelligence, Agent Slate," he says. "I know what I am."

"But it's like you said, you were only reacting. He started the chain of events. Is that what happened with Jessica and the others? Did they disrespect you?"

He begins speaking through his teeth. "I worked on that girl for weeks. *Weeks!*" He gives Judy a shake and she cries out. "We had everything planned. And part of me knew she wouldn't go through with it. That she wouldn't actually tell him off and come to live with me. We were going to head to California. Start a new life together. And you know what? Had she come back to the car and told me she couldn't do it, I would have understood. I really would have. But then she actually did it. And it felt…amazing.

"But when we got to my place, things changed. All of a sudden I wasn't good enough for her anymore. *All of a sudden, I was just poor, white trash to a girl who'd grown up wanting for nothing and I could see the disappointment in her eyes.* When she ran—that's when I could *feel* her disrespect for me. As her teacher, as her friend and as her lover. In that moment I knew. So I made a decision."

"You decided killing her was better than living with the shame you felt when she looked at you."

He shakes Judy again. "*No.* I decided the perfect revenge on Jake Ashford was for his little girl to come back home after all, only he would never even know it. That's what she wanted in the end…to go home. I made that happen." He takes Judy by the neck and moves her to the side so he can get a better look at me, without her in the way. And from the way he's breathing, I can tell he's fired up.

"You want to talk patience, Agent Slate? Patience is going to night school, getting an engineering degree, and becoming a reputable person around town for General Contractors to work with. Patience is keeping tabs on Jake Ashford, waiting for the day when I could get in his house—or in this case waiting until he moved into a new home. And patience was finally pulling Jessica Ashford out of the freezer she'd been in for seven years so she could finally fulfill her purpose. *That's* patience. That's dedication."

Judy chokes on a sob and has gone almost completely limp.

"I bet it felt good to finally get her in there," I say. "Working behind the scenes for all that time."

"You're damn right it did," he says.

"But Ashford never knew," I say. "He couldn't fully appreciate what you'd done to him."

"I considered the possibility Jessica might be found one day," he replies. "But in the meantime, watching the man waste away under the weight of his own hubris was payment enough. I've had the pleasure of witnessing that man destroy himself over the past twenty years."

"What did he do to you?" I ask. "What is this all about?"

Tyler shakes his head. "He never should have gotten that promotion. But he was so headstrong the school board was afraid to say no to him. Despite the fact I had more experience and was a better fit for the school."

"But you were still young, weren't you?" I ask. "You were only a few years out of high school yourself."

"That shouldn't have mattered!" he yells. "I had the same, if not better qualifications. But he couldn't help but berate me for my age, saying I didn't know *how the real world worked*. Telling me that I was better off as a worker bee because I didn't have what it took to inspire people." He turns around, looking away from us. "How's this for the *real world* Jacob, you piece of—"

He doesn't have the chance to finish the sentence because the second he turns away from me I take the opening, rushing forward and plowing my shoulder right into the middle of his sternum. He goes breathless, letting go of Judy as he falls back, with me coming down on top of him. But before I can recover, he grabs my hair with his giant hand, yanks me off him and literally *tosses* me a few feet away. I didn't even have a chance to cry out as I swore my scalp was torn off my head.

Judy tumbles down the steps, and attempts to crawl away as soon as she hits the bottom, but I see Tyler get back up, going for her rather than me. He's quick for a big guy, though

I notice him favor his right leg as he makes his way down the steps for her. I scramble up and go for him, driving my heel into the back of the right knee. He cries out and goes down, but his face is twisted in rage.

"You're not. Going. To. Beat. Me." He pushes himself back up and swings at me as hard as he can. I manage to dodge the hit, though I'm sure had it connected, it either would have knocked me out cold or killed me. The man is like a battering ram. But he's not steady on his feet, and I can see that right leg shaking under his pants. I feint, with both my hands up, causing him to go to the left while I exploit his right side again, this time driving my foot into the knee again, but from the side. There's a sickening crunch and Tyler screams, going down for good this time. He's bleating like a goat as he tries to hold on to his ruined knee. I rub my head a few times, and though I'm sure he pulled out some hair when he grabbed me, I don't feel any permanent damage. Instead, I go for Judy, who is still trying to crawl away as fast as possible.

"Judy, it's okay," I say, reaching her, stopping her from moving. "Are you hurt?"

She looks at me, her eyes red and wet. "No," she says, her voice hoarse like she's been coughing. "But Daddy, I couldn't get him to wake up."

"Where is he?" I ask.

"In the—" She screams and I turn to see Tyler bearing down on me again. Apparently, I underestimated his resolve. He grabs one shoulder, turning me and in the same motion and plowing his fist into my face. Stars explode across my vision and I feel the entire world tilt on its side. For what seems like forever, I can't hear or see anything and part of me thinks he's broken something fundamental inside my head, the thing that connects my brain to my eyes and ears—he's completely destroyed all of my senses with one hit.

But after a few moments I become aware of a high-pitched squeal. Finally, my vision begins to clear and I see

Judy being dragged away by Tyler, holding her by one of her legs as he limps heavily back to the house. I try to get up, but find it takes a monumental amount of effort to even move, much less get back up. Everything feels shaky, and as I'm trying to push myself up my stomach roils and I get so violently sick that I have no choice but to collapse again.

I can't let him get away with it though. He'll kill Judy, just like he killed Jessica. He's probably left Ashford alive, and wants to torture the man by killing his other daughter in front of him. I try turning over again, and my hand brushes against something cold and hard. *My gun.* I grab it, but my vision is so blurry there's no way I could make a clean shot. Still, I point the weapon in the air and fire off a round. It's like a firework going off in my ear and it takes all my strength to keep from falling back over.

Through blurry eyes I see Tyler stop, then turn. He drops Judy's leg, then begins walking in my direction. The man is tougher than I thought. To get up after that hit to his knee means he has a high threshold for pain.

"Let's stop pretending, Agent Slate," he says, approaching me as I try to level my weapon at him. But I find it exceedingly difficult. "This is over. Just give up." I try to say something in response, only to find my mouth not cooperating.

He reaches down and to my horror, grips the gun, still in my hand and turns them both so the barrel of the weapon is resting right against my heart. "Did you know that in Ancient Japan, Samurai would practice something called seppuku— self-disembowelment if they failed in their duty or dishonored themselves? You've dishonored yourself, Agent Slate. And you've come up against a superior foe. One you can't beat. Let's face it, you never had a chance."

An image of Zara flashes in my mind. And another of Liam, Timber, and my parents. Even of Matt. Everyone I've ever loved.

I can feel Tyler's meaty finger pressing down on mine,

crushing it against the trigger to my own weapon. In that second, I know I haven't fought hard enough, and now I've ended up here, about to lose my life because I wasn't prepared. But just as fast as he was there, he's gone. Adrenaline allows me to get up and see Judy has jumped on his back, beating at him with everything she has. Tyler looks like a giant turtle, trying to get a frog off its shell. But the distraction gives me the second I need. I steady the weapon, all my senses dialed up to eleven from being on the verge of death and pull the trigger before he can get to her.

The bullet hits him right in the kneecap and there's a dull thud before he yells again, falling to the ground with both him and Judy. I find the strength to push myself up, staving off the nausea and make my way over to Judy, extricating her from him. He's writhing back and forth, holding his knee with both hands as a crimson stain spreads around the entry point, soaking his jeans. I keep my weapon trained on him, not willing to turn my back on him again.

"Find my phone," I say to Judy, my voice echoing and unsteady. "Call 911."

She nods and runs past me, only to stop short. "I see lights," she says, her voice still hoarse.

I glance out of the corner of my eye and see red and blue flashing lights coming through the trees in the distance.

I guess Reyes got my call after all.

Chapter Thirty-One

"A CONCUSSION, a fractured jaw, swelling in the cheek, one loose tooth that had to be extracted, possible vascular swelling in the brain, and a broken nose." Anna glares at the chart, then bites the inside of her cheek before replacing it back in the little drawer at the end of my bed.

For my part, I've been in surgery and intensive care for two days, recovering from Brodie Tyler's attempt to kill me. I had been right, one hit from him had almost been enough to take me out permanently. "But at least I look good, right?"

Anna chuckles. "You don't. Not at all." I know from her perspective I must look like a mess. Half my face is covered in braces and bandages, and the swelling around my right eye is just now starting to come down enough that I can see clearly out of it again. But I actually feel pretty good. It's the drugs—no doubt. There are going to be some hard days ahead. But I'll take hard days over no days anytime.

"You'll love this. Tyler is on the same floor. Except he's behind a steel door and strapped down to his bed. They don't think he'll ever walk normally again. His kneecap is like a shattered piece of glass."

I swallow, finding it hard. "That was the idea." Anna

reaches over and hands me my cup with a straw and I take a sip. "I've never seen anyone get up like that. I thought I'd broken his knee the first time. I shouldn't have turned my back on him."

"You should have had someone there watching *your* back," she says. I found out yesterday that it hadn't actually been my open line to Reyes that called in the backup. The phone had disconnected almost as soon as it hit the ground. Instead, Anna had gone straight to Reyes as I headed out to Ashford's place and demanded that he send a contingent out to meet me. She'd stood toe to toe with Hodge and gotten him to back down, admitting that he'd taken over the case and taken me off it without Reyes's approval. That had been enough for Reyes to send a couple of black and whites out to the house. Upon finding the carnage there, the officers called in the cavalry.

"What about Ashford?" I ask. "Any word?" I hadn't seen him personally, but apparently Tyler had arrived at the house about an hour before I did, then proceeded to emotionally terrorize Jake Ashford by dangling Judy's life in front of him. Making him admit he never cared about either of his daughters. From what I've heard, Judy suffered some severe emotional abuse at his hands, trying to plead for her father's life while Tyler toyed with them both. Tyler ended up choking Ashford out, planning on coming back to finish him later, after he'd killed Judy. But then I showed up, changing his plans.

"He's awake, but he's not talking yet. He may need some reconstructive work to his windpipe. They're not sure if he's ever going to be able to talk again," Anna says.

I lay my head back and a wave of nausea comes over me again, causing me to close my eyes. "If I'd gotten there sooner—"

"Doing that won't help you or anyone else, *Agent*," Anna says. "You're the only reason both he and his daughter are still alive. Focus on what you *did*, not what you could have done."

"Yes, *doctor*," I say, opening my eyes again.

"Here," she says, holding her hand out. My wedding ring sits in the middle of her palm. "Reyes gave me permission to return it to you. They found a box in Tyler's house, in the floor. It had a trinket from each of his victims, the most recent being this and a master keycard from your hotel."

"Kristin," I say, looking at the ring.

She nods. "They still haven't found her body. But Hodge and Tate will be interrogating Tyler pretty hard once he's out of the hospital. Hodge has assured me he's not going to stop until they have some answers."

"That's good," I say, staring at the ring. "Can you just… can you put that on the side table?"

She sets the ring on the table beside me. I don't take the time to look at it, but knowing it's there makes me feel a little better.

"Knock, knock." I look up to see Judy at the door. A scarf is wrapped around her neck, no doubt hiding the bruising left from Tyler's attack.

"Hey," I say. "How are you doing?"

She tugs at the scarf. "Better. But I didn't come alone. I brought an extra visitor." I can barely sit up, but when I do I notice an older woman with neat, gray hair come in behind Judy. She's dressed impeccably and looks like an older version of my childhood friend.

"Mrs. Ashford?" I ask, incredulous. As soon as I see her I'm reminded of all those times she would make sure Judy and I had everything we needed those times I stayed over. It became so frequent that after a while I started thinking of her as sort of like my mother too. But I'd forgotten about those feelings. Or maybe I just tucked them away.

She gives me a sweet grin and nods. "Emily Slate. Who would have thought?" she says. "If you'd told me back when you girls were running around that one day you'd save my daughter's life I would have said you were crazy." She leans down and gives me a very light hug, minding my injuries. "Thank you," she whispers. "If I'd lost Judy, I don't know what I would have done."

When she pulls away I find myself struck by her. She still looks very much like she did when I was younger. It's like no time has passed for her at all. "She saved me too," I say. "If not for her, I wouldn't be here."

Judy reaches out and takes my hand. "What are friends for?"

"If you all don't mind," Anna says. "I have an…appointment I'm late for." She turns to me. "I'll be back to check on you tomorrow."

I give her a knowing smile. "Tell your appointment hi for me." She flushes with a semi-horrified look on her face and is out of the room without another word.

Judy looks to her mother, then to me with a confused grin. "What's that all about?"

"Apparently…an experiment she's conducting," I say, chuckling.

"Mom," Judy says, looking at her mother pointedly.

"Oh, yes," Mrs. Ashford says. "Judy was telling me about what brought you to Fernview in the first place."

"Oh," I say, looking at my old friend. I honestly hadn't given the letters much thought; with everything else going on I've been out of it half the time anyway. "Right, well I haven't really had much time to—"

"Your mother was a fascinating woman," Mrs. Ashford continues, as if I haven't said anything. "We weren't best friends like the two of you were, but we were close."

"Judy was telling me about that. I never knew you and Mom knew each other."

Mrs. Ashford smiles. "That was on purpose. Not that we didn't think you girls wouldn't get along well, it was just the types of meetings we attended together—they weren't for children or families."

"Wait, meetings?" I ask.

She nods. "Yes. We were in a therapy group together," she replies.

"Like AA?"

"Sort of. It wasn't completely anonymous, we all knew who each other was, but part of the agreement of the group was no association outside of the meetings. It was to help keep our minds clear and to prevent people from forming attachments through the trauma we were working on."

"Trauma?" I ask.

She nods again. "I was there for my years with Jacob. He never physically harmed me but…" She looks wistfully at Judy. "After Jessie left, well…anyway. I had some things to work through. But I wasn't the only one. Your mother had some dark, dark secrets, I'm afraid. Things she never told you or even your father. She used to call it her 'first life', before she met him and had you."

I do my best to sit up, but I'm finding it hard with all the equipment keeping me in place. "I don't understand."

"She was building up to it for months, working through the sessions in an attempt to excise all that old trauma. I think had she made it another month she would have broken through."

"Wait," I say, still trying to sit up. "You don't know what these secrets were?"

"All I know is they involved her family back in Ohio. That's all she could get out before going into a panic. Our therapy leader, he was able to work with her a little more, trying to help her deal with it. Even though it's against the rules, I could…give you his information. He might know more about it."

"Did she ever say anything else?" I ask. "Anything that might tell you what the trauma was?"

She shakes her head, her face drawn. "Just that it involved her family back there. I'm so sorry. I wish I could give you more. Like I said, I shouldn't even be talking about it, but you have a right to know. Especially after Judy told me you received a letter from her?"

"Two letters," I say. "Someone wants me to take notice of *something*, that much is clear."

She gives my hand a reassuring pat. "You'll figure it out. You always were a clever girl. Always with your puzzles."

"See?" Judy says, beaming and squeezing my hand at the same time. "I told you she could help."

I return the smile, but I'm not smiling on the inside. I know virtually nothing about my mother's side of the family. And to find out they were the source of some deep trauma? No wonder she never wanted to talk about them. But at least now I have a direction. At least now, I know where to concentrate my efforts. "Yeah, you were right. Thank you. Both of you."

"I hope you know that you'll always be welcome here," Mrs. Ashford says. "Fernview might not be much, but it will always be here for you if you need it." She gives my free hand a little pat before turning and pulling over the closest chair and taking a seat.

"Now, I want to hear everything. I have quite a few years to catch up on."

"Oh," I say, looking from her to Judy. "I don't want to inconvenience—"

"It's no inconvenience," Mrs. Ashford says while Judy grabs another chair. "We've always been family. Maybe not by blood, but sometimes the strongest bonds are forged beyond blood. The past few days are proof nothing could be closer to the truth." She smiles at me and Judy again. "I think it's high time for a reunion."

"Sounds good to me," Judy says.

"Yeah," I reply, trying not to get wistful. "Me too."

Epilogue

I'VE ALMOST DRIFTED BACK to sleep when I hear rustling outside my room. It's been a full day already since Judy and Mrs. Ashford's visit. I came to Fernview wanting nothing more than to leave again, but now I find the prospect of going back home bittersweet. While I'm anxious to get back and find out what's going on with Zara, I have to admit I'm going to miss this place. Mrs. Ashford made me promise I'd come visit more often, and Judy has already asked when she can come up for a tour of the FBI. But more importantly, they've given me a direction to follow in my own investigation. Maybe Wallace will be willing to give me a few more days off so I can head up to Ohio.

Still, it's frustrating not to be able to do anything from here, other than make vague inquiries on my phone during the one hour the nurses allow me to use it. But Judy promised she would return with the information for the therapy leader as well. Maybe he'll have more for me, once I finally track him down.

"Emily?" I look up to see Liam at the door, his eyes wide.

"Oh," I say. "You're here." I didn't expect to see him, but

as soon as I do my heart nearly bursts from missing him so much. I hold out my closest hand for him.

His face is white as he comes into the room, followed by Anna, who keeps shooting him concerned glances. "Oh, my god." He comes around the bed, taking a seat and placing a gentle hand on my non-bandaged cheek.

"It looks worse than it is," I say.

"They gave me the brief over the phone, but I had no idea it was this extensive," he says, his voice soft.

I give him a smile, then turn to Anna, who is keeping her distance. "Did you do this?"

"I'm…somewhat responsible, yes…" she says, hesitant.

Liam turns, as if noticing Anna for the first time. "I'm assuming you two met?" I ask.

She nods. "Out in the hall, just now."

Liam turns back to me, placing a soft kiss on my lips. "I'm glad you're okay," he whispers. "What can I do?"

"Just be here," I say, taking hold of his hand. "Where's Timber?"

"I left him with the sitter, he's fine," he replies, but I can see there's something he's not telling me.

"What? What's wrong? Is it Zara?" I ask.

He shakes his head. "I'm sorry Em—I didn't come alone."

For a brief second my heart swells even though I don't understand what he's talking about because I think maybe Zara has come back from her assignment and come down with him to surprise me. But when I see SSA Fletcher Wallace stroll through the door that nausea returns, and not from the concussion this time.

"Slate," he says, acknowledging me. He then turns to Anna. "Are you the doctor?"

"I'm *a* doctor, but not that kind," she replies, stepping back.

"Anna, this is my boss, Fletcher Wallace. SSA Wallace, Dr.

Anna Forest. She's the forensic psychologist liaison to Fernview's police department."

He gives her a curt nod, then approaches the bed. "We need to have a word. Alone."

I grip Liam's hand tighter, but I know asking him to stay would be putting his career in jeopardy. "Of course," I mutter.

"I'll be right outside if you need me," Liam says, then shoots Wallace a look that the other man doesn't catch. Good thing too.

"Feel better, Emily," Anna says. They both head out, not closing the door all the way. Wallace waits until they're gone, then heads over and does finally close the door. When he returns, he's removed his glasses and is wiping them with a cloth he's produced from inside his suit jacket.

"I was surprised to get a call from the Fernview Police Captain, telling me what an excellent agent you are and how you fought like hell to find a killer that's been terrorizing this community for twenty years. A killer—by the way—they didn't even know they had," he says, not looking at me while he continues to clean. "Imagine my surprise when I had no idea what he was talking about."

"In my defense, sir, I only came down—"

"I know why you came down here," he says. "Captain Reyes informed me of everything that transpired before and after you arrived." He holds his glasses up to the low light, inspecting them, before replacing them on the bridge of his nose. "You just can't seem to help yourself, can you?"

"I didn't come back in the office, as ordered."

I see the ghost of a smile play on his lips before it's gone again. "Is it your goal to *try* and kill yourself if you're not working?" he asks. "Because you're doing a damn good job of it."

I let out a breath, his presence sobering me a little from

the drugs. "I had a…personal stake in the case. It seemed wrong not to help."

"Your house, I know."

I shake my head. "No. Judy Ashford was a childhood friend. Probably my best friend before I left for D.C. Her sister's disappearance was…it was a big deal…for everyone. And I knew that if I could help her find the answers she needed, then I had an obligation to work the case. Even if I was only assisting."

"And when the ranking Detective asked you to step back from the case? That your help was no longer needed?" he asks, appraising me.

"I decided it was better to finish what I started, rather than hand it off to someone who might not have been as…enthusiastic about getting the job done."

"Right," he says, dropping his gaze and clasping his hands behind him as he paces the room, slowly. "And at any point did it occur to you to notify me that you were helping LEOs on a murder investigation?"

"It did…" I say, maybe a little too fast.

"…but you were afraid I'd have them pull you." I nod. It's the truth. I knew if I informed Wallace of what I was doing he'd more than likely yank on my chain and get Reyes to pull me from the case.

"Slate," he begins before sighing. "I know we don't always see eye to eye. But I had hoped that over the past few months we'd begun to develop something of a working relationship. I see now I was being too optimistic."

"Sir…" I begin.

"I just don't know what to do with you. You seem to refuse to take time off, no matter the circumstances. And you continue to put yourself in harm's way, taking reckless chances when you know better." He places his hands on his hips. "Or maybe you don't, I don't know."

"If I hadn't been there to confront Tyler, more than likely

Judy and Jake Ashford would be dead right now," I say. "That has to be worth something."

"It is," he says. "It's the only reason you're not handcuffed to that bed you're in."

I flinch, like I've been slapped. "Sir. This was a purely personal matter. I was acting as a civilian or a consultant only. I wasn't representing the FBI or presenting myself as a federal officer."

"No?" Wallace asks. "What about when you spoke with Misty Coldwater? Or when you searched for records at the library? Or when you identified yourself to the hotel clerk, asking for a list of his employees who created master keycards? Are you telling me in each of those instances you never showed your badge? Just introduced yourself as Emily Slate, local yokel?"

I flush. He's right. It seems Wallace really does know everything about the case. I did present my badge on multiple occasions, let people think I was here in a capacity for the FBI. Hell, even Tyler thought that, and he'd heard it from the local gossip. Locals talk when the FBI is in town.

"Are you going to fire me?" I ask.

"How can I fire you? You just brought down *another* killer and saved at least two lives." He seems flustered. Like he's dealing with a toddler that won't stop asking him "why." "No. I'm not firing you. But I hesitate to inform you of certain developments because I don't know if I can trust you to maintain your cool."

I sit up a little straighter. "Wait, what developments?" I ask.

"There's a situation in Baltimore. And it involves Agent Foley."

Immediately I'm pulling at my IV, trying to get it out. No sooner do I start before Wallace has slapped the button on the side of the bed for the nurse. "Dammit Slate, can you just listen for a minute?"

"Something's happened to her, hasn't it?" I ask, still yanking and sending wave after wave of pain up my arm due to the needle moving around. A nurse rushes in a second later, followed by Liam and Anna.

"If you don't calm down right now, I'm going to tell the staff to restrain you to this bed," Wallace growls.

Liam rushes over to my side, taking my hand so I can't pull at the IV as the nurse attempts to fix the tape back. "What's happened? Where is she?" I ask. I turn to Liam with accusing eyes. "You knew!"

"I ordered him not to say anything, not until we'd had a chance to speak," Wallace says.

"Fuck your orders, this is *Zara*," I say, silently pleading with Liam to help me out of this bed so I can get back home.

"She's going to upset her injuries," the nurse says.

"Sedate her," Wallace orders. "Now."

"You can't just inject her without her express permission," Anna says. "She's lucid and functional. Emily, do you want to be sedated?"

"*No*," I say, though with Liam by my side I've stopped trying to get up.

"If you can remain calm, I'll leave you be," the nurse says.

"How can I remain calm?" I ask, tears already welling in my eyes. "What's happened to her?"

"She's…missing," Wallace says. He holds up his hands before I can say anything. "We don't think she's dead. If she were, her body would have turned up somewhere."

"What was the assignment?" I demand.

"I can't talk about it," he says, looking at the two non-FBI agents in the room. "But she was making regular check-ins and then went dark. We're still trying to figure out when it happened."

I shake my head. "I need to get back to D.C. You're not going to do this without me."

"I want you back," Wallace says. "You know her best and

you can help us find her. But at the same time you are dealing with a host of injuries, and I'm not moving you until I'm sure you're not going to keel over from swelling in your brain first." He shoots a look at the nurse. "I've spoken with one of your attending physicians. We can't move you for another forty-eight hours, minimum."

"Then bring everything in here," I say, feeling the panic rise in my throat. "I'm not—I can't—"

"Emily," Anna says, placing her hand on my shoulder. "Allow yourself to feel everything that's coming to you right now. But remember to keep breathing."

I take in a deep breath, forcing myself to slow down. "How long since her last check in?"

Wallace checks his watch. "Fifty-seven hours. She's missed three recon checks."

That's not good. Either she's so deep in she's afraid checking in would break her cover, or she's been discovered and is either being held for information or is already dead and we just haven't found the body yet. Even as I entertain the possibility, I feel myself losing control.

"She's hyperventilating," I hear the nurse say. "If she doesn't calm down she's going to crash."

"Get her sedated!" Wallace yells. "Before she gives herself an aneurism!"

All of a sudden I feel a strong urge to slip back into unconsciousness. I'm aware of more people flooding my room, gathering around me, and some part of my brain compares it to a wake as if everyone is coming to celebrate my death.

People are running back and forth, yelling things at each other, but I can't tell if they're wearing white or black and my head goes all fuzzy. I look to my right to see Liam's face, pinched with worry. I want to tell him that it's going to be okay, that he'll be fine without me, but I never get the chance. I'm swallowed by darkness before I can even utter a word.

The End…?

To be continued…

Want to read more about Emily?

BOOM.

Fresh off her explosive return to her hometown, Special Agent Emily Slate finds herself facing her worst fear: the possibility of losing her best friend.

Agent Zara Foley, Emily's ride or die, has disappeared during an undercover assignment. Determined to stop at nothing to find her, Emily learns Zara was infiltrating a known domestic terrorist cell, one who had recently procured a large cache of explosives. Undeterred, and against her boss's wishes, she joins the team tracking the terrorists in hopes that it will lead them back to Zara.

With the clock ticking, Emily must overcome her personal demons and stop butting heads with everyone else on the team if she wants some real answers. But when a series of explosions begin rocking major American cities, Emily will find herself with no one to trust as she tries to uncover the identity of the terrorist leader: a man calling himself Simon Magus.

Will Emily find Zara and stop Simon from enacting his final plan before it's too late?

Or will she end up in the cinders, like all the rest?

Find out in *His Final Act.*

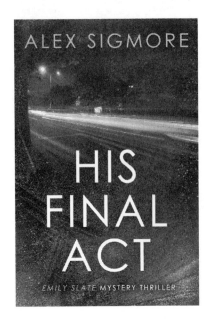

To get your copy of HIS FINAL ACT, scan the code below!

FREE book offer!
Where did it all go wrong for Emily?

I HOPE YOU ENJOYED *THE GIRL IN THE WALL*. IF YOU'D LIKE to learn more about Emily's backstory and what happened in the days following her husband's unfortunate death, including what almost got her kicked out of the FBI, then you're in luck! *Her Last Shot* introduces Emily and tells the story of the case that almost ended her career. Interested? Scan the QR code below to get your free copy now!

Not Available Anywhere Else!

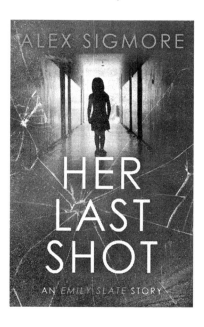

You'll also be the first to know when each book in the Emily Slate series is available!

Scan the code below to get yours!

The Emily Slate FBI Mystery Series

Free Prequel - Her Last Shot (Emily Slate Bonus Story)

His Perfect Crime - (Emily Slate Series Book One)

The Collection Girls - (Emily Slate Series Book Two)

Smoke and Ashes - (Emily Slate Series Book Three)

Her Final Words - (Emily Slate Series Book Four)

Can't Miss Her - (Emily Slate Series Book Five)

The Lost Daughter - (Emily Slate Series Book Six)

The Secret Seven - (Emily Slate Series Book Seven)

A Liar's Grave - (Emily Slate Series Book Eight)

Oh What Fun - (Emily Slate Holiday Special)

The Girl in the Wall - (Emily Slate Series Book Nine)

His Final Act - (Emily Slate Series Book Ten)

The Vanishing Eyes - (Emily Slate Series Book Eleven)

Edge of the Woods - (Emily Slate Series Book Twelve)

Ties That Bind - (Emily Slate Series Book Thirteen)

Coming Soon!

The Missing Bones - (Emily Slate Series Book Fourteen)

The Ivy Bishop Mystery Thriller Series

Free Prequel - Bishop's Edge (Ivy Bishop Bonus Story)

Her Dark Secret - (Ivy Bishop Series Book One)

The Girl Without A Clue - (Ivy Bishop Series Book Two)

A Note from Alex

Hi there!

Thanks so much for reading *The Girl in the Wall*! This was such a fun story for me to come up with and it was a privilege to deliver it to you. I hope you've enjoyed all of Emily's adventures so far. The response to this series has been incredible, and as long as you, the reader, continue to ask for Emily Slate stories, you can be rest assured I will deliver them!

As I've always said, you are the reason I write!

If you haven't already, please take a moment to leave a review or recommend this series to a fellow book lover. It really helps me as a writer and is the best way to make sure there are plenty more *Emily Slate* books in the future.

As always, thank you for being a loyal reader,

Alex